DANTES

THE DARK TRIALS SERIES | BOOK 2

T. JAMES KELLY

INVICTUS BOOKSELLERS, LLC

For Kelly.

1

Hot wind ripped through the Borderlands of Hell. The red sky burned electric with lightning. Thunder threatened to crack the world in half. I ran through the black-charred forest, but not through any part I had ever been before. My leg muscles threatened to untether themselves from my bones as I sucked in hot, biting breaths. Something was chasing me.

Something massive.

A tidal wave of toppling trees nipped at my heels. The monster toppling them roared so loud, the residue left a steady, ringing whine reverberating in my skull. It was gaining on me, and fast.

I stumbled into a clearing, then reached for the sheathe on my thigh, grasped desperately for my sword before turning to face the beast. But instead of my sword, I pulled a long dagger. The blade reflected the red sky, each edge razor sharp, the handle nestled comfortably in my white-knuckle grip.

Adam's dagger.

It wasn't until I pulled in a breath that I noticed my clothing —a black leather jacket with ripped gray denims and heavy boots. These weren't my clothes. This was not my body. Yet, I felt my heartbeat slow, my breathing normalize, and my headspace fill with resolve as if it was. I turned.

The monster crashed into the clearing, stopped, then gurgled a guttural growl.

No more running.

Staring me down with bright red eyes was a creature so horrible not even hellhounds dare go near it. It was ten times the size of a lion. Two bull-like horns jutted out from the mangy mane that framed its head. Folded atop its back were two dragon-sized, bat-like wings. With a low growl, it peeled its lips back to reveal bright green fangs, but those were not what made this monster so deadly. No, what made this thing so lethal was swaying behind its head like a dancing snake—a gigantic scorpion tail that spanned a dozen feet in length and ended in a murderous, black, bulbous stinger that oozed something undoubtedly poisonous from its needle-sharp point.

Myths and legends have long tried to capture the raw horror this beast inflicts on human and non-human hearts alike, but I can tell you, they've failed. Each time I crossed it in a book, its name alone was enough to send me into shivers.

Manticore.

Adam's dagger suddenly felt more like a toothpick.

The manticore lumbered forward two steps which spanned the length of a semi-truck before swiftly ducking its head and launching its stinger. I rolled to my left just before the stinger exploded into the earth where I'd been standing. As quickly as it had struck, it pulled the stinger free, cocking it back like a compressed spring. Legs blazing, heart thundering, I bolted toward the tree line.

Again, the manticore struck as it gave chase. The stinger thudded into the ground behind me, the fibrous hairs coating its stinger tail brushing my heels. I reached a thick tree, turned to face the manticore, then pinned my back against the scratchy trunk.

The monster stepped forward, growling, its eyes boring

hungrily into mine.

There was no escape.

Nowhere else to run.

This was it.

Do, or very literally, die. Forever.

The manticore's stinger swayed lazily above its winged back like a hypnotist's pocket watch. My breath froze as its head dropped. Seconds became hours. Its tail uncoiled and the manticore launched the lethal point of its stinger directly at my chest.

I collapsed to the side.

With an ear-splitting *crack*, the needle end of its stinger stabbed into the thick tree trunk. Scratchy bark rained down on my head, stung my eyes when I peered upward to find the manticore's stinger wedged, stuck. It struggled to pull free.

Before I allowed another heartbeat to pass, I stood, raised the dagger above my head. With a scream that emanated from the depths of where my body's soul used to reside, I brought the blade down hard and severed the bulb of the manticore's stinger from the rest of its scorpion tail.

The manticore wobbled backward uneasily. Its deep roar became a high whine as its fiery red eyes began to flicker out.

I exhaled.

Stepping forward, I flipped the dagger in the air, caught the thin blade's point, then threw it hard. The blade sang, windmilled through the air before piercing its mangy target.

Bullseye. The dagger's handle jutted out directly between the manticore's eyes.

The beast's legs quavered, gave out. The ground quaked when the manticore collapsed, its ribcage rising and falling rapidly beneath scorched fur until, at last, warm wind carried away its final breath.

Finally, the myths and legends were actually right about something. Like Achilles, a manticore had a single, deadly weakness. Separate the stinger from its tail, and you separate a manticore from life.

I approached, pressed one boot against the beast's snout, then yanked the dagger free before bolting upright in bed.

The lucid dream played itself back in my mind as I stood in the bathroom taking in my reflection. Incandescent light illuminated the bloodshot eyes staring back at me from the mirror. Chest still heaving, a bead of cold sweat trickled down from my temple.

It was a dream, Hannah. Just a dream.

Funny how we lie to ourselves sometimes.

I held out my phone again. My finger hovered over the green *call* button, like it had for the last three minutes.

Call Adam. That was my first thought when the nightmare's residue had finally faded. I needed an explanation, and he usually had all the answers. But now, phone in hand, I couldn't bring myself to tap that final button that would connect me to him.

My thoughts raced back to the one-sided conversation we had three nights ago when Adam decided to stop dancing around what had clearly been on his mind for months: That I shouldn't be with Ryan.

That I should be with him—Adam—instead.

Honestly, I knew then what I know now: He was right.

He was always right.

But the idea of pulling my guard down, of letting go and finally giving in to my heart's deepest most longing desire... it scared me to death. Next to Em, Adam was the most important thing in my life. We'd been through Hell together in the most literal sense possible.

I can't lose him.

I love Adam. And not simply "like a brother," like I always told Em, as if repeating that out loud to myself and my sister over and over and over again could negate my true feelings. I am *in* love with Adam Black. And that, more than demons, the Borderlands, hellhounds or even a manticore, terrifies me.

2

Three nights ago, Em and I finally collapsed onto our secondhand couch after a long day of unpacking. I propped my laptop precariously on top of a large cardboard moving box and clicked on the next episode of Vampire Diaries. Poor Em didn't make it through one episode before she started snoring. I closed the laptop's lid softly and carried her to bed, tucked her in, kissed her forehead three times, then made my way into the tiny, bright kitchen.

The floor was hardly visible beneath tossed pieces of crumpled newspaper and plastic bubble wrap. A small, brown box that sat atop the stove was the only box labeled "Kitchen" left to unpack. It held all of my cookware—two whole pans, thank you very much. I pulled out the smallest one, still unsure exactly which narrow cupboard to squeeze it into when someone knocked on our door. Puzzled, I checked the clock.

Nearly midnight, and I had yet to learn who any of our new neighbors were.

Pan in hand, I approached the door and peered through the peephole, then smiled, unlatched the chain and deadbolt and pulled the door open. Adam leaned lazily against the frame.

"Hey," he'd said, nearly a whisper.

"Hi." I motioned with the pan for him to come inside.

Adam let his eyes wander. He peered around corners. His gaze crawled up the walls, all the while a lopsided grin hung loose on his lips. "So, this is the new place. Do you like it?"

Do I *like* it? A momentary flashback to Aunt Sarah's house, my old dingy room, the liquor bottles littered across the hallway floor... Even though Em and I had only moved a couple miles across town, and even though the move was only a few days before, Sarah's house felt like it belonged to another lifetime. I mean, sure, the new place wasn't much bigger than your standard family room, the cacophony of traffic from the highway bled through the paper-thin walls, and the wallpaper was peeling in some places. And yeah, Em and I would be sharing the only bedroom. But it was *our* bedroom.

It was *our* place.

"Yeah," I told Adam. "I guess it's all right."

I could tell by the way he smirked that the uncontrollable, goofy grin spreading across my face belied my attempt at playing it cool.

Adam pulled two things from his jacket pocket: a cylindrical vial, maybe three inches tall, filled with what I knew to be graveyard dirt; and a brown bag of M&M candy from his jacket and tossed it onto the sliver of empty counter space. "She asleep?"

"Yes," I said, "and she'll be happy to see you didn't bring 'the gross peanut kind.'" I swiped the vial of graveyard dirt from his outstretched palm. "Thanks for this."

Shaking his head, he said, "I still can't believe she doesn't like the peanut butter kind, either."

"Plain Jane, that one." I uncorked the vial of dirt and traced a thin line across the bottom of the window over the sink, pinning a mental note to do the same in our bedroom.

Adam raked a hand through his hair and cleared his throat, rocking back on his heels and, weirdly, avoiding eye contact. The way he does when something's on his mind.

"Come on," I said, re-corking the vial and placing it on top of a moving box. "Come sit down."

We settled onto the couch—a thrift store special—which was just big enough for each of us to have our own cushion. I sat back against the armrest and shoved my feet under his thigh.

"They're cold," I said, meeting his confused look with a Cheshire grin. "So, what's up?"

He took a deep breath, which wasn't a great sign. Maybe work wasn't going so well—he'd just taken a job at a warehouse manufacturing knife blades—or maybe his mom had another relapse. He made a sound like whatever words he'd come here meaning to say were clinging for dear life to the sides of his throat, refusing to leave it. Another swipe of his hair, then he watched my hand as I softly rubbed his elbow.

"What's wrong?"

Another deep breath.

"I...," he began. "I don't know. It's dumb." He was always terrible at placing words to match his emotions, but words weren't as necessary as he might have thought. His face was screwed so tightly, I knew that whatever was bothering him was deep, visceral. "I think about it a lot," he finally said, "that last descent to the Borderlands. Standing on the top of that mountain in the hot rain. With you."

"Me too," I said. "Every day." I continued to rub his elbow. His eyes flickered on mine before they fell to the floor.

"Which part?" He asked, nearly a whisper.

Weird question. "Not sure I follow."

"Which part of that time on the mountain top do you think about the most?"

The answer flashed in my mind before I forced it to one side, hoping the lights were dim enough that he hadn't noticed my warming cheeks. "Probably the moment I saw my parents again."

He lifted his gaze to me with a grin, nodding, and for a moment I thought I'd avoided embarrassment.

"That was after we came down from the mountain, though."

Yeah... I was hoping he hadn't noticed that attempt at deflection. But who was I kidding? If there was one person in the whole world I couldn't fool, it was Adam. We'd been through too much.

I faked clearing my throat. "What about you?" I attempted. "Which part do you think about the most?"

Adam ran his palm against his dark, scratchy facial stubble. "I remember the ground breaking apart," he said, "falling away in pieces into the lava. I can still feel the heat on the back of my legs." He shifted, leveling me with those cobalt blue eyes that, once they ensnare you, are impossible to look away from. "I remember standing on one end of the land bridge. Malum stood in the middle, blocking our way. And then..." But he didn't finish. Instead, he wiped his palms across his knees and stood.

I released the breath I hadn't realized I'd been holding.

"Never mind, Hannah. I'm being an idiot. It's just..."

Pressing myself up off the couch, I stepped toward him. "Just what?"

His lips tightened. The color drained from them until they turned ghost white.

"I've never forgotten those seconds you kissed me in the rain under that red sky."

I swallowed. Hard.

"Like I said," he continued, "I'm being an idiot." Adam turned, slowly weaving through piles of clothes and brown moving boxes toward the door.

"Stop," I said, voice weak. "That's... the part I think about most, too." Which was true. No matter how hard I tried to brush the moment off as fleeting, my heart wouldn't allow it.

He turned, faced me. I pulled in a deep breath and spread my hands.

"It's just... I...," I let out a hiss of breath, which did nothing to alleviate the growing heat in my chest. "I'm scared that if we become more than friends, I'll ruin it. And then I'll lose you—*we* will lose you." I motioned toward the closed bedroom door. "I can't risk—"

"I love you, Hannah." His words cut off my breath. "I've loved you ever since we came down off that mountain. And seeing you with Ryan... it destroys me."

Ryan. Suddenly it felt like my insides were wrapped in wire, being tugged in two directions.

"So, I need to know right now," Adam said, stepping forward, each step an electric charge. "Will you give me a chance? Because if not, then... I'll just have to get over it, I guess. But I can't keep hoping if there's no hope."

A flood of jumbled words collided in my brain and mashed themselves into goo. What Adam could not have known was that I'd been struggling for weeks trying to make my heart and my head stop acting like magnets pointing their identical polarities at each other, pressing themselves farther and farther apart. My head said 'Ryan.'

But my heart?

I needed time. I needed to get my head right.

"Adam, I..."

Normally Adam's face was chiseled stone, but right then it looked on the verge of cracking. "I'm sorry," he said. "It's not fair to spring it on you like this. It's just... I've got to know."

His lips split into a thin smile, and my insides became a jacuzzi.

"Think about it. Please."

Adam turned, and with a quick look back, left through the door, shutting it softly behind him.

WE HAVEN'T TALKED SINCE. It's been three days; the longest we've gone without at least texting each other. And the last thing I wanted was to call him to tell him I had something super important to talk to him about, only to tell him about a dream that I suspected wasn't just a dream. I can't help but worry he might take it the wrong way, like I'm avoiding him or not taking his feelings seriously.

Not that he's that sensitive, it's just…

Gripping the edges of the sink, I stared deeply into my own reflected eyes. "The hell is wrong with you?" I muttered, then pulled up my hair and finished applying makeup. Clinking sounds from the kitchen, spoon against bowl.

"Where did you put the bug spray?" Em called, muffled, mouth mostly full of store-brand cereal. I smiled, finished pulling up my ponytail and headed out of the bathroom.

"Back left pocket," I said, tousling her hair as I maneuvered past her into the living room. "Same place it was when you asked me last night." I hefted the daypack that was propped against the couch, patted the left pocket, and set it near the door.

To say Em was excited to experience her first summer camp would be the understatement of the century, especially since she'd be cabin mates with her best friend, Scarlett Reynolds. She'd spent most of the summer at Scarlett's house, which worked out well since I started working full time at Ultimate MMA after graduation.

"Also," I said, pulling a nondescript black flip phone from my pocket, "I know you're not supposed to take electronics with you, but I need you to take this. It's already fully charged. I'll hide it at the bottom of your pillowcase, and you can call me if you need me. My number is already programmed in."

Em smirked and shook her head before releasing a long, "Oh-kayyyy." I'm pretty sure hers was the same look I always gave Mom when I thought she was being overbearing. I smiled at that, then slid the phone to the bottom of her silky pillowcase and set the pillow next to her day pack. To be honest, the phone was more for my peace of mind than for Em's, given everything that's happened in the last ten months or so.

She has changed. I denied it at first, ignored the evidence. But she's just not quite the same Em as she was before I faced the

Dark Trials. I guess she could say the same about me, too, but still...

I first noticed something was different about her when I walked her to the bus on her first day back to school after her stint in the hospital. The day was clear, sky blue, winter wind whipping the trees' bare branches. We went through our regular ritual—a hug followed by wrapping our pinkies together and saying "I love you" before she bounded up the bus steps. She took her seat, and that's when I noticed something odd. Usually, she'd wave at me from the small bus window. That day, though, she seemed transfixed, staring at something behind—or *beyond*—me.

The bus rumbled away, and I turned only to be met by a river of empty sidewalk and road. The world was quiet, the way it gets just before winter's first snowfall. Instead of calming, though, it felt eerie. I pulled my sword for good measure and peered into the Gray.

A yellow-eyed demon peered back, nearly a block away. A shiver ran up my spine. Not because of the demon—I was no longer afraid of them—but because if I didn't know better, I'd say Em had been staring right at it...

I asked her about it when she got home from school that day. She looked at me like I was a crazy person off her meds, which, fair enough.

"No," she said, "I didn't see anything. And why did you ask it like that? All slow and spooky..."

I grinned. "I don't know. It just seemed like you saw something. Promise you didn't?" We re-wrapped pinkies.

"Promise."

I believed her for about a week. That's when she broke the mirror in Aunt Sarah's bathroom. It was like she saw something inside of it, trying to crawl out, trying to curl its fingers around her. She screamed, slammed her palm against the cheap glass. She tried to blame it on a spider.

I was outside the bathroom the whole time. The door was open. There was no spider.

There was no demon, either. At least as far as I could tell. Whatever it was she saw in that mirror, or thought she saw, she wouldn't tell me.

She's had a lot of nightmares since then. About what, I don't know—she keeps it all under wraps, doesn't like to talk about it.

I started blaming myself. I'd rationalize, try to use logic. It's not like she had a weapon from the Borderlands of Hell that would allow her to see across the veil—only *I* had that, so it had to be the fact that she was so close to me all the time that would explain some of the residue rubbing off on her. So, in that sense, sending her off to summer camp for a few days was probably good for her. I thought of saying "no" when she asked to go, but she wanted it more than anything, even more than Christmas.

All I've ever wanted was for her to have as normal a life as possible. But giving her that was really, *really* hard to do, because Mom and Dad were gone and I had to scrape and claw to put food on the table. Scarlett's mom, Tracy, offered to pay Em's camp fee, but my very first tax return ever covered it and then some. My desire for Em to experience normalcy—camping, friends, s'mores—trumped my anxiety about the possibility she'd become sensitive to the supernatural. And besides, ever since I paid her camp fee a couple months ago, she hasn't had any supernatural or paranormal issues. At least not any that I was aware of.

All things considered, life was pretty good. Apart from the occasional run-in with a bottom-feeding demon, that is.

Speaking of, I've learned a lot in the last ten months or so. Between the day I regained my soul and now, I've probably sent twenty-five or thirty other demons back to Hell—assuming that's where they go when they explode into a billion shards of golden light. Maybe they don't go anywhere. Maybe they just drift away into the ether.

They're not hard to spot, even outside the Gray. Signs include a blurry darkness, ice cold blasts of air, and often they're attached to people, following them around like a fuzzy black cloud of hornets. I think my sword has something to do with my ability to see vestiges of them outside the Gray. It's constantly strapped to my hip and invisible to normal people's eyes. In fact, it's even invisible to my eyes unless and until I wrap my hands around its cool hilt and pull it free from its sheath.

Yeah. Don't ask me how that works. It just does.

Also, when I do pull my sword and descend into the Gray, the world outside freezes. If I'm near other people, they freeze in time until I re-sheathe it again. Adam and I experimented in the early days. We thought maybe, in some crazy way, we could... how do I say this? We thought maybe we could time travel. Seeing as the world outside the Gray freezes while we're in it, what would happen if we decided to travel across town before re-sheathing our weapons? That was the question we experimented with one night.

Short answer: no, there's no such thing as time travel. The moment we re-sheathed our weapons, we re-entered reality exactly when and where we'd left it.

Also, Adam can see me when I'm in the Gray without him, and vice versa. It's a pretty wild experience, honestly. Watching Adam, it's like he becomes shaded, in shadow, moving inside a mist. Time doesn't stop for me when he's inside the Gray and I'm not.

Like I said: Don't ask me how that works. It just does. That's what I've figured out so far. Now if only I could figure out my love life, then things would be spectacular.

Ever since Adam walked out the door three nights ago, I knew what I had to do. His outpouring of raw honesty was the push I needed to really inspect my feelings instead of keeping them locked away. It was settled: I was going to break up with Ryan as soon as the time was right.

It wasn't an easy decision, and I had to sift through a lot of emotional baggage. The truth was, Ryan was the stability I needed at the moment I needed it. He made me feel special without taking advantage of my vulnerabilities. That day on the baseball park bleachers, Senior year, when he invited me to the Halloween Fling was the day I realized—truly realized—that I could handle the cards life had dealt me; that maybe our new life in this little Colorado town wouldn't be so bad. And with Gabby gone to college, Ryan was the last vestige of that feeling of normalcy. I clung to it, maybe a little too long.

After graduation, Ryan announced that he'd been accepted to the University of Colorado in Boulder. He had the option to matriculate early, get a jump start, but unlike Gabby he'd opted out. All summer, his number one topic of conversation was just how close Boulder was—about a four-hour drive—and how often he'd visit and how often I'd make the trek through the mountains. He was determined to make the long-distance thing work.

I wasn't so sure. But I'd never expressed any reservations about it to him. In truth, my reason for breaking up with him had nothing to do with whether we could make a long-distance relationship work—we probably could if we tried. But something told me that, *'Hey, you know that guy I hang out with a lot? The one you're kind of worried about but won't admit it? Yeah… I'm actually in love with him, sorry,'* wouldn't go over very smoothly.

Knuckles rapped on the door, barging in on my thoughts. Probably Scarlett and Tracy here to pick up Em and whisk her off to Camp Sego Lily. I glanced at the bright green numbers on the microwave. "Wow," I said. "They're early"

Em trotted to the door, ponytail penduluming side to side. I hefted her pack over my shoulder and followed behind her. When Em pulled the door open, I dropped it with a loud thud.

Adam propped himself up with one hand against the door frame and grinned wide when he saw Em.

"Hey!" Em squealed, then wrapped her arms around his waist. Adam pulled her into a bear hug, then glanced up at me still grinning. A rock settled in my throat.

"I promised Em I'd say goodbye before she left," he said. He rubbed her shoulder. "A whole five days without Em n' Em is a long time."

Didn't I know it... The thought of Em and I being apart for that long had robbed me of sleep, and I didn't think I'd be making up for it while she was gone. I attempted to clear my throat, unsure of what exactly to do with my hands.

"Come in. Please."

"Need help with that?" Adam motioned to the daypack on the floor.

"No. Thanks. They're not here to pick her up yet."

Adam sidled through the doorway, hands shoved deep in his faded jeans pockets. Silence grew long and awkward. Em shifted glances between my face and Adam's, her brow steadily furrowing.

"What's wrong?" she asked.

"Nothing." I faked a smile, then added, "Go brush your teeth and grab your shoes. Scarlett should be here soon."

Still visibly confused, Em slipped into the bathroom without a word.

"Listen," Adam said as soon as the bathroom door clicked shut, "I wanted to apologize. For the other night. That was... I shouldn't have sprung it on you like that."

The rock in my throat dropped and settled in the pit of my stomach.

"Don't be sorry," I said. "I haven't called or texted or anything, and you probably thought..." I pinned two wild hair strands to the back of my ears, then hugged my elbows. "I don't know. I just wasn't sure what to say. And I needed some time to think, and I didn't want to say something wrong..."

Adam's eyes fell as he slowly nodded. I stepped forward and balled a piece of his long-sleeve, gray tee in my fist, raking my short nails softly against his side. That got his attention. I smiled up at him.

"But I've had some time to think," I continued. "I know what I want now."

His eyes sparked. The narrow space between us became charged with warm electricity.

"But," I said, suddenly aware that our lips had begun to close distance, "I still need to break up with Ryan."

Adam smiled, exhaled, nodded. "Let him down easy," he said. I let go of his shirt and took an awkward step back. "I've got one other thing to tell you," he said.

"Yeah? What's that?"

He pulled in a deep breath, then released it quickly. "I decided to join."

This news was a few weeks coming, and it didn't surprise me, but still…

Adam peeled back his left jacket sleeve, revealing a new tattoo-like symbol on his left wrist, the same place Malum had branded him when he'd sold his soul. The symbol was made up of two, opposite-pointing yet overlapping chevron arrows, one pointing away from Adam, the other pointing toward him. Their overlap created a small diamond shape, which was slashed in half by one straight, horizontal line. The symbol shimmered gold like the golden rings that circled his forearm—the same rings that circled my upper bicep; the stripes we earned each time we defeated one of the Dark Trials.

I'd only seen one other person with that same symbol, and that guy wasn't going to let up until I had one, too.

I nodded, attempted a smile. "Are you happy?"

Adam nodded back.

"That's what matters." And I meant it.

Another knock on the door ripped the world back into focus. We blinked, swallowed, then took another awkward step apart.

"Em!" I shouted.

"Coming!" The sink sputtered behind the bathroom door.

I lifted a finger to Adam. "Hold please." He let out a breathy chuckle as I squeezed past him with a grin and pulled open the door to let Scarlett and Tracy inside.

You know that rock that had settled in the pit of my stomach? It flew back up into my throat, and somehow it felt ten times bigger than before, because for the second time this morning, the person I'd expected to see on the other side of the door wasn't the same person that stood there.

Ryan shadowed the doorway with a crooked smile. That is, until he peered past me and noticed Adam standing tall. My eyes darted between the two of them and I tried to formulate words. What's worse? Em came flying around the corner with a massive grin on her face which dissolved the second she saw Ryan. I don't know what was up with her lately, but for some reason she has really soured toward him. Tight-lipped, she turned for the bedroom.

"Did I interrupt something?" Ryan said, still grinning, but with questioning eyes. I finally forced a smile, teeth glued together.

"No, no. What's up?"

Ryan stood still for a moment, surveying the scene. "Not much... just had some extra time this morning and thought I'd walk you to work."

Before I could say another word, Adam slid behind me, out the door and made his way down the stairs outside. "I'll see you later, Hannah."

I wanted to reach out to him and tell him not to leave; that I still had so much to talk to him about—we hadn't even gotten to the manticore in my dreams. Instead, like an idiot, I said, "Yeah. Okay. Yeah, I'll...," my hands flailed, "later."

He turned, winked, and for half a heartbeat I forgot Ryan was even present. Before he could turn and take another step, Em shot stealthily past me, darted halfway down the steps and wrapped herself around Adam's middle. He let out a breathy laugh and gave her one last shoulder squeeze.

"See you, Em n' Em. Have fun at camp. Shakes are on me when you get back."

Em said goodbye and traipsed back into the apartment without even a glance in Ryan's direction. Adam mounted his motorcycle. The bike rumbled to life and carried him away.

I had no words to answer the unspoken questions behind Ryan's raised eyebrows. Thank the heavens and all the angels I spotted Tracy and Scarlett in the parking lot, Scarlett skipping ahead of her mom. I motioned Ryan inside. "Sorry. Crazy morning."

"I can tell. Should I come back later?"

"No, no." I breathed, faced Ryan and finally gave him my full attention. "Just let me see my sister off and then you can walk me to work. That's really sweet of you." With a half hug, Ryan stepped aside and leaned against the kitchen counter.

Scarlett raced through the front door, accosted Em with a hug.

"Scar!" Tracy shouted before she made it to the door mat. "You don't just run into people's homes."

Laughing, I wrapped Tracy in a hug and told Scarlett she could run in any time she wanted to. Em threaded her arms through her daypack straps then grabbed her pillow—cheap phone well-hidden in the depths of the pillowcase—and followed Scarlett out the door.

"Hey!" I said, fists planted firmly on hips. "Aren't you going to say goodbye?"

The adorable bundle of nervous excitement that was Em bounded back to me. I crouched to her eye level, wrapped my arms tight around her middle as she constricted my neck.

"I'm going to miss you more than you know," I said.

"I'll miss you too."

"Have a really great time and take care of Scarlett." I leaned in close, cupped her ear. "And don't forget to call me if you want me to come get you or if you just want to talk or for any reason whatsoever, okay?"

Em giggled. We unraveled, locked pinkies, and after I planted one long, wet kiss on her soft cheek, she was gone, swallowed up in the back of Tracy's SUV. Tracy promised to drive safe and to call if anything came up. I could only nod because I knew that if I opened my mouth to speak, that would be the crack in the dam that broke the whole thing wide open. Up until this point, I thought I'd done a good job at keeping my emotions in check, trying not to think of what happened the last time Em spent a night away from me. But no matter how much I had mentally prepared, the thought of her leaving me for almost an entire week suddenly seemed unimaginable.

"Hey," Tracy said, placing her hands on my shoulders. Apparently, my thoughts were written all over my face, because she said, "Everything's going to be all right. I know it's hard."

"How do you feel about camping?" I managed.

Tracy's face shifted from sympathetic to quizzical.

"I mean, we could share a tent. Camp in the woods just outside of Camp Sego Lily. We could be right there. Maybe bring some binoculars."

Tracy laughed and pulled me in close. Yes, I was joking, but not really. The only thing that kept me from darting to Camp World for an extra sleeping bag and a one-woman tent was the fact that Em had an illegal phone. Tracy gave me a reassuring look, walked over to her SUV. Girl giggles floated out the door when she pulled herself up and in. She started the engine, waved goodbye to me and Ryan—who I sort of forgot was there, again—and pulled away, Em and Scarlett waving from the back seat.

I pulled in a long, deep breath, then said a silent prayer to whomever was listening, followed by a silent threat to whatever dark thing might have been watching from shadows unseen.

3

I slung my gym bag over my shoulder and locked the door behind me and Ryan. Summer had begun bleeding into fall. The August morning air felt crisper than it had in weeks and carried with it that sharp fragrance hinting that the leaves would be turning from green to amber and honey before long.

This summer had been a good one. After high school graduation, business picked up enough for Tyrese to take me on full time. He even asked me to organize a small self-defense night class for girls and women. Truth be told, I still didn't feel fully qualified to teach, but I guess Tyrese saw something in me. Those nights the girls and ladies, usually drenched, always thanked me for teaching them something new. Soon, my night classes became something I lived for. It made me feel... I don't know... like I was contributing to the world in my own small way, making it better.

For the first couple weeks, we pulled in five or six students. But steadily, our little night classes grew to fifteen, then twenty, sometimes more when students brought their friends. I didn't ask for it, but Tyrese thought it was fair to pay me a large cut of the night class fees which, on top of my hourly wage, was what allowed me and Em to get our own little apartment across town, near the gym.

Scarlett's dad, Tim, represented me pro-bono in my case to become Em's legal guardian. As of June twenty-ninth, we had no more legal ties to Aunt Sarah. Since moving, though, I still visited her once a week or so, even restocked her fridge sometimes. She may not have taken the greatest care of us while we lived with her—okay, she may not have taken *any* care of us at all—but, in the end, Em and I avoided the foster care system because she let us into her home. After everything I'd been through for the last year, family was more important to me than ever and despite all of her self-inflicted flaws, she was still my mom's sister.

My nerves bundled themselves up in a tight ball. I hadn't had much time to plan, but here I was, alone with Ryan, mind made up. I guess right now was as good a time as any to break the news to him. My lips opened, closed, then opened again like a fish out of water.

"What are you thinking about?" Ryan said, a wrecking ball through my formulating thoughts. We had nearly reached the bank of mailboxes on the corner and I hadn't said a word to him since we walked out the front door. This was going to be harder than I thought.

"Oh. Just… life stuff." We reached a bank of metal boxes that belonged to our apartment building. I slid my small key into number eleven and pulled out the envelopes. Mostly bills. A few coupons.

"Sounds pretty serious," he said, half joking. It was the other half, his sensitive half, the half that I first fell for that I was worried about. "Want to talk about it?"

That half.

I turned to him, honestly grateful that he'd offer while simultaneously feeling like dirty gum on the bottom of a shoe. Ryan was wonderful. He didn't deserve what I knew I had to do. "I'm," I began, but couldn't manage to keep eye contact.

Returning to the mail, I said, "I'm sorry. It's just, I'm kind of... raw right now with Em leaving, and the move... there's just a lot going on."

Ryan brushed my arm. "I get it. It's cool. Maybe we can talk tonight? You're still planning on it, right?"

The question jarred me. What was tonight? Ryan took in my confused expression and chuckled. "You get all out of sorts whenever you're worried about Em," he said.

"I know," I said and rubbed my forehead as if it would jar loose whatever it was I'd forgotten. "I'm sorry. Remind me."

Why is it that I'm fine with slaying demons on the daily, but breaking up makes me so nervous? But I knew the answer before I even finished the question. I do not like to hurt people—especially people who don't deserve it. And Ryan didn't deserve it.

"I've got reservations at Alfonzo's. Nine o'clock, which I know is late for a Wednesday, but they're usually booked out for a month so I'm glad they even had a spot for tonight."

A wave of nausea hit me. Not at the thought of Alfonzo's— Alfonzo's was amazeballs—but at the thought of breaking up with Ryan on the night of our big date that he'd been planning for weeks. "I can't believe I forgot."

"A lot on your mind..."

I cleared my throat, reaching the end of the mail stack, and—

"Oh, hey, look!" I pulled out the last piece of mail, smiled. On the front, a sprawling downtown city sparkled, illuminated by the millions of hotel and casino lights flanking the main strip of road. A midcentury modern sign superimposed in the corner read *Welcome to Fabulous LAS VEGAS Nevada*. Flowery handwriting on the back side read:

Heyyyy Homeless! I miss you. Like a lot. School is good and I've met some cool peeps but none that compare to my number one ride or die. CALL ME. I love you.

Gabby

I snorted. It was so like her to send an actual post card. I missed Gab so much and would probably never forgive her for leaving me to enroll early at university. Her mom, Miss Johnson, wasn't all too happy at first when Gabby announced she'd be attending the University of Nevada-Las Vegas. She thought it was a party school—and she was probably right. But Gabby had worked hard, and UNLV offered her a full-ride academic scholarship. Gabby's grades earned her tuition, room and board, food, and a stipend worth upwards of fifty-thousand dollars every year. Her mom couldn't argue with that, or with the fact that Vegas was only about a seven-hour drive—a much closer option than the other schools back east that she seriously considered. Little did Gab know, I would most definitely be calling her tonight before what would be my last date with Ryan... and she'd probably be disappointed. She's always liked Ryan. But at the end of the day, Gab would always have my back, and I would probably need one of her patented pep talks to go along with the inevitable pint of moose tracks ice cream.

My heart clenched. Shouldn't I do it now? I mean, waiting for a fancy dinner just to break up with him is kind of a jerk move...

"What did she say?" Ryan asked, pointing toward the postcard. I clinked the mailbox shut and we started walking again.

"Not much, just—whoa." I slid the postcard back into the mail stack, then lifted Ryan's forearm. There, on the underside above his wrist was a large square section of gauze secured with bandages. "What happened?"

"Just a cut," he said, "no big deal."

But if it was just a cut, it had to have been a real gash. The bandages took up nearly half of his forearm. "You sure? Looks pretty serious."

"I'm sure." His answer was sharp, biting. Not like Ryan. I could swear a flash of dark anger swept across his face, but only for a millisecond before he looked normal again. It... unsettled me.

We walked in silence for half a minute, neither of us

addressing the awkward tension that pulled at us. After half a block, Ryan cleared his throat to say something just as my phone buzzed my back pocket.

Another call from another blocked number. For about the tenth time this week, I thumbed the red button and sent him to voicemail. Maybe this time he'd take the hint, though I doubted it.

"Who was that?" Ryan asked.

I stammered. "Probably a wrong number." By the way Ryan chewed his lip and raised his brow, I knew he didn't buy it. Honestly, I didn't like keeping secrets from him, but better to keep secrets than to tell lies, and especially kinds of secrets he simply couldn't understand. How could I explain that my newfound talent of demon-slaying attracted the attention of an international demon-slaying organization that was determined to pull me into their ranks? He'd probably petition to have me committed.

Around a corner, the gym came into sight. It took a few solo steps before I realized Ryan had stopped walking. I turned.

"What's up?" I asked, puzzled. Ryan stood still for a moment sucking on his teeth.

"Are we good?" The look he gave shot daggers into me. Again, that dark flash from somewhere behind his eyes. It almost… scared me, and these days, it took a lot to scare me. Eyes drifting toward the blue sky, mouth slack and hanging open like an idiot, I searched in vain for words. I needed time. I needed to think.

In one fluid motion I reached for my thigh, wrapped my hand around my sword's invisible hilt, unsheathed it and plunged into the Gray. The world whirred, sharp hues of blacks and whites and grays swirling, the outside world trapped in frozen time. My eyes cinched shut. A primal, frustrated scream burned the back of my throat. Ryan stood in front of me, a gray statue, the guy who had been there for me and supported me through my most incoherently insane moments and yet…

I am not in love with him.

There was too much he didn't understand. Too much he *couldn't* understand, ever.

And yet he would always have a grateful, warm spot in my heart. He stopped me from falling when my life was crumbling away beneath my feet. He was a safety net when I needed one most. But as unfair as it might sound... I didn't need a net anymore. I inhaled slowly, then pressed it out through a pinhole between my lips.

There are no convenient moments to do a hard thing, only hard moments when you have to choose between a good thing and the best thing.

But just when I was about to return the sword to its sheath, something caught my eye. There, not far down the road and near the gym's front doors, a lady stood next to a shopping cart full of random items—blankets, large strips of cardboard, a radio. Ill-fitting clothes hung off her shoulders. Her pants were ripped in a few places. Looming behind her was a huge, blacker-than-black mass. It wrapped its smokey tendrils around her, its hooded head attached to her neck. It shifted, sensing me watching, and raised its face.

Two yellow slits-for-eyes set deep within its hood narrowed into a glare, which I returned, my insides burning hot. Unlike most demons I encountered, this dumb oaf didn't try to float away at the sight of my sword. No, this one drew itself up to full height like a bear.

Pure hatred laced my veins.

I sheathed my sword, left the Gray and returned to Ryan.

"Look," I said, "I know I've been acting strange. And I can't really explain why. I promise we'll talk more tonight." I thumbed toward the gym down the road. "I really need to get to work."

I could see the gears turning in his head as he mulled over my words. After a beat, he nodded. "Okay. So, I'll pick you up around 8:30?"

"I'll meet you there. I'm teaching class tonight." And it's

probably best that I have my own way home, but I kept that part to myself.

"Right. Okay."

I offered a tepid hug and said goodbye, then tried to act casual as I headed across the street toward the gym. Ryan turned opposite and made for his truck, and I waited an eternity for him to turn the ignition and pull away. Once he rounded the corner, I crossed the road's double yellow line and pulled my sword again. The Gray was a loud whirlpool of swirling shades. The demon brooded there, waiting for me.

4

S till drawn up to its full height, the black demon hissed as I
stepped across the road. This was the fourth demon I'd seen
in the Gray this week and it was only Wednesday—a serious
uptick from normal. All of them had met the business end of my
sword, bursting into a million flashes of amber. Each one had
tried to escape their fate, but I would not allow it—they should
never be allowed to prey on other people so long as I was able to
send them screaming back to Hell. The hissing demon ahead of
me began unwinding its smoky tendrils from around its homeless victim. I broke into a run.

Unlike other demons, this one floated toward me on a cloud
of noxious fog. The move startled me for a millisecond, but if
there's one thing I know about demons, it's that they will always
try to instill fear in you. That's how they control you. They grab
ahold of it, and as your fear blooms, they grab more, tighter,
until you're utterly paralyzed. Then they can do what they want
with you, and there's almost nothing you can do to stop it.

But fear is a choice.

As the seconds slowed, I chose not to fear. Instead, I chose
rage.

With a primal yell, I double-fisted my sword hilt and brought the blade down hard and fast, aiming to slash the demon from shoulder to hip. The blade, though, never reached its shoulder. Instead, it clanged off something solid; something metallic.

The demon had blocked my blade with a gunmetal gray spike. The spike's bottom end disappeared into the blackness of the demon's baggy sleeve. A flash of lightning in the back of my mind pulled me to the Borderlands, the volcanic mountaintop, to Malum, the red sky glinting off the razor edge of his broadsword. Since that moment, I've slayed dozens of his slimy cohorts. But I've never seen or faced another demon with a weapon since.

Fear wrapped its hot wires around my heart. The demon sensed it, reached out, and forced my body backward.

No! Get a grip, Hannah. Make your choice.

A sharp intake of breath quenched the burning fear. I glowered into the demon's yellow eyes, then stepped forward as it lost its grip.

I whipped my blade toward the demon's midsection, but it blocked the blow. I stabbed hard at its chest only to strike metal, or whatever the underworldly spike was made of. I swiped at its arm but whiffed as the demon stepped aside.

I was throwing haymakers when I needed to throw jabs. Settle, Hannah.

I cocked the sword back, but before I could swing, the demon lunged forward and drove the sharp spike directly toward the middle of my stomach. A burst of electric panic shocked my heart. Red alarm bells wailed in the back of my mind. I sidled right and swatted the spike with my blade. The impact buzzed my hands.

Other demons had tried to escape me, but this one was trying to *kill* me.

What happens if I die in the Gray?

No time. The demon swung again, centimeters from my shoulder. I back peddled, tripped over my own shoes, and landed hard on the asphalt. Crab-crawling backward, my blade skittered as I dragged it against the asphalt road. The demon loomed, pressed forward.

Its eyes became fire.

Slowly, the spike rose above the demon's hood, above me.

With one hand pressed against the asphalt, I sliced my blade through the air between us. It was like swinging a fly swatter to ward off a lion.

The demon growled. The spike descended. I covered my face and shut my eyes.

A whistling sound like a falling bomb pierced the air.

Thunk!

A sucking sound, followed by a popping sound. Before the demon's spike moved another millimeter, the demon and its spike exploded. A million tiny orbs of sparkling light hovered where it had stood, then disappeared.

Something rattled to the ground near my feet. When I looked, I found a black arrow resting on the road. Footfalls approached from behind me. Sword in hand, I quickly stood and turned.

A young woman sauntered in my direction. She wore a black leather jacket over a tight black top, black pants and biker boots. Dark, straight pixie hair covered half her face. The uncovered half revealed a sharp jaw, high cheeks, and dark eyes. She slung a bow over her shoulder, passed me without making eye contact, then bent down for the arrow lying in the spot where the demon had nearly killed me. Fingering the sharp tip, she tightened her lips and shot me a sideways glance.

"Don't ever try to take on a Reaper on your own." Her voice was silky smooth and laced with impatience.

A 'Reaper?'

I swallowed hard. I hadn't ever talked to anyone inside the Gray other than Adam. Besides him, there was only one other person that I knew of who could enter the Gray at will and kill demons. This girl was very obviously not him.

"I... who..."

"Talk to Crew."

She slid the arrow over her shoulder where I assumed her quiver rested. With one final, sharp glance, she released it and left the Gray.

Reeling, I sheathed my sword and plunged back into the full color, real world. But the black-clad girl that had saved me wasn't there. I spun, peering side to side, searching. Then a blaring car horn electrocuted my senses. A guy behind a minivan windshield spread his hands, his face turned up in a what-the-hell-are-you-doing look before I realized I was still standing in the middle of the road. I waved him off and made for the far sidewalk when I finally spotted the girl slipping her thin frame into the driver seat of a matte black muscle car. It roared to life, then peeled off. She flipped a loud U-turn, then disappeared around a corner in a flash.

"Out of the road!" minivan guy shouted as he passed.

"Yeah," I mumbled, "sorry."

The homeless lady outside of Ultimate MMA watched me intently as I approached the gym doors in a daze. I would've dubbed her *the homeless lady I had saved from a demon*, but had I? I mean, the demon almost took me out and probably would've returned to feed on her if the girl in black hadn't shot it through with a Borderlands arrow.

What did she call the demon? A 'Reaper?'

'Don't ever try to take on a Reaper on your own...'

Lost in thought, I floated through the gym's front doors. The entrance bell rang. But it wasn't the bell, or the stringent odor of sweat plastered on leather, or the staccato snaps of boxing gloves striking heavy bags that brought my mind out of the fog. It was my phone buzzing again, and again a blocked number flashed across the screen.

'Talk to Crew...'

A heavy exhale, then I sent the call to voicemail. Not that Crew would ever leave one.

5

"You all right, Hannah?" Tyrese popped his head into the front office at the end of the day and startled me out of a daydream. I had no idea how long I'd been staring mindlessly at the computer monitor, mentally running through the sequence of events between me and the demon—Reaper—and the girl in black who saved my life. I couldn't get her out of my head...

"Yeah, sorry," I said, "just a little distracted today." I shuffled through a few pages of bills that sat haphazard on the small office desk. "Busy today, huh?"

Tyrese wiped a towel across his gleaming brow with a smile. "Very. Feels good. You gonna be ready for class in...," he checked his digital wristwatch, "ten minutes?"

Ten minutes? Where had the day gone? Sure enough, the wall clock pointed to 5:50. The sinking sun cast long shadows over the road outside.

"Yep! Better go change." I straightened the papers one more time for good measure and started the computer's shutdown process. Tyrese rapped his knuckles musically on the doorframe.

"You good with flying solo tonight? Me and George have a few things to take care of, some errands." He must've noticed the surprise splash across my face, because he chuckled and added, "You got this. It's not like you ever need me anyway. You're doing a great job, Hannah. The ladies really like you." The bell above the door chimed and two women in active wear sidled through the door. Tyrese winked, knocked on the door frame once more, then turned to greet them. "Hello, ladies! You're here for self-defense tonight?"

They simultaneously nodded and undressed him with their eyes like most women did when taking in Tyrese for the first time. He was dark, tall, and cut, with a deep voice coated in a smooth Jamaican accent. I couldn't help but snigger imagining the subtle devastation in their hearts the moment they realize Tyrese had a very lucky husband waiting for him at home.

"Well then, I leave you in Hannah's very capable hands." Tyrese motioned through the glass pane separating gym from office. I waved and smiled as they tried hard to suppress their obvious disappointment. With a bow and a thumbs up, Tyrese scooted out the door and into the evening air. I introduced myself, told them to make themselves comfortable, feel free to stretch, and I'd be right back.

The bell above the front door chimed six or seven times while I was in the women's locker room changing into my gear— leggings, sports bra, Nikes and four-ounce MMA gloves, pink and black. With a few deep, nasal breaths, I told myself to focus, to clear my mind, to do my job.

There were more women waiting for me than there ever had been on a Wednesday night. There had to be around twenty-five, ranging from teenagers to middle-aged moms. They filled the small mat-covered sparring area to capacity, chatting and stretching their arms and legs. I was about to call for their attention when I noticed, standing in the far corner, two tall men. One wore an all-too-familiar black leather jacket and dark gray denims with long brown hair and piercing blue eyes, and I couldn't help but smile. Adam cocked his head and smiled back.

The guy next to him was about the same height, also had long hair, but his was somewhere between sandy brown and dirty blonde. A denim jacket overlayed a dark, unzipped hoodie over a bright white shirt—I mean, was he not aware it was still warm outside? His black pants were tight and ripped at the knees. A sharp toothpick danced across his lips, flicking the edges of the short-cut beard that lined his chiseled jaw. His dark eyes flashed, his mouth forming a tight smile.

This was Crew. I wasn't all that happy to see him, and less happy to see him alongside Adam. I began weaving my way through the thicket of chatty women toward them when Adam caught my eye, waved me off.

I guess we'll talk later then.

With a sigh, I turned, jogged along the wall, and welcomed all the ladies to self-defense. Tonight was all about close-quarters escapes. "But remember one thing," I said softly. The women edged their faces closer. "No matter what new tricks and techniques you learn here tonight, you're never above kicking a guy in the nuts."

They laughed. A few of them stole awkward glances toward Adam and Crew, but Adam nodded with smiling eyes, tongue firmly in cheek.

I could tell the hour-long session had gone well by the fact that each lady was grinning, drenched and out of breath. That, and also by the full, rich warmth that filled my chest. I had taught them something valuable and, like I often told Tyrese, it felt so good, so fulfilling, that I would've done it for free. As the last of the students filtered out through the front doors and into the night. I gripped each end of the towel slung across the back of my neck and faced the inevitable.

"You're a hell of a teacher," Crew said. His voice matched the ambiance outside the window, dark and low.

"Thanks." I brushed past him and stood next to Adam. "Hi."

"Hey."

"That elbow strike looked nasty," Crew continued. "Bet it hurts."

"Maybe someday you'll find out." I cocked a half grin.

"Don't butter me up, Crew. What's on your mind?" But I already knew what was on Crew's mind. I already knew why he'd been blowing up my phone with blocked numbers for months ever since high school graduation. It was Crew who Adam and I had seen in the Gray that graduation day near the bleachers, when I told Adam about the sign my parents sent me—three knocks on my bedpost, each representing a letter, each letter representing a word. I-L-Y; I Love You.

As it turns out, Adam and I were not the first, and most certainly would not be the last to face the Dark Trials in the Borderlands of Hell to reclaim our sold souls from the demon who took them. Crew was like us. He'd been there and back and pulled his soul from the brink. With one tug of the underworldly weapon he'd earned by conquering his Trials, he could plunge into the Gray and see the other side. Like us, the weapon strapped to his side gave him the ability to tell when something or someone stirred inside the Gray. And apparently there was another one of our kind in town—the girl who had saved me from the demon she called a Reaper. The one who told me to talk to Crew.

I guess I at least owed her that much as a thank you.

"One chance," Crew said, eyes gleaming. "That's all I ask. Come see what we do, then think it over."

I wanted to tell him that he'd already explained to me what 'They' do—more than once—and that for the love of all I was not interested in joining Crew's crew, pun intended. But if I said that, I knew he'd just blow up my phone again in the morning. I checked the time. With two hours before I had to meet Ryan at the restaurant, I sighed, nodded, and told the guys I needed a few minutes to change.

I USUALLY HATED locker room showers. In high school, most girls tried not to look like they were looking, judging, raking over your exposed body for any sign of imperfection. Or maybe that's just how it felt to me, and maybe that's because I had P.E. with Alice and her gaggle of mean girl wannabes. But now, whenever self-defense class ended, the last lady gone and the front door locked tight after hours, I had the showers to myself. Steaming hot water blasted from all six shower heads at once, filling the tiled space with a thick, humid vapor cloud.

It was a little weird knowing Crew and Adam were waiting outside the locker room door. It was also satisfying to know that if Crew tried anything, Adam would be sure to separate his arm bone from its socket. Not that Crew would try anything like that. At least, I didn't think he was the type. If I had to compare Crew to anyone, it would be Adam anyway—stoic, quiet, resolved, principled. And loyal, but not necessarily to people. Loyal to a cause—*the* Cause, with a capital "C." Ever since graduation day when we saw Crew in the Gray next to the bleachers, weapon in hand, he's been trying to recruit me.

"You see," he'd say, "there aren't many of us out there; people who have been through the Dark Trials and made it back. You can pierce the veil. You can see the dark things on the other side and, most importantly, you can destroy them. People like you, like me, like Adam—we have a power almost no one else has. And with great power…"

You'd better believe I gave him so much crap for trying to use the quote from Spiderman against me. And besides, I truly, honestly was not interested in joining his merry band of demon hunters. Especially now that I've finally started to get my feet under me. Is it too much to ask for a normal life? Or, at least normal-*ish*. I already told him I'd slay any demon that crosses my path, which for some reason has happened more and more frequently over the last few weeks.

I wonder what's up with that…

Why else would Crew be here? It can't be solely to recruit me and Adam to join Crew's Crew—I really should trademark and copyright that. Plus, Adam already joined. At least that's what he told me this morning and I can't blame him. I mean, it's Adam after all, and joining a secret group of demon hunters is right up his ally. But you'd think Crew would get a clue after roughly five thousand 'noes' from me. And now there's another one like us in town—black leather badass chick, and I mean that sincerely. The way she carried herself, like it was her against the world and the world didn't stand a chance...

Post-shower, I wiped steam droplets from one of the mirrors, pulled up my hair and applied a little makeup before stepping out to find the boys right where I'd left them, holding the wall up in the corner near the entrance. A quick glance at my phone showed a text from Tracy with a picture of Em and Scarlett, arms around each other in front of their camp cabin with a caption that read, *'They're going to have so much fun!! XO.'* I smiled, tried to ignore the heart pangs, and slipped the phone into my back pocket.

"I hope this is quick," I said, approaching the boys. "I have a..."—a quick, awkward glance at Adam— "something I have to get to, tonight."

"Shouldn't take too long," Crew said. We stepped out into the darkening evening. I pressed the metal door firmly shut behind us and keyed the lock.

"Lead the way, then."

We piled into Crew's Jeep, which looked less like a Jeep and more like a matte black, jacked up, four-by-four monster truck. The knobby tires alone topped out just above my waist level. The engine rumbled to life and probably caused a minor earthquake somewhere. I slid across the slick leather back seat and settled on the driver side behind Crew. Instead of riding shotgun, Adam slid into the back next to me. Crew peeled off the curb and drove toward... well, wherever we were headed.

"How far are we going?" I half-shouted over the engine's roar.

"Not far," Crew said, and the way he eyed me in the rearview sent a thin, cold shiver down my spine. Since the Trials, I never liked the feeling that things were outside my control. Moments like these made me uneasy. Adam tapped my knee, leaned toward me.

"Hey, I hope that my being here doesn't add any pressure or anything. You don't have to join."

"I know," I said. In fact, I was very glad that he was there with me. And the fact that his hand rested on my knee was... nice.

"And if you feel uncomfortable during any of this, just say the word," he continued. "We'll bolt. No problem." I smiled and nodded, rejecting the urge to slip my palm beneath his and weave our fingers together. I still had a boyfriend, after all. At least for a couple more hours.

Streetlights drifted away as we reached the outer edge of the city limits. Houses became more scarce, more spread apart.

"So, where exactly is this thing you guys want to show me?" But before Adam could answer, Crew pulled the Jeep onto a gravel driveway and cut the engine, then placed one hand on the back of the passenger seat and turned to us.

"Both of you need to be on your guard here," he said. "I don't expect we'll run into anything we can't handle, especially with three of us, but don't hesitate to shout for another's attention if things start to go sideways or you're backed into a corner." With that rousing pep talk, and before I could raise a question, Crew leapt from the driver seat, his boots crunching gravel.

I shot Adam a questioning stare. "What in the world is he getting us into?" But Adam only smirked and shook his head.

"He talks tough. I'm sure it's nothing major. Come on." Adam slid out the door, onto the gravel, and held out a hand that I slapped away with a sly grin.

"I'm good."

"I know."

Tall, dangling tree branches hung over the drive and blocked out most of the moonlight. What light crept through the branches left thin, silvery slashes across the ground. A house loomed at the end of the gravel drive, two stories tall and very old from the looks of it, though the shadows made it hard to tell. Light danced behind the drapes of two windows, both on the second floor, like two yellow eyes above a dark shadowed porch eager to gobble up any approaching strangers.

I didn't like it. At all. And after my earlier run-in with what black leather badass chick called a Reaper, I'd be lying if I said I wasn't nervous. I squelched my nerves with a heavy swallow before we reached the groaning, wooden porch steps.

The front door screeched open before we knocked. A young man, my height with messy dark hair and matching-colored bags under his eyes stepped aside and let us pass wordlessly. Crew thanked him, moved inside, and headed directly up creaking wooden steps to the second floor. Trading glances, Adam and I followed.

Halfway up the dusty staircase, something banged hard against the floor above our heads and I suppressed a yelp. Dust specs floated like snow from the ceiling to the floor below. The young man watched them fall, then met my eyes with what I can only describe as pure desperation.

What have I gotten myself into?

I took a breath, ascended, and met Crew at the top of the staircase. We padded slowly down a dark, narrow hallway. Yellow light crept from beneath one of the doors. Someone behind it was speaking. More than one person. Muffled voices, then a growl, like an animal, followed by more banging.

Crew pressed a flat palm against the door. With one final steely look at both of us, he twisted the knob. The door whined open.

Faint light capered across the room's walls. One small candle set on a small table flickered in the corner, along with two others in the windows—the one's I'd seen from outside. The closet door stood halfway ajar next to a small dresser. There were other people, the voices we'd heard. One was dressed in a dark robe that draped from his shoulders to his ankles, all black except for the small white rectangle set just below his Adam's apple. He held a large, leatherbound book in one hand, a vial in the other. He looked relieved to see us.

Two other people, a man and a woman, stood, holding each other, each gazing down at the bed. On the bed lay a boy who didn't look any bigger or older than Em. He was tied down with leather straps around his wrists and ankles.

All at once I realized exactly what this was, and I did not want to be there.

This was an exorcism.

"Thank you for coming," the man in the black robe—a priest of some kind—whispered. He was older, but not old—maybe fifty-something. He waved the three of us over to the corner. I could not take my eyes off the boy on the bed.

He looked peaceful. Serene, even, like a life-sized doll, except that his chest was rising and falling quickly, his breathing labored. Something dark, fuzzy surrounded him. I knew what that something was. I'd seen it dozens of times. The woman—his mom, I guessed—buried her face into the man's chest who stood tall, holding her. His eyes met mine. I quickly looked away.

"It's not often we have to call you in," the priest whispered. He draped his arms around Adam and Crew like he was about to call a very important fourth down play in the huddle. He even smiled, which seemed wholly inappropriate given the circumstances. "I'm glad you could get here on such short notice."

"We are too," Crew said. "Always happy to help." He nodded at Adam, then more slowly at me. I realized that all three men were looking my direction, apparently waiting for a reply for some reason.

"Yeah," I said softly, then cleared my throat. "Happy to help." Whatever that meant. But it was good enough for the priest, who broke the huddle and spoke a little louder as he re-approached the bed.

"Mister and Missus Ramirez," he said, spreading his hands,

"these are the specialists of whom I spoke to you about. We're very glad to receive their assistance whenever we can."

They took in the sight of us. I mean, if I were told that the three of us were "specialists" of any kind, I would've looked just as skeptical as the Ramirezes. By the looks of us, we were just a few newly minted adults wearing, in my case, street clothes, and in Adam and Crew's case, borderline goth chic.

"If you would," the priest continued, sidling close to the boy's parents, "please bow your heads with me in prayer."

The second they bowed their heads, the boy released a dark, guttural growl that shook my bones. His small frame yanked on the leather straps, lifting the bedposts and slamming them to the ground. A whimper came from either his mother or father—I couldn't tell which—before they wrapped their arms around each other, lowered their heads, and prayed aloud.

The priest glanced at us, nodded, then joined the Ramirezes in prayer.

Crew turned to me and Adam, then reached for his thigh. Adam followed his lead. I took the cue and wrapped my palm around the invisible hilt of my sword. Simultaneously, we pulled our weapons and dove into the Gray.

The scene that greeted us was vapid and bleak. No fewer than six different demons surrounded the bed, looming over the boy. Two were attached by the mouth—if it was a mouth underneath those midnight hoods—to either side of the boy's neck. The others slowly leaned inward, a pack of black wolves licking their chops above a wounded juvenile deer.

"Hate to interrupt," Crew said. All six of their inky hoods whipped in our direction. "Fun's over. It's about time you all head back to wherever in Hell you came from."

One demon in particular stood tall next to the boy's head. It must've been the one in charge, because it hissed and growled in a way that, if I had to guess, sounded like it was giving orders to the others. My guess was confirmed when the ringleader stood back as the others charged, screeching, robes flapping.

We formed a phalanx—Crew in the middle with Adam and me on his left and right. It didn't take long to realize that the demons charging weren't made of the same stuff as the one I'd met outside the gym. These were the standard, run-of-the-mill parasites that preyed on the weak and vulnerable—the one's I've grown fond of demolishing over the last year. Hateful heat rose in my chest, and with a roar I slashed through the middle of the demon closest to me and sent it to Hell in a flash of glittering, golden light.

It felt good. Really good.

I took my time with the next one. It hurled itself, arms flailing toward my shoulders. I ducked. It flew past me in a rush of gray air. Just as it turned, I landed a heavy front kick right where a normal person's sternum would hang, knocking it backward, then shoved my blade deep into the recesses of its hood. It hit, then went through, something solid. One dog-whistle scream before it folded in on itself and exploded into a billion embers.

I realized my cheeks hurt from smiling.

Adam and Crew simultaneously slashed through two demons when I first noticed Crew's weapon—some kind of double-sided dagger with bright blades that curved like licking flames on either side. He spun it like a rock star drummer spins his sticks after a fast song, crowd screaming. We caught each other's gaze. He nodded, grinning, impressed. The sound of metal grating against bone ripped our eyes back toward the bed where the last, lone demon loomed. Out of its long sleeve slid a craggy blade, not much different from Malum's that day on the angry mountain.

So, you must be a Reaper.

My beating heart was blood in the water, the Reaper a shark. It leaped, flew through the air, the point of its blade aimed for the thrumming bullseye inside my heaving chest.

I fanned my sword between us and knocked the Reaper's blade off course, then slashed toward its chest. It dodged, floated backward, assumed a wide stance and raised its blade.

'Don't ever try to take on a Reaper on your own,' the black leather badass chick had told me. But when I glanced to my right and left, I saw Adam white knuckling his dagger and watching intently, and Crew who took a step back, holding his double-bladed weapon at his side. Before I could scream, "Well, aren't you going to help me out here!" the Reaper lunged again.

Our blades clanged, slid off each other, then clanged again as the Reaper advanced, intent on slicing me into ribbons. My back hit the wall so hard I was sure it would leave a dent in reality. The Reaper swung for my neck and I dropped, rolled, then slashed upward and through where the Reaper's arm would be —a move I brought with me from the Borderlands. A sucking sound, but I wanted one more piece of the Reaper before the inevitable. Quickly, I rose and plunged the end of my blade into the void where no heart had ever beaten. The Reaper dissolved in a flash of golden embers which floated slowly to the floor and burned away.

Crew's slow claps reverberated through the Gray, But I ignored him. I wheeled on Adam, white hot. "The Hell was that! Where were you? Why didn't you back me up?"

Adam's patented half-cocked grin split open. "Come on. You know I would've stepped in if things got too hairy. You didn't need my help."

"Had to make sure you were made of the right stuff," Crew began before I shifted from Adam and pointed my ire, along with a middle finger, at his smug face.

"What," I said, "so this was some kind of test?"

"No," Crew said so calmly that it raked my nerves. "Adam here has always given your skills high praise. Just wanted to see you in action myself is all. Like he said," Crew motioned toward Adam, "if it got too serious with the Reaper, we would've stepped in. You didn't need help. Pretty damn impressive if you ask me."

I realized I was huffing like a bull about to charge and forced myself to draw in a long breath. "A little heads up would've been nice." I turned back to Adam, leveling my sword's pointed end dangerously close to his chest. "You should know better than to piss me off."

He nodded and reached for my shoulder, but when I backed up, he ran the hand through his hair with a wince.

"Well, let's see how this turns out, shall we?" Crew held his open palm out toward the boy on the bed. I settled, nodded, and each of us returned our weapons to their sheathes.

The world snapped from whooshing gray to darkened color. The priest and the boy's parents stood near each other, heads bowed in prayer. I shot Crew a *what now?* glance, and his return nod said to *be patient and watch*. Half a minute passed in awkward silence. Then, the boy moved.

He coughed, then sucked in air like it was the first time he'd ever tasted it. His eyes fluttered open. "Momma?"

The boy's mom carefully crumbled into a heap of emotion onto her boy. The look on his dad's face rivaled a blind man's first sight. He looked to the Priest, to the three of us, then curled around the bed and pulled all of us into an awkward embrace.

"Thank you," the boy's dad managed, sobbing into the Priest's collar. "I don't know what you did but thank you. Thank you." The Priest held the man at arm's length and nodded with a smile.

Crew began unclasping the boy's ankles. Adam worked off the wrist cuffs. The boy, delirious, asked, "Momma, what happened?" But the boy's mother couldn't keep from sobbing long enough to answer. She pulled her son into the warmth of her breast.

The young man who had let us through the front door bolted into the bedroom. "He's okay? He's okay!" Then joined his mom on the bed.

"We will leave you now," the Priest said to the father. "Please call me tomorrow with an update on his status."

Mister Ramirez took the Priest's hand in both of his. "I will. How can I thank you?"

"Don't thank me," the Priest said. "Thank the Lord." A single tear glimmered in the lamplight as it rolled down Mister Ramirez's cheek. He turned, taking each of our hands in his, shaking and thanking. It was only then that I truly realized what we had done.

His boy had been oppressed by six demons, including one bad Reaper. There was nothing he could do. He needed a miracle. Would Mister Ramirez have sold his soul to the Reaper if it meant saving his boy? Would his mom, or his brother?

I already knew the answer.

But now, his family would never know the absolute haunting horror that comes with trading their soul for someone's life or losing their son to madness.

We saved him.

We saved all of them.

Crew clapped Adam on the shoulder and motioned his head toward the door. "Time to go."

"Thank you," the boy's mother managed between hitching sobs. "Thank you."

OUTSIDE, the air was crisp, clean, light. The gravel crunched under our feet as we made our way back to Crew's Jeep, each of us internalizing what had just happened. Well, at least that's what I was doing—sifting through competing emotions as the adrenaline burned off.

"I'm a little jealous of your weapon, Crew," I said. "Classic story. Give a woman one blade to do the work of a man who needs two…" I winked. Adam held back a laugh. Whatever his quick response was going to be, Crew smiled and bit his tongue instead.

Smart guy.

"It's called a haladie," Crew said. "And thanks. I'm pretty

fond of it." Behind us, the front door creaked open and the Priest called for us to wait.

"Be right back," Crew said, signaling for Adam and me to hang tight. He met the priest halfway between the Jeep and the house. They exchanged muffled words that I couldn't quite make out, then the Priest handed Crew something. They shook hands, the Priest headed back into the house and Crew headed back toward us tapping something against his open palm.

"Hop in," he said to me in passing, then climbed into the driver seat.

"Are you taking me home?"

"After one more stop." When I tried to protest, he added, "It'll be very quick. I swear."

Adam and I slid into the back seat just as Crew cranked his engine, then he pulled out of the gravel drive and onto the sparsely lit road and headed the opposite direction of the way we came. I knew better than to ask where we were going, knowing I'd only be tossed a meaningless filler phrase like, '*You'll see.*'

"So, Hannah." My eyes met Crew's in the rearview mirror, his flashing in intervals with each passing streetlight. "What did you think?"

I wasn't sure whether I knew the answer to that question yet. Still working it all out in my head. The way he asked the question though, was like he'd asked how I liked a horror movie we'd just finished.

"Is that what you... your group does, then? Fights demons? Because you know I do that already. There's not a demon that crosses my path that doesn't get to meet the edge of my sword."

He smirked at that. "That's part of it, yes. But tonight was just a sample." Normally hard as stone, his gaze softened in the rearview. "We do a lot of good in whatever little corner of the world we're called to, Hannah. I hope you could see that."

I could see that. I had to admit that even if whatever Crew's gang of demon hunters really did was still shrouded in mystery,

I felt satisfied at having helped that family back there. Especially knowing how it could've turned out if we hadn't shown up to take out the demon trash. Thinking back to the sullen looks on their faces, those demons had to have been tormenting that family for who knows how long. Weeks? Months?

And what did Crew mean about being called to different corners of the world? It's not like I could up and leave if I decided to join. I'm finally getting my feet under me. Life is finally turning a corner. I have a job I like and that I can't just leave it all whenever demon duty calls. And that's without even mentioning Em—there's no way I would ever leave her just to help them off a few demons.

But Adam already joined. Does that mean he'll be leaving me? Leaving us? A strong hand gripped my heart and squeezed.

Crew tossed the thing the Priest had handed him into Adam's lap. It was a white envelope, bulging to the point of ripping at the seams. Adam slowly pulled open the top tab.

"Is that…" I began, but with only the dull orange flashes of passing streetlights to see, it was hard to tell exactly what was tucked inside the envelope. When Adam pulled out its contents, my breath caught. He fanned through a stack of newly minted one-hundred-dollar bills. I mean, there had to be a few *thousand* dollars stuffed into that envelope; more cash than I had ever seen before in one place. If Adam was surprised to see it, he didn't show it.

"Hannah can have my third," Crew said. "She more than earned it." Adam though, knowing me and anticipating my response, simply glanced up at me with steepled eyebrows.

"Where did this money come from?" I demanded. "It better not've come from that family. That's wrong and I will never—"

"It's not from the family," Crew interrupted. I turned back to Adam and found him smiling, sympathetic, like he'd been through this conversation once already but was letting me work it out for myself. "Churches and other organizations all over the world understand the value of what we do," Crew continued.

"Ridding the temporal world of demons is no small thing, and they gladly pay for our... very unique set of skills."

If I had to guess, I'd say there was five or six thousand dollars in that envelope. Crew offered me his third, so that would mean three or four thousand dollars—more money than I've ever handled, and all for about fifteen minutes of pretty enjoyable work if I'm being honest. The money thing still nagged at me, though. Something still felt wrong about taking money for saving that mother's son. Then again, that Reaper gave me a pretty good run. Plus, wasn't ridding the world of dark, bad, demonic things the mission of every religion? As for return on investment, I'd say this envelope was full of money well spent as far as they were concerned.

I suddenly had a clearer understanding of why Adam joined. It was a life-changing opportunity. He'd get to jet-set around while exploding demons *and* getting paid well for it—what could be better than that?

A normal life, maybe; a life far from a world riddled with demons and Reapers. The problem, of course, was that that world seemed intent on finding me wherever I was...

We rode in silence for a while. One question still niggled the back of my brain.

"What would've happened to that little boy if we hadn't shown up?" I asked.

Crew contemplated my question in silence for a few moments. "I'll explain it all inside," he said, then turned into another driveway, this one paved with stamped concrete that led up to a well-lit, big brick house. A few other vehicles—nice ones —littered the drive, including Adam's Harley that stood propped on its kickstand near a three-car garage.

"Home sweet home," Crew said, killed the Jeep's engine and managed a look back. "For now, anyways." Adam's hand met my knee.

"No pressure, Hannah. Really." Our eyes met and I tried to slow my reeling mind. We exited the monster truck and made our way up the drive, up white wooden steps, onto the white wooden wrap-around porch—complete with porch swing— where Crew stood sentinel, holding open what looked to be a solid oak front door.

"Mi casa, su casa," Crew said with a wink. "Come on in."

6

Adam entered first, comfortable, like he'd done it a dozen times. Maybe he had. I tentatively followed. Inside, the house was dimly lit and, from what I could tell, nearly devoid of any furniture. Wide wooden planks striped the floors and creaked underfoot, old yet sturdy. The heavy music coming from somewhere in the house didn't jive with the Victorian fixtures, but I didn't mind. The band rattling the walls was Architects, which I only knew because they were one of Adam's favorites. They had grown on me, too.

The music grew louder as we followed Crew past an ascending staircase and down a long, narrow hallway passing both a sparse living room on the left and a kitchen on the right. Ancient-looking books seemed randomly strewn throughout the house. Some lay open on the floor, others on the stairs and countertops. I ran my fingers along an open page of one that lay precariously on a kitchen countertop's edge. It showed a crude drawing of a horned, fanged, lizard-like creature. A chill crawled up my spine like a spider up web line.

At the back of the house, the hallway opened up into a large, open room framed by high windows. The centerpiece chandelier caught the flames from the crackling corner fireplace and reflected their orange and yellow flickers across the high walls. Beneath the chandelier, a single round table littered with a few twenty-dollar bills. Two people sat on opposite sides of the table, facing each other—one I recognized, and one I didn't. Each glowered at the other over a fanned hand of playing cards.

"Want to turn that down?" Crew asked in the table's general direction.

"Not really." But the girl—the one I'd affectionately nick-named the 'black leather badass chick'—was already reaching for her phone. She tapped it a few times which brought down the Bluetooth speaker's levels.

Crew gestured to the guy sitting opposite from her. Even sitting, I could tell he was tall. Dark skin, dark eyes, and very short black hair was all I could make out other than the fact that his face was screwed up in a grimace. I really hoped for his sake they weren't playing poker.

"Someone I want you to meet," Crew said." Jordan, this is Hannah. Hannah, Jordan."

The guy named Jordan laid down his hand and said, "Fold." The girl across from him grinned, chuckled, then wrapped her hands around the loose bills and raked them to her side of the table. Jordan shot me a gleaming smile which caught me a little off guard, jumped out of his chair and put his hand out. "Good to finally meet you, Hannah. We've heard a lot." We shook.

"Yeah... it's good to meet you too."

Jordan clapped Adam on the shoulder with a nod. "What's up man, you good?"

"Good." Adam nodded back.

"And this," Crew cut in, "is Sloane. I think you two have already met."

Sloane apparently couldn't be bothered to look up from her winnings and instead shot a two-finger salute in my direction. "Hey Reaper girl."

So, she had a nickname for me, too. Fantastic.

"Hey... Sloane. And thanks again, you know, for earlier."

"Don't mention it." Sloane folded the twenties into thirds and stuffed them into her bra strap. She finally looked up, but not at me. Her steely eyes landed squarely on Adam, and the way they widened while the corners of her mouth curled ever so slightly lit a match in the pit of my stomach. I cleared my throat and tried to pretend I hadn't noticed.

Each of them seemed a little older than me, though not by much. Maybe it was the intimidation factor that made them seem older, I don't know. I couldn't help but wonder what the three of them—Crew, Jordan and Sloane—were really doing here in this little Colorado town that didn't have much action or, really, anything going for it. They seemed more out of place here than a priest at an Architects concert.

"This is HQ," Crew said, a single finger circling the air above him to indicate the house.

They each shared a knowing glance, obviously aware of something that I clearly wasn't. Jordan grabbed a couple of folding chairs that had been propped against the corner, unfolded them and pulled them over to the table. Crew, Jordan, Sloane and Adam each took a seat. One remained unoccupied between Jordan and Adam. I wished it was between Adam and Sloane—I didn't like the way Sloane had ever-so-slightly scooted closer to Adam when he took his seat. Crew motioned for me to join them. I did, as I checked my phone.

"I only have a few minutes, guys."

Crew motioned for the envelope still in Adam's hands. Adam slid it across the table. Crew opened it and peeled off a few grand, straightened the bills then slid the stack of hundreds over to me. To be honest, it felt a little like a trap, like the money came with some pretty serious strings attached. I didn't reach for it and kept my eyes squarely on Crew.

"HQ for what?" I asked. Crew pulled in a deep breath and started in.

"You've noticed a spike in demonic activity lately." It wasn't a question, but I nodded. "Stronger demons and... other things... are coming through. There are reasons for that; reasons I can't really get into here and now. But it's steadily gotten worse here, and it'll keep getting worse until we fix the problem."

My eyebrows shot up. "We?"

"Let me back up." Crew leaned forward, placed his large hands on the table. "You know as well as anyone that the veil between this world and the underworld is very thin. Much thinner than most people think. There is a war going on, Hannah; a war for souls that affects every person whether they believe it or not."

The rest of the table nodded in sync, except for Adam. He was trained on me, reading my reactions which I tried to keep from spilling onto my face. If this were a poker game, I didn't want to pull a Jordan.

"There are very few people in the world who can go where we go, who can cross that veil and take the fight straight to the demons and send them back to Hell where they belong."

The Gray.

Sloane leaned back in her chair. Jordan sucked on his teeth and nodded like Crew was preaching the gospel.

"There is a name for people like us," Crew continued.

"Yeah?" I tried to sound casual. "And what name is that?"

"We're the Dantes."

That name sounded so familiar, but I couldn't quite place it. Adam could probably see the wheels turning in my head.

"After Dante Alighieri," he offered. "He wrote—"

But suddenly the answer sparked all at once in the back of my mind and I cut him off. "Dante's Inferno," I said. "About Dante traveling through the seven circles of Hell and returning."

"Nine," Jordan said. "It was nine circles."

Jordan smiled warmly and winked. I cracked and smiled back.

"Dantes," I said. "Because you've gone through Hell and back."

"And so have you," Crew added. He stood, shed his jacket,

revealing three golden rings encircling his left elbow, identical to the golden rings that wrapped around my upper bicep—one ring for each of the Dark Trials completed. Jordan pulled up one sleeve. His rings encircled his forearm, just like Adam's did. In a huff, Sloane fingered one of her black leather jacket sleeves exposing the golden rings encircling one wrist.

Adam and Jordan were both grinning. Sloane looked like she'd rather be anywhere else in the world. "It might not be what you want to hear," Crew said, "but like us, you have unique abilities. Not only are you able to cross the veil between this world and the underworld, but you're a pretty badass fighter. You definitely held your own tonight, and we could really use you."

"Seems like there are plenty of you here," I said, shifting glances between them. "What are you all doing here, anyway? I know you're not from here. This town is too small for me not to have noticed you."

Sloane and Jordan chuckled at that. "I'm from L.A.," Sloane said, "Jordy there is from Seattle." Jordan nodded. "And Crew... where are you from again, grandpa?" she asked with a knowing wink.

Crew rolled his eyes. "Phoenix. And I'm *maybe* five years older than you."

My head swam. "Okay, so... why are you all here, again?"

Crew straightened up. "We go where we're called to go. Usually, where there are some major supernatural issues that need to be fixed."

"Called? Who 'calls' you?"

"There's a governing body," Crew said. "They're called The Ring. They keep their ears to the ground, keep tabs with all the churches and other groups and let us know where we need to be and when. If we're able to go, we go."

"Usually it's pretty quick," Jordan added. "Get there, kick some demon butt, get out."

"'Demon butt?'" Sloan said, scoffing. "You are so adorable, Jordy." Jordan tipped an invisible cap toward Sloane.

"I'm still trying to figure out why you are all *here*, though. In this town. All of you. Is it really necessary to have three..." I snapped my fingers, trying to remember the name...

"Dantes," Adam said.

"Thanks. Is it really necessary to have three Dantes in one little town to deal with one exorcism?"

While Crew, Jordan and Adam were visibly patient, allowing me to work through and process all this new information, Sloane sighed and rolled her eyes. She may have saved me from a Reaper earlier, but she was really beginning to get on my nerves now...

"There are four of us now," Crew said with a nod toward Adam, "and there's more at stake here than one exorcism. A lot more."

"Okay, like what?"

Crew tightened his lips and glanced at the table for a few beats, then spread his hands. "Dantes are obligated to follow a certain code, Hannah, which means there are things that we can discuss only with other Dantes. Unless you decide to join up, like Adam here"—he thumbed in Adam's direction—"you'll just have to trust me." He motioned around the table at the others. "There are some things we can't disclose to you just yet."

I cracked a couple knuckles and rested my elbows on the table. "Other Dantes?" I tried to keep the impatience from lacing my voice, but that was becoming more difficult by the second.

Crew turned his hand over, then gestured for Jordan, Adam and Sloane to do the same. Each of them had the same symbol on their left wrist—the symbol Adam had shown me at my apartment earlier this morning: Two intersecting, opposite-facing chevron arrows slashed through with a horizontal line.

"All Dantes carry this symbol," Crew said. "And until you have it, there are some things we can't tell you."

"Even though I can come and go through the Gray, just like

you?" My voice rose louder than I meant it to, but it was fueled by the rising heat inside me. I didn't like to be strung along, to be kept in the dark. "Even though I slay demons, just like you? Just because I might not want to join your little club doesn't mean the things happening here—whatever they are—don't affect me. They do. Probably more than they affect you, seeing as you will all go back to wherever you came from sooner or later. So why don't you just spill exactly why the hell it is you're all here and we can all be on our way?"

Where I'd expected to see surprise or maybe even anger on the others' faces, there were smiles all around—except for Adam. He knew better. Even Sloane, who made eye contact with me for the first time in a while, wore a tight grin.

"I get it, Hannah," Crew said evenly. "But there's an order to these things. And while we no doubt appreciate all of your contributions and your willingness to fight based solely on your own passions, there are curtains that can only be peeled back for those of us who take an oath to become a Dante."

I clenched my jaw. This was going nowhere, and I had places to be. I scraped my chair across the floor and rose. Adam matched my movements, but the others remained seated, relaxed.

"And if I don't take an oath to become a Dante?"

Crew's smile never faded. "Then we part as friends."

"Keep in mind," Sloane chimed in coolly, "there are more and more Reapers out there by the day." *Don't ever try to take on a Reaper on your own*, she didn't have to say. For the first time, I got the impression that, despite the hard exterior and body language, she wanted me to join up just as bad as Crew did.

Maybe I was the one with the leverage here...

I nodded and scanned the faces around the table one final time, then pulled in a breath. "I need time to think it over."

Crew nodded, eyes narrowed.

"Come on," Adam said, breaking the tension. "I'll take you home." He wheeled around the table and placed a hand on my back, leading me through the narrow hallway and out the front door. Before he shut the door behind us, Crew called out, "Hurry back, Black. It's already time to head out."

"Will do," Adam called back, then winced as he met my questioning gaze.

———————

BEFORE HE HAD the chance to answer my silent question, I said, "Let me guess; It's classified. If you tell me, you'd have to kill me because unlike you *Dantes*"—I gestured vaguely toward the house as we descended the porch steps—"I'm not special like you're special." Adam didn't deserve to be the target of all my confused ire, but alas, there was nobody else walking next to me.

"It's not like that," he said.

"Oh, really?" I said as he placed his helmet in my waiting hands. "Then where exactly are you heading out, tonight? Secret demon hunting mission, I suppose?"

"No. I don't know. Maybe."

Oh, thank you so much for clearing that up for me, 'Black,' is what I wanted to say, but bit my tongue. Why was I even mad? And why was I mad at him? Maybe because facing and beating the Dark Trials and entering the Gray and sending demons back to the underworld was *our thing*. We were unique, special. Of course, there had to be more than just us two who had beaten the Dark Trials but... but why in the world did they have to come here? Why did they have to barge their way into our thing and...

And take Adam from me?

In the midst of all these thoughts thundering across my brain, I realized I was breathing fast and heavy. Adam rested a gentle hand on my shoulder, his face a mask of sympathy.

"I know it's a lot to take in," he said. "And... I don't know, maybe I should've talked to you and gotten your thoughts before jumping in, myself. I'm sorry about that. But I couldn't pass up the opportunity to fight back against the darkness that took hold of us and is trying to take hold of so many others. And to be able to do that *and* not worry about holding down a nine-to-five? Like I said... I couldn't pass it up." Like usual, Adam's deep voice served as ointment to my inner burning.

"Don't apologize," I said, releasing a wave of tension through a long sigh. "You did what's right for you, and I'm happy for you. I mean that. It's just... it's a lot."

He nodded knowingly, tapped my shoulder.

"Come on," I said, "I've got a... thing to be to and you've got a... thing to be back for." Adam released a breathy chuckle, handed me his helmet.

"Yeah, best not to keep Sloane waiting." I meant it sarcastically, but by the way Adam's eyes widened, it was like I hit a darts bullseye from a hundred feet. "What?"

"That thing I'm doing tonight," he said. "It's with Sloane."

And... the hot fire returned to my guts. I flashed to the moment when Adam and I entered HQ and Sloane gave Adam that look, like she was a hungry wolf and Adam was a steak dinner. I slammed the helmet on and snapped the black visor shut.

"What?" Adam asked.

"Just drive."

Resigned, Adam straddled the bike and ignited it. The engine's heavy rumble matched my own inner growling as I slid onto the back. Adam throttled, weaved through the other cars on the driveway, turned onto the road and bolted for home.

IT TOOK the entire ride back to my apartment to cool myself off. When Adam killed the engine, I remembered what I'd been burning to tell him ever since he came over this morning to say goodbye to Em but never had the chance. Even now, it had to be quick or I'd be late for my last supper with Ryan. The thought cinched my nerves. I pulled Adam's helmet off and raked fingers through my wind-whipped hair.

"Do you ever dream about your time in the Borderlands?" I asked. He seemed to ponder that for a few moments as we ascended the steps toward my front door.

"All the time," he said softly. I dove deeper.

"Do you ever have dreams—memories—about the Borderlands that… aren't your own memories?"

Adam halted on the top step and turned to me. The way his jaw muscle rippled told me the answer was 'yes.'

"Do you?" he asked.

With a deep breath, I launched into the quick summary version of last night's dream, about nearly being killed by a manticore yet somehow knowing that if I could just cut off its stinger, it would die. "What's even stranger," I said, "is that I didn't have my sword with me. I had your dagger. And even that's not the weirdest part."

Even in the dim moonlight I could tell most of the color had drained from Adam's face. He raised his eyebrows, urging me onward. After a quick glance around to make sure the space was devoid of neighbors, I leaned in.

"I had your dagger, *and* I was in your body. It was like I was experiencing your actual memory. But… I mean, did I? Is that even possible?"

Adam took a few moments to mentally gather himself. I could almost see his inner wheels turning as he swallowed, opened his mouth to say something, then shut it again.

"What is it?"

"I…" he began, shifting his feet. "A few nights ago, I had a dream like yours. I was bolting through the forest, away from the door and chest and toward one of the three pillars. I ran up the front side of a hill. The back side was covered in this black, glassy rock—really sharp, like giant arrowheads."

Obsidian Hill. I couldn't believe it, but he was describing Obsidian Hill.

"I tried to step down the hillside carefully," he continued, "but the ground shifted and suddenly I was caught in an avalanche of sharp, black rock. One cut my arm open. When I finally rolled to the bottom, I panicked because I had lost my…"

"Your sword," I said. "*My* sword."

Adam nodded. We locked in on each other. "And you were…"

"I was in your body," Adam finished. "I'm guessing that's something that happened to you while you were down there?"

"My first Trial," I said, "before I got to the hellhound's cave."

We stood silent for a few heartbeats, and I could tell by the droop in Adam's shoulders that he'd been thinking about his dream—my memory—for a while but wasn't sure how or whether to bring it up. To be fair, I was a little nervous that I'd sound crazy bringing up my dream—his memory.

"What do you think it means?" he asked, which caught me off guard. Usually, I was the one asking questions, and Adam almost always had the answers.

"I have no idea," I said. "And that's not the first time it has happened to me, either."

"Same." Then after a moment, Adam smiled. "The way you used that poisonous tree sap to blind the hellhound was…," then he brought his fingers together to make a chef's kiss motion. An embarrassed grin pressed against my warming cheeks. I turned and slid my key into the door then twisted it open.

"Since we're being all open and honest about stuff, there's one other thing," I said. "I think something is up with Em."

Adam drew his eyebrows together. If there was one person who could rival my over-protective leanings toward Em, it was Adam. "What is it? What's wrong?"

"Nothing major," I offered. "At least, I don't think it's anything major. I think she's a sensitive or something."

Adam's stony demeanor didn't change.

"I mean, I think she can see things without crossing to the other side. Kind of like how you and I can see that fuzzy darkness hanging over someone when there's a demon attached to them. Just... the way she acts sometimes, or some of the things she says... I don't know."

Adam's features softened. "I guess that shouldn't surprise us. She was touched by a demon too when you traded your soul for her life. Maybe all of that left some residual effects on her."

"Yeah. I've had the same thoughts." I felt a sudden urge to jump into the old Civic and rush to Camp Sego Lily just to check on her. Or I could call the cheap burner cell I gave her, but that would probably end in the phone getting confiscated and then I'd *really* be worried, since Em wouldn't have any way to reach me on her own if she needed me.

Take a breath, Hannah. She's fine.

"You good?" Adam asked, pulling me back to reality.

Deep breath.

"Good. Just, you know... worried about her." I pushed the door fully open and took a step inside. "Sorry, I've got to get going. But can I call you later?"

Adam tried to hide a smile as he took one step down the stairs, but then both of us seemed to simultaneously remember that he'd be on a super-secret demon hunting mission with Sloane. I sighed, tried not to scowl.

"If I don't answer," Adam said, "then I'll call you back as soon as I can."

"Okay. And hey," I said and took a step toward him, "please be safe. Promise me."

The corners of Adam's lips pinched together.

"I promise."

7

Forty minutes after Adam left my apartment, I pulled up to Alfonzo's feeling guilty, and not only for showing up late. So much craziness had happened today that I hadn't had time to stew over Ryan and how I might let him down softly, which in hindsight is probably a good thing since I tend to over-think situations like this. Still, my heart thumped like a drum and my stomach felt like it had been filled with a million overanxious butterflies.

The maître d'—I think that's what the hostess is called in a fancy restaurant, right?—welcomed me and led me to a table for two in the corner. Sounds of clinking silverware and classical music flowed softly, muffled by the fine, cream-colored linen tablecloths draped carefully over each table. Even though I had changed out of my street clothes and pulled up my hair, I suddenly felt very underdressed as I took in the other patrons in their suits and dresses. At least I wasn't wearing a pirate costume this time though. The memory of last year's Halloween night—Ryan dressed as a zoot suit gangster, Jake as Dusty Henderson from Stranger Things and Gabby as an Egyptian goddess—made me both chuckle out loud and fill me with a sense of longing.

I missed Gabby. She would've known how to handle this little situation. I had planned on calling her before all of this but… well, between clothes and makeup, it was a mad dash.

"Your table, ma'am."

Turns out, I need not have felt guilty about showing up a few minutes late, because Ryan hadn't made it to the restaurant yet, either.

"Thank you." I sat across from Ryan's empty chair, fiddled with the very real silver silverware, and checked my phone. He was almost fifteen minutes late, which was not at all like Ryan. While I sat there, waiting and avoiding judgmental glances from the other patrons, I felt a sudden, sharp pain, like someone was jabbing a sewing needle against the bottom of my stomach. The needle became a knife. The knife became a sword. I suppressed a gasp, bit my bottom lip and gripped my midsection. And then…

It was gone. As quickly as it had come, the pain disappeared.

Nerves, maybe? I told myself it had to be, even though something in the recess of my mind told me pain like that didn't come from being nervous. It came from… somewhere else. Still gripping my stomach, I swallowed hard and exhaled slowly.

"Your table, Sir."

"Thanks." Ryan slid into the seat across from me, hands raised in the surrender position. "I'm so sorry. I had this thing come up and I couldn't get away in time. You're mad, I can tell."

I wasn't mad, but I wasn't surprised to hear that I probably looked mad, or at least uncomfortable. I tried to wipe the lingering grimace from my face with a smile and a, "No, no. Actually, I just got here a couple minutes ago. I was afraid you would be the one here waiting for me."

Ryan grinned, stood, wrapped me in a warm hug, then returned to his seat without bothering to ask why I was late, and if everything was all right—also not at all like Ryan. My eyes fell to the large bandage wrapped around his right forearm that I'd noticed during our walk to the gym this morning. That time, when I'd asked him about it, he snapped at me for asking and said it was nothing to worry about. I had been so distracted by sending Em off to camp and trying to formulate words to break up with him right then and there that it hadn't really hit me how strange he'd acted. Ryan was not—*is* not—himself.

His eyes were bloodshot, like he'd just pulled an all-nighter, yet his mannerisms were those of an adrenaline junkie who'd just B.A.S.E. jumped off a skyscraper and straight into Alfonzo's. Usually so quick to strike up a conversation or ask me how my day had gone, Ryan just stared into the beyond, fiddling with his knife and obviously stewing heavily over something. He was there, sitting across from me, but he wasn't present.

I took a careful look around his edges. It would explain quite a bit of his strange behavior if he had a demon attached to him, but I didn't see any sign of that dark, fuzzy outline usually floating around the oppressed. I pulled my sword hilt anyway and shifted into the Gray.

Nothing. No demon, no dark matter enveloping him, sucking out his energy or whispering into his ear. Ryan was a gray statue, his eyes focused on the knife in his hand, jaw set hard enough to ripple that small ball of muscle under his ear. I turned slowly, surveyed the rest of the restaurant. As far as I could tell, no other patrons had brought any demons to dinner, either.

I sheathed my sword and re-entered the world of clinking silverware and classical music.

"Everything okay?" I asked. It nearly startled him. He cocked his head to the side questioningly.

"I don't know," I said. "You seem a little... off, I guess. Like something's on your mind. Is something bothering you?" Again, my eyes drifted toward the large bandage covering the bottom of his forearm. Ryan noticed my gaze, slid his arm beneath the table and tightened his lips before opening his mouth to speak, then closed it again. Shifting in his chair, he tried again.

"I—"

"What may I get the lovely couple to drink, tonight?" A perky young woman had materialized next to our table and looked between us expectantly, leatherbound order book in hand, pen at the ready.

"Uh," I cleared my throat, "just a water for me, thanks."

"Same," Ryan said, low and soft. Without bothering to write our drink order down, she left with a tight, insincere smile. I turned back to Ryan and leaned in, eyebrows raised. He released a weighty exhale.

"Is it school?" I asked. "Are you nervous about leaving?"

"What do you want out of life, Hannah?" He asked abruptly.

Not what I was expecting. The question took me aback, literally. My chairback creaked, and if Ryan noticed the confusion on my face, he didn't mention it. He only stared, bloodshot eyes unblinking.

"I guess…" I started, but wavered. He had asked the one question I was trying to avoid even asking myself. Do I want to be a Dante? Or do I want a normal life, or at least as normal as I could get? What do I *want*?

Ryan still stared.

"I guess I want to have peace of mind that whatever I decide to do with my life is the right choice," I said. And it was true. "I'm starting to think that that's too much to ask for, though. Seems that kind of peace of mind only comes with hindsight." My gaze had wandered, drifting down. I was talking more to myself than to Ryan. I looked up. Ryan hadn't moved; hadn't even shifted an eyelash. My nerves began tightening up again.

"What about you?" I asked. Finally, his eyes narrowed a little. A small bump ran along the inside of his upper lip as he raked his tongue across his teeth, lips sealed shut.

Wait. Something sparked at the back of my mind. Was he… was Ryan about to break it off with *me*? Is that why he'd been acting so strange? I'd been so introspective that I hadn't even thought of that possibility until now. Honestly, I wouldn't blame him—I've probably seemed so standoffish with everything that's been going on. And selfishly… well, it would make things much easier for me if I wasn't the one having to end things. Ugh, I felt so guilty all of a sudden. A heavy pit formed in the bottom of my stomach.

"I want so much more than what this little town can offer, you know?" Ryan said, and suddenly his voice was full and strong, a little too loud for a quiet restaurant. He raised his bandaged arm from underneath the table, balled a fist. "I want people to respect me, to know that I've made it. I want to leave my mark on the world."

The pit in my stomach sank deep as I glanced around uncomfortably.

Ryan was ambitious. He always had been. If I had to peg anyone with the ability to get out of this town and leave their mark on the world, it would be him. Yet, as he spoke, I suddenly felt uneasy. But maybe it wasn't the way he spoke at all.… Maybe it was the cocktail of anxiety and newly-formed spark of pain blooming in the pit in my stomach—that same sharp, needle-like jab I'd felt before Ryan arrived.

"But yeah," Ryan continued, and I willed myself to focus on his words. "Something has been bothering me lately. It's been on my mind a lot." Ryan combed one hand through his sandy hair, then slid his arm across the tablecloth, took my hand in his, his serious face crumbling into a crooked smile. "Hannah. I want you with me, every step of the way."

Oh… Oh no. This was sounding less like a breakup and more like a…

I suddenly wanted to puke.

"Ryan, I—"

"I know, I know. Your sister," he said, which wasn't fair. Em wasn't some excuse for me not to run off with him. She was my life. She came first, before everything, always, and he knew that.

The needles in my stomach became a pile of charcoal, and his words were lighter fluid. I swallowed hard, but before I could gather the right words, he plowed onward.

"We've already talked about trying the long-distance thing, and look, we could do that. It's not like Boulder is all that far away, anyway—you could come see me all the time and I could come see you, but... well, what if you and Em come with me, instead?"

That burning charcoal in my stomach became a five-alarm fire. He must've noticed the heat rising to my face because he added, "Hannah, it's okay. You don't need to worry. I will take care of you; of both of you. I just... really want you with me." He squeezed my hand lightly, leaned in closer. "I love you, Hannah."

I tried desperately to ignore the blooming pain engulfing my insides as he spoke. His eyes, despite the bloodshot, sparkled with sincerity. I had to remind myself that even if he'd been acting strange, even if we've slowly drifted apart, it was still Ryan sitting across from me—that sweet boy who made me feel less alone in the world when I needed it most. I pulled my hand from his grasp and tried to gather myself, tried to breathe. "Ryan, listen..."

Ryan leaned in, but just as he did, the fire inside me solidified into a thousand thumb tacks. All of their pointed ends jabbed into my guts at once, stealing my breath. I gripped my midsection with one hand, gripped the edge of the table with the other, and tried desperately to hold in a scream. I doubled over.

"Hannah? Are you choking?" The table rattled. "Hannah!"

But I wasn't choking. I wasn't breathing, either, because I knew somehow that if I sucked in breath it would act like oxygen to a flame and the pain would grow and grow until it consumed my entire being...

Then, blackness. But not unconsciousness. A dark room. Cold. Not empty.

Screams. But not mine. Not my body. Deeper.

Crude straps wrapped around wrists and ankles. Mine?

Hot breath. From above me. More than one.

People?

No.

Soft light burned away the dark room.

String music covered the screams that were not mine but came from me.

One hand around my wrist, one hand on my back.

"Hannah," a voice said. I opened my eyes. Ryan knelt above me. Another man, much older, crouched beside me.

"Ma'am, can you speak?" the older man asked. "Tell me what you're feeling. I'm a doctor. I can help."

I realized I was on the floor. The pain in my stomach subsided, but lingered. With the doctor's help, I sat up, then managed to get to my feet. Every single eye in the restaurant was trained on me, and suddenly I flashed back to that moment in English class when neon words announcing *YOU DIE* flew off the chalkboard and drifted toward me. Malum was behind that.

Deep down, I knew something just as sinister was behind what had happened just now.

"Ma'am?" the doctor repeated.

"I'm okay," I managed. "I'm sorry. I must've fainted. I don't know…"

"Ma'am, you may need to lie back down—"

"I'm good. Really."

I gathered my things from the table, kept my head down and slowly made my way out the front door, trying to outrun all the thoughts that trailed after me like moaning ghosts. I was most of the way to my car before Ryan caught up, took me by the arm.

"Hannah, what happened in there? What was that?"

The pain began blossoming again, slowly.

"I don't know," I said, because I didn't. "I can't explain." I couldn't. "I just need to get home."

"I don't think you being alone is a great idea," Ryan said, then tried to pull me into an embrace, but instead his chest met my open palms as I stepped back. His brow drew together. "What, Hannah?"

"I need to go." I needed to call Adam. Something told me he'd know what it all meant. I turned toward my car, and Ryan made no attempt to stop me. He only stared as I pulled out of the parking lot and sped away.

8

Twice I had to pull over and scream away the pain. I barely made it up the stairs and into my apartment before collapsing onto the cold kitchen floor, writhing. Once the pain again subsided, I reached for my phone and held down the center button until it chimed.

"Call Adam," I said between panting breaths.

"Calling Adam Black," the robotic female voice responded.

There were no rings. Instead, the call went straight to Adam's voicemail. "Hey, it's Adam," his voice said coolly. "You know what to do."

After the beep, I said, "Adam, call me. Something's wrong." It was all I could manage before the pain began to bloom inside me again.

It came and left in waves for I don't know how long. Hours, and every second I begged for Adam to call me or come to me and make it all go away because, somehow, I knew he could. I called out for him, whether with my voice or only with my mind I couldn't be sure.

As the black sky outside began giving way to the grays and purples of sunrise, something impossible happened. I swear I could feel Adam calling back to me. Not with words, though. It was as if he reached out from somewhere, some other place I couldn't see, and touched me until the pain diminished from harrowing, to dull, to… gone.

For the first time all night, I breathed in deep.

I uncoiled myself and sat up on the kitchen floor where I'd left a pool of cold sweat. Leaning heavily against a lower cabinet, I sucked wind like I'd just finished a marathon. My mind was covered in dense fog, clouding any semblance of sense.

Someone pounded on my door. I nearly jumped out of my skin.

"Hannah? You in there?"

A deep voice.

Adam?

I wrapped a shaking hand around the edge of the countertop and pulled myself upright, hobbled to the door, unlatched the deadbolt, and pulled it open.

Crew, Jordan and Sloane didn't wait for an invitation to come inside. I looked past them expectantly. Adam was not with them.

"Have you heard from Adam?" Crew asked pointedly.

"I… no… what—"

"No phone calls? Nothing?" That was Sloane, who, unlike the other two, looked like she'd been in a fight with a bear and lost. Dried blood hung in drapes below her nose. A nasty, dark half-moon had formed below one eye. Panic rose inside of me where the pain had been.

"Wasn't he with you?" I asked Sloane.

Sloane cracked her neck, broke past me and out the door, slamming it behind her. Jordan sighed and followed after her. Crew took me by the shoulders.

"Adam is missing," he said. "He was taken."

9

C rew's words failed to register in my numb mind. I heard them. I didn't understand them.

"What do you mean, Adam was taken?"

Someone outside—Jordan?—called for Crew. "Hurry up man! We got to go!" Crew turned back and leveled me with a deadly serious stare.

"Hannah," he said. "Something happened last night. We're trying to piece it together. Sloane and Adam were jumped. Sloane made it out, barely, but Adam was taken."

"By who?" My voice cracked and I realized I was desperately gripping Crew's jacket sleeves, feeling like if I let them go, I'd tumble off a cliff. "Who would do that?"

Crew grimaced, and I knew exactly what he was about to say.

"Don't you dare say you can't tell me." I shook him as hard as I could. "Crew!"

"We'll find him," he said impatiently. He tried to lead me toward the living room couch, but I wasn't having it.

Adam was taken.

Adam was... gone.

A cocktail of dread and panic and adrenaline spun my world into a whirlpool.

"No!" I shouted at Crew. "You're not leaving me here. I'm coming with you, and you're going to tell me what happened! It's *Adam* you're talking about and he…" I choked down a sudden onrush of emotion. "He means everything to me."

Crew sighed. Outside, a car horn blared. "There are some things happening right now that you can't know, and I'm sorry that's hard to hear, but—"

"I want to be a Dante." The words flew out of my mouth before my thoughts could catch up to them. I released Crew's jacket sleeves and he took a step back, eyes trained on me.

"I don't think this is the right moment for you to make that decision," he said.

For two full, long seconds, I closed my eyes and focused, tamping down the enormous wave of panic that had washed over me. "I had already made my decision," I said. "I made it last night." Something clicked in the far recesses of my mind, the part that connected with my soul. What I was saying was true, even if it took until this very moment for me to realize it. I met Crew's trained gaze and refused to flinch.

Finally, Crew offered a slow nod.

"All right, then." He walked into the kitchen, pulled out a pen and scribbled on the back of a bill envelope that sat on the countertop. "Address to the HQ house, in case you forgot how to get there." He motioned with a thumb out the front door. "I'll let them know what's going on. I need to make some calls. Meet us there in about half an hour."

I slid the envelope off the counter and stared at the address, fighting the urge to rip the paper in half. "That's not what's important right now," I said, exasperated. "Adam is missing. He's out there somewhere, and we don't have time for—"

"Half an hour," Crew said, then left and shut the door behind him. Through the slatted blinds I saw him jog to his Jeep. Silhouettes of Sloane and Jordan shifted once Crew climbed inside, then Crew started the Jeep and pulled away.

I wanted to scream. So, I did. So hard and so violent that my throat burned with bile. The insane thought that maybe if I just called him one more time, he would answer and tell me where he was and who took him and why this happened and why in the hell they didn't take *Sloane* instead. I scraped my phone off the kitchen floor, pressed the button. It was dead, screen black.

If only I had joined the Dantes yesterday, he would've taken me with him. I could've stopped this.

I should've followed them. Adam and Sloane.

Adam is gone and Gabby is gone and Em. I'd never felt so alone. Not since Mom and Dad died.

I screamed again. This time it sounded like an elongated smoker's cough. It rattled my skull just enough to clear some of the mental fog away. I plugged a charger into my phone and gathered a fistful of dishrag to dry my soaked, hot cheeks.

"Come on," I said, staring hard at the red *charging* symbol on my phone's screen. I dropped the dishrag, rubbed my sweating palms together then brought my hands to my face, wiping away fresh moisture that threatened to spill over my bottom eyelids. What seemed like hours later, my phone finally buzzed to life. With a weighty exhale through a pinhole, I brought up the home screen.

There were three missed calls. All from Crew.

None from Adam.

One text from Ryan.

None from Adam.

I quickly pulled up Adam's contact information and called. Like before, it went straight to voicemail. 'Hey, it's Adam. You know what to do.'

The sound of his voice crushed me.

"Adam…" I said after the beep, on the verge of weeping. "Adam, please. If you get this…" I sniffled and cleared my throat as warm, angry fire burned in my chest. "Adam, you… you promised me you would be careful. You *promised* me!" A few silent seconds passed, and then, "I'm coming to get you." I pressed the red button and barely stopped myself from slinging the phone—charger and all—across the kitchen, shattering it into a million pieces against the wall.

I'm coming to get you.

10

I changed, splashed my face with icy water a few times, then swiped my phone and keys and left for the HQ house. On the way, I texted Tyrese that I'd been up all night sick and wouldn't be into work. Outside, the day was clear, crisp—a morning I would usually enjoy if not for the storm raging inside. A noxious concoction of panic, anger and fear of the unknown brewed and bubbled during the drive through town. I couldn't have cared less whether anyone saw what a lunatic I probably looked like by smacking the steering wheel over and over.

'Adam is missing,' Crew had said. 'He was taken.'

Who could possibly want to take Adam, and what could they want with him? Whoever it was, they'd better pray I don't find them. A horn blared, knocking me back into reality where I had accidentally drifted over a double yellow line. Grimacing, I corrected. The lady I'd nearly run off the road flipped the bird as she shot past. Her face, screwed up in anger, reminded me of the woman who ran *me* off the road last fall. It was after I returned from my first Trial and I had decided to drive to Saint Mark's to visit Em who was lying memory-less in her hospital bed.

In the most literal sense, the lady that ran me off the road that day was possessed. Dark matter floated around her. Hatred lined her bloodshot eyes. She took a lead pipe to my taillights before I peeled away and left her screaming in the wake of my dust.

What if that was who took Adam? Not that lady exactly, but someone with her same condition? Someone possessed?

The thought briefly terrified me before I told myself that, no, it couldn't have been. One possessed person against two Dantes? The demons inside wouldn't have stood a chance.

But what if there were more than one? What if there were ten possessed people?

I swallowed hard and forced myself to breathe and focus on the one thing I could control: getting to the HQ house and getting there fast.

I sped through the suburbs to the outskirts and pulled into the HQ house's long driveway. My heart fluttered when I saw Adam's motorcycle propped on its kickstand near the garage until I realized he and Sloane must've taken her car to wherever they'd gone last night, to do whatever it was he couldn't tell me about. I hated the secrecy, especially from him.

I killed my engine and bounded up the front porch steps and into the front door without knocking. Jordan was propped against a wall in the entryway. He welcomed me with a subtle nod, then cocked his head in a *follow me* motion toward the back room where I'd met him only yesterday.

The pain in my stomach began to manifest again.

"You good?" Jordan asked when he noticed I had stopped following. One hand resting against the hallway wall, I breathed deep and relaxed my core until the pain subsided. I would blame it on the situational stress, except I wasn't aware of the Adam-being-taken situation when the pain first manifested during dinner last night...

"Yeah," I said, then pressed off the wall and followed him into the back room. Crew was bent over the center table, poring over a note pad. Sloane was propped against the fireplace in the corner, looking like she hadn't changed or showered since...

since what? Since she and Adam were jumped? The frustration of not knowing boiled over.

"Tell me what happened. Now." My words were a record scratch. All three Dantes came out of their heads and gave me their attention. Crew cleared his throat and walked across the room, fresh mug of coffee in hand. I had a mind to slap it out of his hand, watch it shatter across the wood floor and tell him I didn't want anything but to know *exactly* what happened last night. Then again, after a brutal all-nighter, some caffeine to slough away the mental fuzz wouldn't hurt. Glaring over the rim, I took a sip, then set the mug on the table. Sloane and Jordan took a seat.

"First things first," Crew said. "Your induction."

"Guys, for hell's sake, we don't have time for—"

"You need to be a Dante if you're going to help us," Crew said, his voice sharp. "Period. Now draw your weapon."

"Do it," Sloane added, reaching over her shoulder. Jordan reached for his waistband. Each of them leveled me with a stone-serious gaze.

"Fine." I pulled my sword as the others pulled their weapons—Crew's a double-bladed long knife called a haladie, Sloan's a black arrow nocked in a sleek black bow, Jordan's a long hatchet. The Gray swirled. I could hear their breathing, their swallows, their grips tightening over weapons. "Now what?"

"Hold out your left wrist," Crew said. It was the same wrist that Malum had branded with three rings, which disappeared one-by-one each time I returned from the Borderlands having beaten a Trial. When I hesitated, Crew added, "You're going to have to trust us going forward. Best to start now."

I held out my wrist.

"You've made this decision of your own free will and choice?" Crew raised his eyebrows.

"Yes."

"Then you will take the oath, like we all have." He scanned the others. "Once done, you will carry with you all of the privileges, along with all of the obligations of a Dante. Do you understand what those obligations are?"

"I think so."

"To fight the Dark at all costs," Crew continued. "Whenever possible, you will answer the call to render your unique services anywhere in the world. You will support your fellow Dantes, and you will answer to the Ring. Do you understand?"

The Ring... What was the Ring again? They're the people in charge... I think...

"Yes," I said, "I understand."

"You'll repeat the oath in Latin. But I'll state the oath in English first, so you understand."

I nodded. Crew's eyes narrowed as he leaned in.

"You'll state your full name, first. And then, 'This oath I take as a warrior of Light: From this moment I shall answer the call to destroy the servants of darkness in all their forms, be they demon, devil or fallen angel. The gates of Hell shall be closed before me, Hell's fires on Earth quenched by my blade. To this, my life is dedicated.'"

The oath's final line rang in my head like a gong. *'To this, my life is dedicated....'* I swallowed hard, looked each Dante in the eye. Each peered back expectantly. It all felt eerily similar to that moment I sold my soul to Malum. I guess, in a way, I was selling my soul to them, or to the cause, but I brushed that thought away before it stuck.

"Okay," I said. "I'm ready." Whether that was true or not no longer mattered. Adam needed me.

I'm coming to get you.

Crew nodded to the other two. He, Sloane, and Jordan each lightly placed the tip of their respective weapons on my wrist. Knowing how sharp my own blade was, I wasn't surprised to see a small bead of blood bubble to the surface. But I didn't flinch.

"Your name," Crew said.

"Hannah Michelle Church," I said.

"Repeat after me. *Tolle hoc sacramento miles lucis.*"

"*Tolle hoc sacramento miles... lucis,*" I said, trying to match his timbre and accent.

"*Ego ex hoc momento nobis respondet,*" he said, and I repeated. Something warm began manifesting in my chest. Not the pain returning. More like a warm candle in a cold room.

"*... ut disperderet cultores tenebras in omnibus suis formas...*"

"*... ut disperderet cultores tenebras in omnibus suis formas...*"

"*... sive daemonium, Daemonis, aut angelus lapsus.*"

"*... sive daemonium, Daemonis, aut angelus lapsus.*" Each word was another candle, each candle a little larger, a little warmer than the last.

"*Panduntur portae inferi non clausit coram me, ignes in terris cessit extinctus est mei ferrum inferos.*"

"*Panduntur portae inferi non clausit coram me, ignes in terries cessit extinctus est mei ferrum inferos.*" Every ounce of angst, every bit of anger, every remnant of exhaustion was replaced by needle-sharp focus.

"*Ad hoc quod vita dedicated.*"

These final words poured out of me with vigor. "*Ad hoc quod vita dedicated.*"

For a beat, silence. Then, suddenly, their blades glowed red as if they'd been pulled from a blazing fire. A tingling, burning sensation covered my wrist, then shot up my arm and through my body until, one by one, each Dante removed the point of their blades to reveal a golden tattoo matching each of theirs. Two chevron arrows intersected each other, one pointing toward me, one pointing away, forming a small diamond shape in the middle, intersected through the center by a solid horizontal line. Jordan gently gripped my hand and ran his finger softly across the horizontal line.

"This represents the veil," he said, then ran his finger along the arrow pointing up and away from me. "This represents your life above the veil, meaning your normal life." He traced the downward-pointing arrow. "And this represents your ability to descend below the veil, to the other side, where we are now."

I blinked, nodded, still humming with warmth running through my veins.

Crew moved to sheathe his haladie. "Let's talk," he said. Each of us sheathed our weapons, left the Gray, and pulled up a chair.

"There's obviously a lot you'll need to learn about how we operate," Crew began, "but that'll all come in due time. We need to find Adam, and now that you're inducted, you need to be brought into the loop." Arms folded, he leaned back in his chair. "So, why are we here? I'm sure you've noticed an uptick in paranormal and supernatural activity. You've also come face to face with different classes of demons."

"Classes?" I asked. Crew looked to Sloane, who leaned forward.

"You've got your run-of-the mill haunter that finds weak people to attach to," she said. "They're basically scouts. Pull your weapon and they either run or try to scare you off, which usually leads to them getting exploded."

I nodded, familiar.

"We call them Phantom Demons, or just 'Phantoms.' Above them... well, you've met a couple now."

"Reapers," I offered. One corner of Sloane's mouth curled upward.

"Exactly. They're a little gnarlier. Not sure what the protocol is, but we assume that after a while of skulking around as a successful Phantom, they're promoted. 'Reaper,' because they're usually the ones who make deals, reap souls."

So Malum had been a Reaper, then.

"Phantoms and Reapers will sometimes team up to possess a person. If they're successful, they can take control, make that person do things. Bad things. We call those people Vessels."

Again, I flashed to the possessed lady who assaulted my car last fall, and to the security guard in the Saint Mark's parking garage whose eyes turned black before he tried to shoot me. They were the reason I still always carried a vial of graveyard dirt in my car. 'Vessels.' My toes began involuntarily tapping the ground, hands tightening around my elbows.

"We cast away demons before they're able to fully possess a person," Crew said. "Like that young boy you, me and Adam saved. Once someone becomes fully possessed—a Vessel— there's not much we can do at that point other than turn them over to the Ring to be…" Crew didn't finish. His eyes wandered, searching for words.

"Exorcised?" I offered.

Sloane shook her head. "Common misconception," she said. "Once someone is fully possessed, once they become a Vessel, they're a goner. Yeah, the Ring can extract however many demons have possessed a person and usually cast them back to Hell, but… the person never survives."

I swallowed, remembering the young boy on the bed covered in a cloud of black robes trying to break their way in.

"There is no way to destroy the demons within a Vessel without destroying the whole person they possess," Crew added, solemnly. "The longer a Vessel lives, the stronger the demons inside of him or her get." Crew's eyes traced the table's wood grains. Pain, maybe grief, hid behind them.

Sloane cleared her throat. "So, you've got Phantoms, Reapers, Vessels," she bulldozed on. "Then you've got the daddy of them all. The Arch Demon. Better pray you never meet one of those."

Suddenly inundated with new information, my head started pounding. Sloane had sounded all too calm relaying all this demon knowledge. I grabbed my mug and gulped black coffee like it was water, then wiped my lips.

Jordan chimed in. "We refer to all demons, Vessels, and anyone in league with them simply as 'the Dark.' Not the cleverest of names, I know, but it's efficient."

"What does any of this have to do with Adam?" I said, maybe a little more forcefully than I'd meant, but while I was at it... "And how is it that he got taken, but you got away?" I set my mug on the table and turned to Sloane.

Sloane's lips tightened, eyes narrowed, but I didn't let up.

"You *were* with him, right? Was it a... what did you call it? An Arch Demon? Is that what this is about?"

"She's just giving you the lay of the land," Crew interjected calmly. "It'll all make sense if you listen."

I brushed a few loose strands of hair behind my burning ears, turned back to Sloane expectantly.

"Yes," she said, tone sharp. "I was with him. No, it wasn't an Arch Demon who took him. And...," she looked away, then down at the floor and rubbed her palms against her pants. "I don't know why he got taken and I didn't. Everything happened so fast." She rubbed the back of her head. "They threw my keys into the desert. Smashed my phone. I got hit. Knocked out. I woke up and they were gone. So was Adam." Sloane's eyes remained glued to the floor.

"Who's they? Vessels?"

"Maybe a couple," Jordan said, "but probably not."

My intestines tied themselves in knots as I clenched a fist. "Would you please—*please*—just tell me exactly what happened. Talk to me like I'm five years old if you have to, but quit making me guess. Quit dancing around it."

Jordan and Sloane looked to Crew.

"A portal to Hell has been opened somewhere near here," Crew said. "That's why there's been a spike in activity, and why you're starting to see more, stronger, and higher-ranking demons."

"But," Jordan added, "a portal to Hell has to be opened topside, meaning the demons can't open the portal themselves. It has to be opened by someone who wants to let them in."

"Someone has opened a portal nearby," Crew said. "Someone who is in league with the Dark."

"Who—"

"People become entangled with the Dark for all sorts of

reasons," Crew said, anticipating my question before I could finish asking it. "Usually, it's in exchange for power. Not super-powers or anything like that. More like prestige, fame... the type of power we mortal humans tend to think is the most important. The type people might even sell their souls for."

I shut my eyes, processing. "So, this person... who opened a portal to Hell and is in league with demons... took Adam?"

Crew fielded the question to Jordan. "Not a single person," Jordan said. "Multiple people. A secret combination of people engaged to bring about the same dark purpose in exchange for... well, like Crew said... whatever they deem most valuable."

"Like a secret society. Devil worshippers, that kind of thing?"

Both Crew and Jordan nodded. I jumped when Sloane slammed her forearm against the table next to me. Shocked, I looked at her face, but she gestured with her eyes for me to look down at her arm. The normally pale bottom side of her forearm faced upward, but it wasn't pale now. It was the color of copper, covered in dried blood. I followed the dull copper streaks from the inside of her elbow up to her wrist.

Her golden Dante mark was shredded. Someone had carved what looked like a crude circle, but on closer inspection I could tell that one end of the circle opened up in a small V-shape, like a mouth swallowing the circle's end. Something else I noticed: Sloane had another tattoo, a black fletched arrow on the outside of her hand, running the length of her outer palm to the top of her pinky finger.

"Ever seen this symbol?" Sloane asked in staccato breaths. She had to have meant the bloody circle shape on her wrist. I glanced up at her and shook my head. "It's a snake," she said, "eating its own tail."

Now that she'd described it, I could make it out. And yes, it was a symbol I'd come across before, maybe in one of my books... But I couldn't pin down its significance.

"What does it mean?" I asked. Crew chimed in.

"There is a particularly bad occult society, with roots that spread all across the world. They're called the Order of the Snake."

For a few beats, everyone remained silent, staring. My eyes shifted between the three of them. Did they expect that name to mean something to me?

"And this...," I glanced down at the snake eating its own tail carved into Sloane's wrist. "This Order of the Snake. They took Adam?"

"Yes," Jordan and Crew said together. "At least," Jordan added, "that's what the mark on Sloan's wrist would suggest."

Sloane pulled her arm back, rose to her feet and walked heavily out of the room toward the kitchen. "I'm washing this off," she said. The blood, I guessed she meant—those cuts would take more than a wash before they disappeared, if they ever did. She might have the scars for the rest of her life. The kitchen faucet squeaked, followed by the tinny sound of water beating the sink, followed by the swishing sound of cloth against skin. Then, there came a sound I never imagined I'd hear out of the black leather badass girl who'd saved me from a Reaper.

Soft, hitching sobs.

Neither Crew nor Jordan made a move to get up, to go to her. And maybe that was okay.

A rush of guilt as I realized she must've felt extremely shaken, having been through what she'd been through—jumped, assaulted, knocked out by a group of demon-worshiping lunatics in the dead of night. They left their mark on her, but it could've been worse. They could've killed her. They could've killed both of them.

My guilt was soon replaced by slow-burning alarm. I'd been operating under the assumption that Adam is still alive. What if...

No, Hannah. Don't go there.

"Why would they have taken Adam? What would they want with him?" I asked, scared of the answer, but I had to know. I had to go into all of this with eyes wide open if I had any chance of saving him. Both Crew and Jordan let out a collective sigh.

Not a good sign.

"Let me shoot you straight," Crew said.

"Please."

"They either want to kill him or turn him over to the Dark. Now, I don't think they took him to kill him—they would've done it on the side of the road." His eyes wandered toward the kitchen. "They would've done it to both of them. No, I think they made a deal."

"A deal?"

"A trade. You have to realize that a Dante would be a demon's most valued prize. They're satisfied possessing regular people, sure, but a Dante... just imagine. With a Dante's body and a Dante's ability to cross through the veil and into—what do you call it?"

"The Gray."

"Right. With a Dante's ability to enter the Gray, they would be able to open portals to Hell anywhere, at any time."

"Wait," I said. "What? We can do that?"

"Yes, although we never open them, for obvious reasons. We're much more interested in sealing them shut once they've been opened."

So much to take in. Too much.

"So, they want to turn Adam over to the Dark to be possessed by demons and wreak havoc."

They nodded solemnly.

The explanation both exacerbated my dread and opened a small pocket of hope. They would've killed him if they wanted him dead. They wanted him alive to trade to their demon over-lords for who-knows-what, not that it matters.

He's alive. He has to be.

Somehow, somewhere deep down, I'd known that was true all along. Chair legs scraped across the wooden floor as I stood.

"You said you had to make phone calls when you were leaving my apartment," I told Crew. "Did you find anything?"

"I had to inform the Ring about what happened." He probably noticed my screwed-up expression when I tried to recall who, exactly, 'the Ring' was, because he added, "You'll remember that the Ring is our governing body. The ones in charge, and the people who tell us where to be and when."

"Right. And what—"

"Let's go," Sloane's voice came from behind me. Crew and Jordan both stood as I turned to see her nod toward the front door, then turned and walked that direction. The boys began to follow.

"Go where?" I asked.

"Scene of the crime," Crew said. "Not sure what we'll find, but it's where we start."

11

We split up—Jordan took Sloane in his slate gray BMW, and I rode with Crew.

"Do you know where we're going?" I asked as we followed the BMW onto a southbound highway heading out of town.

"Generally."

I waited for a more thorough explanation, but Crew stared forward and gripped the steering wheel.

"What was this 'mission' that Sloane and Adam were on last night?"

"We had a lead on where the portal might be," he said. "They were headed out to investigate when they got mobbed." Not once did he look over at me as he explained, and his tone was nearly devoid of emotion, like he was bottling it all up inside and the merest hint would break the dam.

"If that all happened in the middle of the night," I said, "why did it take Sloane so long to get back? I mean, you guys weren't at my door until, what, seven-thirty? What—"

"Did you not hear the part where Sloane said they smashed her phone?" Crew said, near shouting. He finally turned to me and I wish he hadn't—his eyes were fire. I almost regretted lighting the spark, but only for half a heartbeat. "They tossed her keys. Did you not hear that part either?"

"Don't you dare get mad at me for asking questions," I shouted back. "Adam is almost all I have. One week as a Dante, and he was taken by some occult group to either hand him over to Hell or have him killed, so you can take your righteous anger and shove it up your ass for all I care. I need answers." The hot words left my burning chest quicker than I could think, and for one fleeting moment, Crew's face shifted, eyes narrowed, like my words were salt on an open wound. He re-focused on the road and pulled in a deep breath.

"You're right," he said, voice tempered. "And I'm sorry." Another quick breath, then, "It's just that nothing like this has ever happened under my watch before. The Ring's not happy, obviously. I have to make this right." He turned back to me. "I will make this right."

My tension eased a little as understanding dawned. He wasn't mad at me. He was shouldering the burden that what happened to Adam, happened under his supervision. In his mind, it was his fault.

"We're all frayed," I said. "Sorry for snapping. I just... we have to find him."

Crew nodded. We rode in silence as the houses dotting the outskirts of town faded away, replaced by oceans of brown desert and wilderness on either side of the highway. Jordan's BMW signaled right, then slowed and pulled off the highway's shoulder, kicking up clouds of dust before coming to a stop. We followed, parked behind him. The landscape outside the window was desolate. Desert stretched for miles in each direction, sliced down the middle by straight black road and pock-marked everywhere with sagebrush and weeds. A few yards from the highway shoulder, a barely-legible sign hung half-tilted on a crude, barbed wire fence that read: *Private Property—Trespassers will be shot and survivors will be shot again.* I say barely legible because, ironically, the once-white sign was peppered with bullet scars. Just as I slid out of the passenger seat, my phone buzzed. I frantically yanked it from my pocket, still hoping beyond hope Adam had escaped and found a way to contact me.

It was a text, but not from Adam. It was from a number that... I mean, could I even call it a phone number? It was six zeros, no area code, no dashes.

Strange. I clicked open the text box.

000000: *IMPORTANT: Do not show this or the following message to anyone. Do not discuss this or the following message with anyone. Follow-up message imminent.*

What in the world...?

My confusion grew when I watched the message I had just read disappear. I opened the text app and, sure enough, the message was gone—wiped from my phone's memory. The phone buzzed again and the screen populated with a new message.

000000: *We welcome you, newest Dante. Based on intel, we believe you to be trustworthy. There is a mole within our organization which has led to the culmination of current unfortunate events. A Dante within your inner circle is compromised and cannot be trusted. There may be others within your inner circle who are also compromised, and for this reason we are reaching out to you and you alone. Please be careful. Do not act conspicuous. Following these instructions will result in finding the Dante Adam Black sooner and safer. You cannot text or reply to this number to get in touch—we will contact you. In confidence—The Ring.*

The... the Ring? What intel? How would they know my—

"Something important, Hannah?" Crew barged in on my thoughts before I could finish them. I fumbled for my phone's lock screen, but noticed that the second message had already disappeared, like they—the Ring—already knew I'd read it. *A Dante in your inner circle is compromised... There may be others within your inner circle who are also compromised... Do not act conspicuous...* I glanced up at Crew and cleared my throat.

"No," I said, trying to keep my voice level. I shoved the phone deep into my back pocket. Crew's eyes narrowed, but I avoided his gaze and shouldered past him toward the others.

"Right here," Sloane said, pointing just beyond Jordan's car. "This is where we were run off the road." But while everyone else inspected the tire marks that slashed through the dust, I couldn't help but train my gaze on Sloane.

'A Dante within your inner circle is compromised and cannot be trusted...'

My breath quickened, fanning the red-hot anger that slowly grew, making my chest warm and my fists clench tight.

"Which direction?" Someone asked. Jordan, I think.

"I was passed out somewhere over there." Sloane pointed lazily toward the barbed wire fence. "By the time I woke up, they were already gone."

Right. Passed out. Pretty convenient...

"Doesn't look like they drove into the desert," Crew said, scanning the landscape for other tire tracks, "which leaves two possibilities: north or south."

"What do you think, Sloane?" I said. My voice was a scalpel, sharp and precise. "North?" I stepped toward her slowly, reading the expressions on her face. Did her eyes move? Someone once taught me that if a person moves their eyes down and to the left when asked a question, it was a sure tell that they were lying. "Or south?"

Sloane pursed her lips, blinked, but didn't unlock her gaze from mine. "Like I said, I was an unconscious crumpled heap in the dirt. So, I wouldn't know." Either she was telling the truth, or she was a really good liar. Given her other skills, I'd put money on the latter.

Other than a few loud cars rushing down the highway, a looming silence grew between us that weaved a thick wire of growing tension, tightening by the millisecond until one of the boys cleared their throat.

"Where did you find your keys?" Jordan asked Sloane.

Oh, that's right. I'd forgotten that part of the story. She'd been knocked out and their "attackers" tossed her keys somewhere into the desert, stranding her without a phone on the side of the road. That's why she couldn't get to Crew and Jordan to tell them Adam had been taken until morning. Or so the story goes…. I cocked an expectant eyebrow, awaited her answer.

If it was true that Sloane was a mole, a traitor, and that she'd turned Adam over to the Order of the Snake, why wouldn't the Ring arrest her? Do they arrest people? Maybe they're more of the dispose-of-traitors-quietly type of organization. In any case, it was taking everything I had not to lash out and take her down in a choke hold until she spilled every little bit of information leading to Adam she had. The sarcastic smirk she gave me when she turned to Jordan, then toward the desert expanse behind the barbed wire fence, nearly freed the inner, prowling lion from its cage.

"Over here," she said, then deftly slid one leg between the two lower wires and slid through. Jordan, Crew and I followed as Sloane scanned the ground until she found the ghosts of her midnight footsteps. They led her to about twenty yards into the desert where a thick patch of sage opened up to an island of craggy dirt. "They were right about here, in the middle of this little clearing."

"Lucky break you found them," Crew said.

"Yeah," I added. "Lucky."

Sloane wheeled around, leaving a wake of rising dust like smoke as she stomped toward me. "You got something to say? Huh?" She stopped a few feet from me, her eyes hot coals, but I didn't budge. "Go ahead then, say it!"

The flame inside became a bonfire, but I kept my voice level. "Just seems awfully convenient that you got 'knocked out,' that you 'woke up' without knowing what direction they took Adam, and that you found your keys in the middle of the desert. And why would they only kidnap Adam when they could've had two Dantes for one?"

"Oh, so I was in on it! Is that what you think?" She pulled her jacket sleeve up her forearm and shoved the underside of her wrist underneath my nose. Fresh blood trickled from the deep, circular wound. "You think I did this to myself, too?"

That was the one thing that didn't really add up. That mark… it would take a mixture of guts and a whole lot of crazy to do that to herself. The thought made my stomach queasy.

Crew stepped between us. "Guys, I get that tensions are high right now, but this is insane."

If only he knew what I knew, he'd be on my side. *Do not discuss this message with anyone… Don't act conspicuous… Following these instructions will result in finding Adam Black sooner…*

I have no choice but to trust the mysterious messenger. At least for now.

"You're right," I said and heaved a heavy sigh. "This is all too much, and I'm not in the right state of mind. I'm sorry, Sloane."

The acting job must've been convincing, because the apology seemed to soften her. She nodded. "Forget it. Can we stop with the bullshit and work on getting our Dante back?"

"Sounds good to me," Jordan said, joining the circle.

My phone buzzed again, but this time I didn't frantically pull it out. Somehow, I knew it was them again. 000000. The Ring. And I was right.

As the others slid back through the barbed wire fence and onto the highway's dusty shoulder to look for any clues the tire tracks may have left behind, I snuck a glance. On the lock screen, a bubble message.

000000: *Meet. Clark's Diner, 2PM. Come alone.*

12

C rew and I drove north, back toward town, while Sloane and Jordan headed south searching for anything out of the ordinary that could clue us in to Adam's location or tell us anything about his captors. As we drove, I couldn't help but let the thought that not only could I not trust Sloane, but I couldn't trust any of them, not even Crew. He drove silently, white knuckling the steering wheel as cold sweat dribbled through the small crater that was his temple.

I thought it was the anxiety of the entire situation that made my stomach hurt, but I realized it was that same feeling that had incapacitated me overnight creeping into my guts again. I gripped my stomach with a groan.

"You okay?" Crew muttered without taking his eyes off the road.

I held my breath for a few long seconds. "I don't know," I said. "Ever since last night, this sharp pain has been stabbing at my insides. It's like..."

It's like when Malum pried through my ribs and pulled out my soul. In fact, it was almost *exactly* that same feeling, but I kept that thought to myself.

"Like what?" Crew asked. I grimaced.

"I think you need to drop me off at my apartment."

"No way. No Dante can be left alone until we figure this out."

Through gritted teeth, I sucked in painful breaths. "I'll be fine. I just need to lie down and let this pass, whatever it is. I'm no help to you otherwise and I don't want to hold you back."

"Hannah, no. It's—"

"Take me home, then go out and look for Adam. I'll text you when I'm done puking my guts out and we'll find each other. I promise."

Despite his shaking head, he huffed and turned off the town's main road and headed toward my place. As quickly as the pain had come, it began to ebb, but I gripped my stomach harder and breathed through a pinhole so Crew became none the wiser. If he didn't know better, he'd probably think I was about to go into labor. And honestly, if this whole mess with Adam hadn't happened I'd probably be much more concerned about what felt like someone trying to knife their way out of my stomach. But for now, with Crew, I had to keep up the façade.

Meet. Clark's Diner. 2PM. Come alone. The now-disappeared text bubble crawled across my foggy mind like a stock ticker. The time was 1:40 p.m. when Crew pulled into the parking lot and dropped me off at the foot of the steps leading up to my door.

"If I don't hear from you in an hour," he said, low and serious, "I'm coming back here. Rest up for a bit and I'll let you know if I find anything." I nodded, slid off the passenger seat and climbed the stairs. Before I closed the front door behind me, I glanced back at Crew who still idled. The utter concern on his face said he had a mind to follow me in and sweep the place for any Order of the Snake goons lurking in the shadows. With a wave, I shut the door, pressed my ear against it, relieved to hear his engine finally rumble away.

Either Crew was the best actor to ever live, or he was not the mole the Ring warned me about. My instincts said to bet on the latter. But after an all-nighter and some serious brain fog, trusting my instincts probably wasn't safe at the moment.

I plugged in my phone, pulled out a Red Bull from the fridge then popped five extra-strength Tylenol pills before firing up my laptop. Clark's was around the corner, no more than a two-minute walk, so I had a few minutes to kill before heading over to meet the mysterious texter. Clicking the browser icon, I pulled up Google and typed *Order of the Snake* in the search bar.

Not much came up. Mostly cheap-looking wiki sites tied to the occult. If this was a real secret society, they sure didn't have much of an internet presence. But then again, would a secret society really be a *secret* society if it had a prominent website? I clicked one of the wiki hyperlinks, and an early two-thousands era webpage loaded. It looked like one of those old Myspace pages—black background overlaid by pixelated, sparkling star graphics. A short description in white letters was framed in a text box under the title *Order of the Snake*. It read:

```
Who knows how long this will stay up.
Probably not long. O.O.T.S. seems to
keep a pretty short leash on what gets
posted online about them.
```

The amateur author had a good point. I took a screen grab of the page, then resumed reading.

```
O.O.T.S. (Order of the Snake) is an
ancient secret society, like the
Hellfire Club or Skull and Bones, but
much more sinister. It's said they deal
directly with the Devil in exchange for
power and glory. Members are usually
identified by a tattoo of a snake eating
```

its own tail—a pretty common occult symbol. Some say the symbol's origins lie with the O.O.T.S., but I haven't been able to verify that claim. The symbol represents chaos—the eternal round of human nature destroying itself. Because human nature demands chaos, they bring balance to the world by introducing more chaos. Meaning, they make a deal with the devil for power, and once they have power, they at least partially do the bidding of the one that put them there. Or something.

To be honest, it's all a little weird and there's not much out there to go on, but that's how I understand it. Hopefully they don't kill me now. Or worse, initiate me. Click the links below for my sources and other info.
    - Howard

Thanks, Howard. I hope that's not your real name.

A few links hung beneath the last paragraph, sizzling orange. I clicked each one, and each of them led to a different dead page. Not unexpected, but still disappointing. I shut the laptop's lid with a sigh and checked the time. Better to be early than late. At least then I could choose my seat and see who walks through the door.

You sure you want to meet with a total stranger who claims to be from the Ring, Hannah? What if it's the Order of the Snake leading you into a trap? You're a Dante now, too—wouldn't they want to turn you over to the Dark like they've probably done with Adam?

Head swimming, I pounded the entire can of Red Bull

swiped my phone and headed out before I could talk myself out of it.

CLARK'S CLAIMS TO be the home of the World-Famous Grilled Chicken Sandwich, which is funny for two reasons: First, nobody outside of this little town has ever heard of it; Second, because it's gross. The underside of two mostly soggy buns was lathered in mayo which dripped off the thin, gray-colored chicken. That was it. Mayo and chicken. I ordered the sandwich so I wouldn't appear conspicuous and picked the corner table where I could easily see who would come in and out of the door while also remaining close to the other patrons and restaurant staff, just in case something weird was about to go down.

The only other people were two high-school aged couples— one a few tables down from me, the other on the restaurant's far side. Luckily, I didn't recognize any of them, and I hoped they didn't recognize me. I had only served time at Eagle Ridge High for my senior year and didn't get to know many juniors or sophomores, who were all seniors and juniors now. Still, I kept my head down, eyes trained on the door, my heel tapping involuntarily against the cheap linoleum floor.

Whoever was on the other end of the disappearing texts had all of thirty seconds before they'd be late. I checked my phone, refreshed the texting app, checked my missed calls, wondering if this was all some kind of distraction to separate me from the others; wondering if my coming here, alone, was a massive mistake. Then the old tin bell above the entry door clinked.

A man in pressed slacks and a navy-blue sport jacket strode with authority toward the corner table. His light, cropped hair was spiked in front, his face free of even a hint of stubble. In a smooth, one-handed motion, he removed his aviator sunglasses, folded them, then carefully tucked them into his jacket pocket and pulled out the chair across from me. Before either of us said a word, the same server who'd brought my world-famous chicken sandwich approached the table. The man waved her off wordlessly and without even a hint at breaking eye contact with me.

"Thanks for coming, Hannah." His voice wasn't as deep as I'd expected. On closer inspection I could make out thin slivers of wrinkles fading away from the corners of his eyes. And speaking of closer inspection…

I gripped my sword and plunged into the Gray. I needed a second to think, to plan out what to say. I mean, I had a plan coming in, but it floated away in a foggy wisp the moment he bore into me with his intense gaze. Just a second to collect myself, and then—

A shock ran through me when the man broke through my thoughts and into the Gray, holding what appeared to be a short sword similar to mine.

"You're…" I began, startled. "You're a Dante."

The man pulled the sleeve of his sport coat up toward his elbow, exposing the same mark I now bore on my wrist; the mark of a Dante. "I'm with the Ring," he said coolly. "I couldn't be with the Ring without first being a Dante." He covered the mark, shifted his sword, then held out his right hand. "Name's Michael. I'm sorry for the secrecy, but it was the only way."

Skeptically, I shook his hand. It made sense that the Ring would be made up of more experienced Dantes. A tight cord began to unwind, my muscles relaxed.

"I'd like to discuss something with you, if you're comfortable."

I pulled in a breath, nodded, then returned my sword to its sheath. Michael matched me. A millisecond later we were back in reality, sitting across from each other. I glanced around, then leaned forward.

"What is this about?" I whispered. "Do you know where Adam is?"

Michael broke my questioning gaze, fished a smartphone out of his jacket pocket and set it on the table between us. "How much do you know about your fellow Dante, Sloane?"

My cheeks warmed, my muscles began re-tightening. "Not much," I said. "What does this have to do with Adam? If you can't help me find him, I'm going to have to—"

"Please," Michael said, palm outstretched. "Keep your voice down." He swiped the smartphone's screen and quickly entered a long numeric password, then opened an app. With one hand, he pressed the phone toward me. With the other, he produced a pair of earbuds.

Whether he registered my expression—a mixture of utter confusion and hot frustration—or not, I couldn't tell because he didn't move a single facial muscle. Not even a twitch. The screen he was holding out to me was black except for one, small white triangle exactly in the middle. I swiped the earbuds, plugged them into the phone jack, stuffed them into my ears and tapped it. The screen brightened, but only barely. I caught a shaky glimpse of the night sky, then turned up the volume.

Footsteps. Heavy breathing. Laughter, but not innocent laughter. Sinister laughter. When the video finally came into focus, my hand shot to my mouth, my throat closed tight. I could barely suppress a shriek.

Adam knelt on top of dirt and weeds on the highway's shoulder—the same place Crew and the rest of us had just visited—coated in dim yellowish light from a car's headlights. Five or six people surrounded him. Even though the video was shaky, I could see that each of them were dressed in mostly black, and all of them were wearing matching masks—bone white with a small, dark circle centered on the portion covering their foreheads. Adam's hands were bound with what looked like heavy-duty zip ties. He spat, and what hit the dirt looked ominously dark.

"You want some more?" one of the masked figures asked, voice dark and deep. The others laughed.

Adam's long hair drifted back as his head rose up to face the masked figure looming directly in front of him, apparently the one who had spoken. Adam's cheeks were bruised, swollen. A gash above his left eyebrow gushed a steady dark stream down his temple and cheek.

The masked man in front of Adam crouched, then cocked his head to the side. "Trust me," he said, "you don't want some more."

Adam spat again. A thick, dark streak splattered across the man's white mask. One tense, silent second passed, then the masked man pulled back a heavy fist and drove it hard across Adam's bruised cheek, knocking him sideways to the ground. Others joined in, kicking his stomach and ribs and shoulders. Each thudding strike was a spike through my heart. I paused the video and ripped out the earbuds, unable to take anymore.

I couldn't breathe. Fingernails dug fissures into my palms.

Michael's hand wrapped around one of mine. "I know," he said. "It's difficult to watch. But I need you to watch to the end."

I swallowed, tempted to rip my hand away and bolt for the door. Michael squeezed ever so slightly.

"It's important," he said.

I wiped the moisture from my eyes and somehow managed to pull in a breath. I couldn't be sure, but something in the back of my mind whispered that Michael was showing me this for a reason. Maybe it would help us find Adam, or at least find who took him. With trembling hands, I pressed the earbuds back into my ears and tapped the white triangle.

The beating continued. I forced myself to watch blow after bone-crunching blow until…

"You know," a female voice called from behind the person filming, "your bosses won't be too happy with you when you bring them a dead Dante."

The beating ceased. Plumes of dust curled around Adam in the dim car light as each of the assailants slowly turned their white-masked faces toward the camera. The speaker stepped forward into the frame.

"Something tells me you'd all try to pin it on me if this one didn't make it down to Hell alive. And we all know I wouldn't let that slide."

I could only see the back of her. The black boots. The black pants and leather jacket. The hair… Forget her face—I'd know that pixie cut anywhere.

Sloane.

Rage isn't a strong enough term to describe the feeling that took over me. My vision reduced to one pulsing, black tunnel. The video played on.

Someone chuckled awkwardly. "Well," Sloane said, "load him up and do whatever you're going to do with him. And someone punch me in the face a couple times for good measure." Three white-masked assailants wrapped their arms around the nearly lifeless heap that was Adam and hauled him into the back of a waiting van, then slammed the doors.

The video cut off.

I couldn't feel.

I pulled out the earbuds. The only sound was blood pulsing, pounding against my eardrums.

Then a thought.

"How did you get this video?" I think I said.

Michael slid the phone off the table without looking up. Within a couple seconds, he'd taken a screen shot of the video's final frame showing the back of Sloane's pixie haircut while she watched the masked kidnappers shove Adam into the back of the van and texted the picture to me. "A show of good faith," he said, slipped the phone back into his jacket pocket, then began wrapping the earbuds in a neat circle around his fingers. "We have moles in many organizations that provide us information."

"Like in the Order of the Snake?"

"Yes." Michael didn't flinch, didn't act surprised. "And

again, I ask you: What do you know about your fellow Dante, Sloane?"

I slid my phone screen open and glared at the screenshot Michael had texted, then saved it to my pictures before it disappeared. "All I know," I managed through gritted teeth, "is that she handed Adam over to those... those...," but I couldn't grasp the right word to describe those featureless people in white masks.

Michael quietly rose to his feet.

"Where are you going? We need you. We need help. Adam—"

"We're doing what we can."

"No!" I slammed the table. The plate holding my chicken sandwich crashed to the floor. The small restaurant turned eerily quiet, the few patrons glancing our direction. I didn't care. "You *will* help me find him," I seethed.

Michael pressed a soft hand on my shoulder. "I am helping you," he said. "And as hard as it may be to accept, you're just going to have to trust me." Something flashed behind his eyes. He leaned forward. "I'll be in touch."

With that, Michael turned and left out the front door without a backward glance.

Eyes clamped shut, I tried to regain my composure. When I reopened them, the server came by with a broom to sweep up the shards of broken plate along with the splayed buns plastered to the floor.

"I'm so sorry," I said.

"It's okay," she said with sympathetic eyes. Who knows what she thought she'd witnessed... Domestic abuse? A lovers' quarrel? Whatever it was, I appreciated her look of concern.

My phone buzzed. Michael, I guessed. But when I flipped it over, I saw a text bubble from Crew.

Crew: *Jordan and Sloane are back. We're meeting at HQ. Should I come by and grab you?*

I shot back a few words.

No. Meet you there.

I gathered my things and left the diner.

There's one person who knows who took Adam. One person who knows exactly where they took him.

Time for Sloane to tell me what she knows, by any means necessary.

13

Every quarter mile closer to the HQ house was a fresh coat of kerosene on my flaming nerves.

I knew it. I knew something was off with her ever since I first met her. I had mistaken the look she'd given Adam at the table for attraction. Oh, she was a hungry wolf staring down a platter of fresh, red meat all right, but not for the reasons I had thought. She didn't see him as a meal. She saw him as a meal ticket—a way to get in good with the enemy. And for what? What did they promise her?

Doesn't matter. Of all the Snakes in the video Michael had shown me, Sloane was the slimiest, slithering across the ground on her traitorous belly ready to strike at the most opportune time. She was poison. Venom. And the best way to deal with deadly snakes? The same way I'd dealt with the two-headed, slithering monstrosity waiting for me in the midnight black of the hellhound's lair where I'd found my first key.

Chop its head off.

I peeled into HQ's driveway. All the cars were there. I slammed mine into park and marched toward the front door, a human bonfire.

The front door was locked. I knocked. The quick steps that

approached the door's other side matched the pace of my heavy breathing. The bolt flipped. The doorknob twisted. The door swung lazily open. Sloane stood in the doorway, then propped herself against the door frame, narrowed her eyes and licked her teeth.

"Heard you decided to take a nap while the rest of us went looking for—"

But I shut her jaw hard with a solid right hook before she could finish. The fleshy *thwack* sound reverberated through the entryway, followed quickly by the *thud* of her shoulder meeting the entryway wall.

"Traitor," I spat. "Snake." I advanced, this time pulling back a haymaker with my left. Like I anticipated, Sloane lifted both arms to cover the right side of her face, leaving her left side wide open for the quick right jab she never saw coming. She winced, her cheek turning an angry shade of crimson.

Dull commotion came from the back of the house. I gripped Sloane by the shoulders.

"You sold him out," I hissed, then slammed her against the wall. "You know where they took him, you poisonous bi—"

She rammed a knee hard into my stomach. The blow doubled me over. I let go, backed up a few paces, searching for breath.

"What is wrong with you!" She screamed.

I stood tall. Sloane reached over her shoulder where I knew she kept her invisible arrow, her ticket into the Gray. "Oh," I managed, "so that's how you want to play it?" I reached for my sword.

The Gray seemed darker, more ominous than usual. I double-gripped the hilt. Sloane nocked the arrow in her bow. We circled.

"This isn't going to go well for you," Sloane said, sneering.

"Why? You going to hand me over to your buddies in the Order of the Snake like you did Adam?"

"What?"

"Don't play stupid, Sloane. Not with me." I stepped forward. She parried back. I lunged, slashed, smacked her arrow with my blade. By the way her eyes flew wide, she'd finally realized that, yes, I was deadly serious. I took advantage of her momentary surprise and jumped forward, dodged the bow and pinned her neck against the wall with the sharp end of my elbow. "You're going to tell me where he is," I spat, "or I'll beat it out of you."

I pulled my elbow off her neck just far enough to launch it at her jaw. On contact, the back of her head drove a dent in the wall. She tried to spin out, but I had her pinned in a clinch. A trickle of dark blood escaped the corner of her mouth.

"Whoa, whoa!" someone behind me called. I felt hands vice my shoulders, trying to peel me off of Sloane. I ducked, spun the hands off me, turned and landed a front kick square in the middle of Crew's chest, driving him backward.

Sloane jumped on my back, but I still had all the leverage. I leaned forward, wrapped my hands around her arm, launched her over my shoulder and drove her onto the hardwood. All the air that had occupied her lungs rushed out in a wheeze. I raised my sword.

Sloane's eyes grew wide.

I drove the blade down hard.

"Hannah," Crew called. "No!"

The sword's razor point hit with a solid *thud* exactly where I had aimed.

When I let go of the hilt, the blade warbled side to side, the point stabbed deep into the hardwood floor barely an inch from Sloane's left ear.

Her eyes drifted to her reflection in the blade. Mine drifted to Crew. His were saucers.

Jordan entered the Gray, only to be met with silence. None of us breathed for a few long seconds as he took in the scene. "What in the world…"

I yanked the sword from the splintered floor and faced him while keeping the business end pointed at Sloane. "She's a traitor," I said. "She was in league with the Order of the Snake to hand over Adam. And I can prove it."

Both Jordan and Crew kept their eyes locked on me during the seconds it took for my words to sink in. Then, they slowly looked down at Sloane who finally struggled to prop herself up on an elbow.

"She's insane," she said. It sounded like someone had run her voice box through a heavy cement mixer.

"Maybe," I said, "but I'm not wrong." Electric adrenaline coursed through my veins, pulsing with each pump of my drumming heart.

"Let's, uh..." Jordan began. "Let's put these away and talk. How about that?" He motioned toward the hatchet in his right hand.

"That's a good idea," Crew said, and made to sheathe his haladie.

"Fine." I glared at Sloane, then sheathed my sword. Jordan stepped between us. Sloane left the Gray, and Crew helped her up off the floor. She wiped blood from her lips with the back of her hand.

"What the hell is this all about, Hannah?" Crew demanded.

I fished my phone out, pulled up my photos, then clicked the screenshot Michael had sent. "Here," I said, handing the phone to Jordan. Crew peered over his shoulder. Sloane, curiously, didn't seem interested in what I had to show them.

Jordan and Crew both raked their eyes over the screen, taking in the picture that showed Sloane's back in the foreground while Adam was being lifted and forced into the back of the waiting van in the background. Their faces screwed up tighter with each passing second. By the way Crew finally looked back at Sloane, I knew the picture was convincing.

"What's this about, Sloane?" Crew asked while pointing at the phone's screen. Sloane crossed her arms.

"I don't even know what you're looking at," she said. "And besides, I don't care. Whatever *she*"—Sloane spat the word 'she' out like it was a piece of rotten fruit—"says shouldn't be taken seriously. She's a psycho."

Crew turned back toward me and held his hand out. "May I?" He took the phone, then pointed the screen toward Sloane without a word. Instead of looking, though, Sloane decided to keep her scorching glare trained squarely on me. I returned the favor.

"Sloane," Crew broke the tense silence. With a hot breath, Sloane looked. Her brow furrowed as she took in the scene. She cocked her head to the side, the way a curious bird might look at a worm. Her hands dropped. She took a step forward.

"That's…" she started, but swallowed whatever she'd meant to say next.

"You?" I offered, the word a sharp barb. "That's you. And that's Adam being kidnapped by your friends in the white masks. And you're going to tell us where they took him, unless you'd prefer that I cut out your tongue."

Sloane, normally so cool and collected under pressure, balked. Her lips opened, closed, opened again but no words came out. To their credit, Crew and Jordan didn't try to break the tension this time. They stood sentinel, listening.

Good. Give her some rope. Let her hang herself.

Finally, Sloane found her voice. "That's not me," she said, her voice a step higher than normal. "You guys,"—her eyes pled with Jordan's and Crew's—"you have to believe me. I don't know what this is. I mean… that's… I was knocked out. They threw my keys. I…"

"Cut the bull," I said, stepping toward her. Lucky for her, Jordan grasped my arm. "Tell us where the Order of the Snake took Adam."

"She has a point," Crew said, and for one brief second, I felt vindicated. Crew was on my side. Except he wasn't looking at Sloane anymore…

He was looking at me.

"Where did you get this?" He asked, motioning toward the picture on screen. Heat rose inside me again, white, intense.

Now Crew's questioning me? After what I'd just shown him,

what he's seen with his own eyes? My jaw flexed, clamping down until my teeth buzzed.

"From a trusted source," I managed.

"Who?" This time it was Jordan asking.

I nodded toward Sloane. "I'll tell you when she's not around. She can't be trusted."

"And you can?" She spat back. "You come crashing in here with some picture from last night, trying to accuse me of being a traitor. Who's to say you didn't take the picture yourself?"

I rolled my eyes. "We don't have time for this. You're in the picture. You're handing Adam to the enemy. The longer you stall without telling us where they took him, the more likely they kill him." I couldn't be sure whether killing Adam was the Order's ultimate goal, but surely they wouldn't let him go free once they pulled whatever information they sought from him.

The inner heat turned to pain. Whatever it was that made my insides feel like they were engaged in a civil war with needles and thumbtacks began rearing its head again, but I fought the urge to grip my stomach and double over. Still, Jordan must've noticed my grimace.

"What is it?" he asked, his eyes traveling rapidly from my head to my waist and back.

"Nothing," I managed through gritted teeth.

"Jordan," Crew cut in, "take Hannah and wait for a few minutes. Sloane, come with me."

"But—"

"Now, Hannah," Crew interrupted. He led Sloane through the front door and onto the porch. "I need some time to figure this out." He tossed my phone and I caught it, then he shut the door behind them.

I could've screamed if it wasn't for the fact that my stomach felt like it was trying to escape through my burning throat.

"You don't look too hot, Hannah," Jordan said. "Come on."

He led me to a small folding chair in the front room. I sat, then gave into the pain. With one arm across my stomach and the other across my smoldering chest, I viced my eyes shut and folded myself in half.

"How long has this been going on?" Jordan asked.

"I... I don't know," I managed. "She's probably been in league with the Order for a while..."

"No," he said, "the pain. How long have you had it?"

I glanced up briefly and caught the intense concern that masked his face. "Since yesterday. After I left here. After Adam left." Sizzling agony flared through my chest, forcing out a high, painful moan.

"Hang on," Jordan said, "I'll grab you some water."

Rushing blood pumped through my ears in intervals. The edges of my vision began fading into a dull, gray fuzz. I was halfway out of the chair when Jordan returned.

"Whoa, whoa," he said, then helped me lay flat on the hardwood. I avoided deep breaths, as breathing seemed to fan the inner flames that seemed ready to burst out of my pores at any moment. I caught sight of Jordan as he pulled another chair over, set a full glass of water on the floor, then sat. He had something in his hands, something large, rectangular. A heavy book—one of the dozens strewn across the floor or countertops.

"I have a theory about this... this pain, or whatever it is you're feeling," he said, turning over piles of pages. "Me and Adam were looking at it the other night."

My ears thrummed. He sounded much farther away than he was. Despite the pain, I had craned my ear toward the house's front wall hoping to catch whatever Crew and Sloane were discussing. But even when Sloane raised her voice, it was only muffled notes.

Jordan pulled the cover open and scanned the first couple pages until he apparently found what he'd been looking for, then flipped to the book's middle. He read, hummed, nodded. "Interesting," he said.

Whether it was the hard, cold floor against my back or the

mere passage of time, the shards of inner pain started ebbing again. I breathed a little deeper.

"Oh," Jordan said. "Oh, wow. Okay this *is* interesting."

"Spit it out," I managed hoarsely.

"Okay, okay, correct me if I'm wrong," he said, "but you and Adam were tied to the same demon, yeah? You went through your Dark Trials together, didn't you?"

I guess Adam shared more about me—about us—with the Dantes than I'd thought.

"Not exactly," I said. Embers burned in my chest and stomach, but the flame had died. I pressed myself up with a grunt until I reached a sitting position. My mind flashed to Adam, his long hair plastered to his face, panting in the mud when I pulled him from the cliff's edge, then the light smile that crept across his face once he realized I'd sent Malum flying to the raging lava lake below. The race down the mountainside, through the burning forest to the Circle. Seeing my parents. Twisting the third and final key in the chest's keyhole. "Just the third Trial," I said. "We finished it together."

"Your souls re-bonded with your bodies at the same time?" Jordan asked. Not sure where he was going with all this, I nodded.

"We both woke up in my bedroom, yeah. We got our souls back, and that's where we found our weapons. That's when we learned we could enter the Gray, though I guess we didn't know what that all meant at the time."

Jordan nodded, then seemed to closely re-read a passage, smirking.

"What is it?"

"Well," he said, "if I'm right about this, then it could be both good and bad news. And if I'm wrong, then we should probably get you to the hospital."

"About what?"

"Says here," Jordan said, "that if two or more people are

bonded to the same demon, their souls may become bonded to each other."

I remembered the look Adam had given me that morning after I'd sold my soul to Malum to save Em, and when he realized that we were branded with the same mark on our wrists indicating that we were tied to the same demon. That's why both our keys were on the volcanic mountaintop with Malum, and why both of us earned our souls back after defeating him.

"So," Jordan continued, "when you and Adam defeated your demon, you both were re-bonded with your souls. In theory, at least, you received the souls that had been taken from you but were then bonded to each other, linked by the same demon who took them."

My head swam. "Okay…"

He forged ahead. "Meaning that you and Adam might… share things. Like feelings, emotions, or maybe even thoughts."

"Or memories," I said. The shock of realization cleared the clouds from my mind. I hadn't just dreamt of Adam's Trials, of taking on that manticore—I had lived it. Through Adam. Just like how he had re-lived mine.

"Yeah," Jordan said, "probably. I mean, it doesn't mention 'memories' here, but—"

"Let me see that," I said, reaching for the book as I pulled myself back up onto the folding chair. Jordan passed the tome, open to where he'd been reading.

"Right there," he said, tapping a paragraph in the middle of page 309. It read:

> Though extremely rare, two souls may be reunited simultaneously with their human bodies. When that unique event occurs, the two souls become, in a manner, linked. And when two souls are linked, the bodies they occupy may share some of the same feelings, the same emotions, and sometimes even the same thoughts. This is a phenomenon some call *anima circulo,* or "soul circle,"

meaning two souls, linked in one eternal round without beginning or end.

That would explain some of the weird things that've happened over the last few months—the memories, the way at times it seemed each of us knew what the other was thinking. But what would a 'soul circle' have to do with the physical pain I'd been suffering?

"Did you get to the part about 'anguish?'" Jordan said the word 'anguish' like it had left a literal bad taste in his mouth. I read on.

Although *anima circulo* may sound like the trappings of any number of romance stories, the truth of *anima circulo* is far less appealing. Those very few with the condition describe shared suffering, between themselves, especially when one member of the *anima circulo* is experiencing a particularly excruciating bout of anguish.

My thoughts went to Adam that day Em and I had moved into our new place, and the look of pure... well, anguish on his face as he expressed his true feelings for me. The same feelings I had been feeling for him but holding them back, locking them away until they literally made my heart ache. To think that, maybe, we'd been dividing the heartache between our souls, or maybe even exacerbating it, doubling it. But still...

"What does this have to do with anything, Jordan?" I asked. His jaw slackened and his head dipped like he'd just told me a joke but the punchline flew directly over my head.

"Two souls," he said, slowly, "when linked, may share the same feelings... the same 'anguish...'" He leaned forward and looked at me expectantly.

The meaning finally landed hard and square in the center of my chest.

"The same pain," I said and pressed a hand softly against my quivering lips. Jordan nodded. My hand dropped to my chin. "So, these pains I've been having... they're... connected? Shared? With Adam?"

Jordan pulled in a breath, then said, "It's just a theory. But it would make sense. You started feeling it after Adam was taken."

If Jordan's theory was true, that meant I'd been experiencing a piece of the pain, the anguish that Adam was feeling. The thought was a heavy weight threatening to drag me through the floor.

Then another thought: If I could feel his pain, or at least a portion of it, that meant Adam was still alive.

"Jordan," I managed. A deep well of heart aching emotion began to overflow. "We have to find him."

Crew came through the front door. Sloane, though, was not with him.

14

"Where is she?" I demanded.

"She'll be back," Crew answered. Out the window, I caught the image of taillights pulling onto the road, heading away from town.

"You let her go?" My voice rattled, my eyes shooting from the window to Crew. "You... she's the only one who knows where Adam is!" Crew stepped to me, calm, yet resolved.

"Who gave you the picture, Hannah?"

Are we really going to do this again? Right now? While Adam was suffering?

"The Ring," I blurted. "They... he wanted to meet me. He knew he could trust me." I shouldn't be telling them these details, but if it meant moving beyond their skepticism and finally getting to the matter of finding Adam, then I'd do whatever it took. Crew and Jordan split skeptical glances, and I anticipated Crew's follow-up question. "Michael," I said. "His name was Michael. He's a Dante with the Ring who has a mole in the Order who sent him the video that showed Sloane handing Adam over. The picture is a screenshot from the video." I breathed, forced my voice into a less frantic, lower register. "He asked what I knew about Sloane. I told him I didn't know much. He said I shouldn't trust her."

Crew and Jordan digested my explanation for a few long, silent seconds.

"Why you?" Crew asked. "The Ring always comes to me."

"Sounds like a question you should ask them," I said. "But right now, we need to find Adam and you just let our best and only lead drive away."

Crew padded slowly to the fireplace, rested his arm on top of the mantle.

"Something's not adding up," Crew said, tapping his fingers. "I've known Sloane ever since she was initiated. I initiated her, just like I initiated you. There's just no way…"

Jordan kept silent but nodded in agreement.

"Look, guys—"

"I called them," Crew interrupted. "I called my contact at the Ring. They confirmed that there's an operative here, in town." A ray of hope pulsed in my chest as he spoke. "The thing is… I just don't get why he would contact you, the newest Dante, and not me. Everything is supposed to run through me."

"If that's true," Jordan offered, "that the Ring is here in town, then it's safe to assume they have eyes on Sloane if she really is the threat they say she is. But I'm with you," he said to Crew. "There's no way she's a traitor. After what she's been through? No way…"

"And if they do have a mole inside the Order, then the mole would've told them where the Order has taken Adam, right?" Crew asked. They both looked at me.

It was a good point—one I hadn't thought of. Were they waiting on information from their mole? Or were they simply waiting for the best moment to strike? I could only shrug, shake my head. The mystery of it all made my head throb.

Jordan glanced past me, toward the house's front window where Sloane pulled away minutes earlier. "I don't like that she's on her own, though," he said. "Even if the Ring has eyes on her. Too many things are going sideways."

Crew lowered his head. "I tried to stop her."

My phone buzzed, shocking my senses. I pulled it out of my pocket expecting to see another text from **000000** in a soon-to-disappear text bubble. The phone buzzed again, and I realized it wasn't a text at all; it was a phone call. The number flashing on the ID made my heart sink.

"Em?" I answered. "What's wrong?"

Em didn't answer right away. Instead, I heard muffled sounds, heavy breathing. Was she crying? My heartbeats picked up speed.

"Em, talk to me. What's wrong?"

"Hannah," she finally said. Her voice was high, quiet, near a whisper. "Hannah, I don't... I... There's something..."

I swallowed hard. "Take a breath. Are you okay? Tell me what's going on. Did something happen at camp?"

"I saw ghosts," she said. "In the woods. Real ghosts. They... they could see me too. I'm in the closet. I think something followed me. Help me, Hannah."

Jagged ice curled itself around my spine. "Don't move," I demanded. "And stay on the phone. I'm coming right now."

I pressed past Jordan and Crew, pulled open the front door and flew to my car.

"Wait!" one of them shouted. But I wasn't about to wait for anyone. Em was in danger. I could tell by the timbre in her voice. She said she saw ghosts, and I believe her. It made sense—she'd been touched by a demon last fall. That had to mean something, leave some kind of residual effect on her, give her some abilities to see into the other side. But something deep down told me that what she thought were 'ghosts' in the woods weren't actually ghosts at all. They were something much, much worse. *They could see me too,*' she'd said. *'I think something followed me.'* Crew's hand gripped the top of the driver's side door before I could slam it shut.

"Let go! I have to get to my sister, and I have to get there *now*."

"No Dante travels alone," he said, eyes steely. "Not until we figure all this out."

Without a word, Jordan slid into the passenger seat with an apologetic expression. I had no time for this.

"Fine," I said, exasperated, then yanked the door hard until Crew finally let go. I turned over the ignition and Jordan lowered his window.

"What are you going to do?" He asked Crew.

"Find the Ring," he said, voice fading as I reversed down the driveway. "Then find Sloane."

I turned south, away from town, and mashed the gas pedal to the floor.

THE SUN STARTED SINGEING the horizon. My headlights capered along the highway as I weaved between vehicles. "You still there?" I asked.

"Yes," Em answered softly. Houses and buildings disappeared with time until all that remained was dusty, bleak desert on either side of the highway. Traffic thinned, and as we sped past the highway shoulder where Sloane had taken us hours ago —where Adam had been taken—Jordan finally spoke up.

"Where we headed?"

The white stitching that made up each side of my lane began to blur. I clenched my jaw. I didn't want him here. I didn't need him here.

I didn't need any of them.

A lot had changed in the last twenty-four hours. I glanced at the barely visible brand on my wrist. Maybe becoming a Dante was a mistake. Maybe the reason the Ring reached out to me was because *none* of the others could be trusted, Jordan included.

"Hannah?" Jordan said.

"We're going to get my sister," I said, and that was all he needed to know.

"Um," Em's voice squeaked from the phone's speaker.

"What is it?" I asked.

"The phone you gave me," she said. "It's about to run out of batteries."

I mentally shuffled through every swear-word in existence. "Tell me where you are, and that way if your phone dies before I get there, I can come find you."

"I'm in the front, by the main cabin." Her voice was a rattle. "There's a shed next to it. I'm in there."

"Okay," I said, trying to picture the description in my mind. "You hang on, Em. I'm coming." But Em didn't answer back. Half a second later, my phone beeped. A small text box on the screen read: CALL FAILED.

"No..." I tried re-dialing. No rings. Instead, a robotic message that the person who I was trying to call had a voicemail box that had not been set up yet. "No, no, no..." This time, I let the swear-words fly, barely holding myself back from launching the phone into the dashboard. Moisture threatened to spill over the corners of my eyes.

Then a thought... Where was everyone else? Scarlett, the other campers, the camp counselors... I pulled up Camp Sego Lily's front office number and dialed it. The other end of the receiver rang ten times before an automated message picked me up. I mashed the red button in frustration before the beep.

First Adam, now Em. At least I'd heard her voice. At least I knew where she was. Nothing in this world or the next would deter me from reaching her, but as we raced down the highway, I wished I could feel a hint of that hot, needling pain I'd felt before. Strange as that sounds, I needed a sign that Adam was alive.

"Look," Jordan said, barging in on my thoughts, "I don't know what's going on, but I'd like to help if you'll let me."

"There's nothing you can do," I said, checking my speedometer. It felt like two miles were tacked onto each mile driven. Despite pushing the small Civic as fast as it could go, we were still over sixty miles away from Camp Sego Lily, from Em.

A few silent seconds passed before Jordan spoke up again. "Do you think I could take another look at that picture? The one you showed me and Crew?"

I gripped my phone tight and considered the question. Of all of them, Jordan did seem the most willing to help, the most concerned about my well-being. He'd opened my eyes to *anima circulo*, and even if he didn't believe that Sloane could've double-crossed the Dantes, he never questioned my sincerity either. I unlocked the home screen and handed it over, then choked the steering wheel with both hands as if squeezing it would coax the whining Civic beyond its apparent maximum speed of eighty miles-per-hour.

Jordan started making the same annoying sounds he'd made when he was studying about *anima circulo*; humming, saying the words 'okay' and 'interesting.'

"Holy crap, Jordan," I said. "What is it?"

He held the screen in front of me. I split my focus between the picture and the road.

"Yeah, I've seen the picture a thousand times. What about it?"

Wordlessly, Jordan pinched then expanded his fingers to zoom in on Sloane's butt.

"Are you serious right now?"

"Oops," Jordan said, then shifted the picture slightly, centering on Sloane's hand resting against her waist. I looked, then looked again.

"What am I supposed to be seeing?"

"Sloane has a new tattoo," Jordan said. "Do you see it?"

I looked again. "No," I said. "I don't see any tattoo."

"Exactly."

Confused, I racked my brain. Sloane had plenty of tattoos. What was I supposed to see? Jordan apparently wanted me to discover that answer for myself, because he still held the phone out, the picture zoomed in on the side of her hand that rested against her waist...

It hit me in a flash. The arrow.

Sloane had lain her arm on the table to show me the damage to the Dantes marker on her wrist. Someone had tried to cut it out, replace it with the circular symbol for Order of the Snake. That's when I'd noticed Sloane had a narrow tattoo of a fletched arrow that striped the side of her hand beneath dried blood.

I peered at the screen again to make sure, then triple checked. "There's no arrow," I said. Jordan nodded and pulled the phone back. "You sure that's the correct hand?" I asked him, unsure myself.

"I'm sure," he said. "Something isn't adding up." His words matched my thoughts.

Jordan pulled out his own phone and called Crew, then informed him in detail of what we'd discovered. "Yes, I'm sure," he said quietly into the receiver. "Something's up. Have you found her?" Crew must not have found Sloane, because Jordan quickly followed up with, "Well, let us know. We'll keep you posted." Then hung up.

Something strange was happening. Something the Ring didn't want us to know. Or was it the other way around?

Roughly one million miles later, I pulled off the highway, following a large brown sign that announced CAMP SEGO LILY in white letters with a white arrow pointing west. The raw desert landscape had transformed into wooded wilderness miles ago. The narrow road ascended, winding through a mountainous canyon fenced by tall, thick trees.

One arrow points to Em. The lack of another arrow seemed to point away from Sloane.

Was I wrong? Had I attacked her, accused her of being a traitor, on bad intel? Was Michael aware that the girl in the video may not have been Sloane at all?

Who was the mole?

Every single question was a thread tied to a dead end. I forced them into a lockbox in the back of my mind and focused on the road that led us into the dark woods. Asphalt disappeared. The road became bumpy, narrow, dusty. Large trees loomed in the darkness. Their arching branches became a tunnel which, in the dark, looked less like tree branches and more like spindly skeleton hands reaching out.

Headlights danced over wood-carved signs along the road's shoulder, each carved in the shape of a Sego Lily flower. Each wooden flower had one yellow word etched in its center like 'Friendship,' 'Fun,' and 'Adventure.' They seemed almost comically out of place on the dark road in the dark forest. It wasn't until we passed 'Responsibility' before the first cabin finally came into sight.

WHERE WAS EVERYONE? The car rattled as I bumped along the dirt road toward it, headlights bouncing off the dark, empty windows. Sure, it was getting late, but I expected to at least see a light on. I shoved the transmission into park and killed the engine. The dust wake we'd created caught up and enveloped the car in a cloud as we exited.

"She said she was in a shed next to the main cabin," I told Jordan.

"I'll take this side." Jordan went right. I went left. As I peered into the darkness ahead, I couldn't fight the uneasy feeling settling heavy in the bottom of my stomach.

Something's wrong. Something is way off. No lights. No people...

"Hey," Jordan called just before I'd rounded the cabin's front left corner. "Check this out." My anxiety tried to yank me around the corner, to look for the shed, to find Em and to find her *now*. But the look on Jordan's face told me that what he had to show me was important. I jogged over.

He pointed to a makeshift paper sign duct-taped to the cabin's front door. It read:

IT'S CAMPING NIGHT! ALL CAMP COUNSELORS ARE ROUGHING IT WITH THE GIRLS ON CRAIG'S MESA. IF YOU HAVE AN EMERGENCY, CALL CAMP DIRECTOR RIGGS: (970) 555-4563

I dialed Director Riggs. He didn't pick up. I cupped my hands around my mouth to call for Em, but before I could, Jordan wrapped his hand hard around my wrist.

"I don't know, Hannah," he said. "Something's up. Not sure what." He released my wrist, then added, "Probably best that we find your sister and get in and out without drawing too much attention to ourselves."

He was right, and I was glad I wasn't the only one of us feeling uneasy. Jordan nodded, then made his way around the cabin's right corner. I returned to the left side, scanning for a small shed or outhouse, or anything matching the description Em had given.

Fog nestled along the forest floor. I hated it. It reminded me of the Borderlands. But I hated even more that there was no obvious outbuilding on my side of the cabin. Jordan hadn't called for me either, which I know he would do if he'd found something.

I can trust him. Right?

I swallowed and rounded another corner. If there wasn't a shed in plain sight along the cabin's back side, I'd have to call out for her, attention be damned. Jordan rounded his corner at the same time. We met each other's wide eyes, then scanned the cabin's back wall, walking slowly toward each other. There was nothing there except split and stacked firewood and a couple of wheelbarrows. My anxiety shot into the red, and just as I was about to scream for Em, a narrow section in the middle of the wall of stacked firewood revealed itself. A narrow, wooden door with a tiny metal handle was so well disguised, I nearly missed it.

A shed.

I exhaled, rushed to the door and pulled the handle.

"It's locked," I told Jordan. "From the inside. Bolted. Em!" I called through the sliver of space between door and frame. "Em, it's me!" I tried the handle again, but the door wouldn't budge. I pressed my ear against the cold wood and listened hard. The only sound I heard was my thrumming heart like pistons in a massive engine.

'I saw ghosts. In the woods. Real ghosts. They… they could see me too.'

I called again through the crack, then listened.

Silence.

I took a few steps back, ready to bust the door open with a front kick when I heard a small *click*. The door creaked slowly open. Em's pale, terrified face peered out of the darkness, around the door's edge. When she saw me, she flew, crashing into me with such force that we both ended up on our knees.

"Em… Em… It's okay. I'm here. I'm here." I brushed one hand through her hair, then held her face. It was shaking, rattling like a dead leaf and white as the moon. Even in the darkness, the pure terror that laced her damp eyes sent an icy shiver down my own spine. "Hey," I said, rubbing a tear from her cheek with my thumb. "Don't be scared. There's nothing to be afraid of. Not while I'm here."

"I saw things," Em managed. "You won't believe me." I pulled her in tight, then glanced at Jordan who was hanging back, hands in pockets.

"I will always believe you, Em," I whispered into her ear. "I promise. I've seen things too. Awful things. You're not alone."

Em pulled back, wiped her nose with the loose sleeve of her hoodie. "You see things, too?"

'You see,' she'd said. Present tense.

"Yes," I answered. "I see things." I nodded, trying to hold

back the rush of emotions that battled for supremacy inside me; Relief that I could finally be honest about myself with her, and dread at the fact that she carried a burden no young girl should ever have to carry. She had sight. She could see beyond our world. To what extent, I didn't know yet, but that didn't matter. Hers was a curse, a remnant of having been touched by the demon Malum. I hated him more in that moment than I ever had.

"Where's Scarlett?" I asked her.

"Probably still asleep in the tent. Our campsite's about a couple miles that way," she said, motioning toward the dark woods beyond. "When I... saw things... I remembered the phone you gave me. So I ran back here, away from those things, to call you."

'*Those things...*'

What had scared her so badly that she left her sleeping camp mates, including her best friend, and ran through miles of dark woods all alone?

"Come on," I said, standing, then lifted her up to her feet. "We have a lot to talk about, but let's get you home first."

"Who's that?" Em asked, turning toward Jordan.

"That's my friend, Jordan. He's like me. You'll understand more about that later, I promise—"

"No," Em interjected, then pointed a trembling finger toward the dark woods behind Jordan. "Who is *that*?"

15

I swallowed hard, then peered into the thick darkness just beyond Jordan. Three silent beats passed before I spoke up. "Em, I don't see anyone. Are you sure you're—"

But before I could finish the question, Em gripped my arm, stepped quickly behind me and buried her face into my back. "Don't," she said, trembling. "Don't let it come closer."

Jordan, who was now standing beside me and also peering into the woods, shot me a questioning glance. On instinct, I reached for my sword. As I pulled the blade from its sheath, Jordan followed my lead, and both of us plunged into the Gray. The sight ahead was an icicle through my heart.

Directly in the middle of two craggy trees loomed a massive figure—a Reaper, based on the long spike it held directly between its slitted yellow eyes in front of its ink-black hood. But the Reaper's weren't the only yellow eyes floating in the woods.

Two—no, three—other pairs peered out from beyond the trees, deep in the foggy forest.

"Do you see them now?"

My heart nearly burst from my chest when I realized it was Em who'd asked; Em, who wasn't affected by the Gray but could see the demons ahead; who could see me as I held the handle of my short blade firmly. I turned, dropped to a knee and held her in front of me by the shoulders.

"You can see me? You can see the de—the things out there?" Through the whirling ash-colored air that made up the Gray, Em nodded, her eyes heavy and apologetic as if she'd been caught breaking a camp rule. Tears threatened to spill over her bottom eyelids when I pulled her to me again, raking my free hand through her hair. A pang of guilt gripped my stomach. Had she suffered like this ever since she'd gotten her memories back? Or had this curse gradually come to her? How have I not noticed until now?

"Everything's okay" I whispered into her ear. "You've done nothing wrong. I bet you have a lot of questions, and you'll probably have a lot more, soon."

"Hey, uh, Hannah?" Jordan spoke up behind me. But before turning, I held Em out in front of me and held her wet eyes with mine.

"I'll give you all the answers as soon as I take care of a few things, okay?"

"What are you going to do?" She asked, wiping her nose across her sleeve. I stood, and when I did, I saw Em's gaze fall over my sword, eyes widening.

"Stay right here, and don't move" I said, then turned and stepped toward Jordan. The three pairs of yellow slitted eyes had multiplied. At least six now hung in the air like thin blowtorch flames that narrowed at the sight of us. None of them burned hotter than the flame blooming inside of me, spreading like wildfire through my chest as I stepped toward Jordan.

"What should we do?" Jordan asked when I reached him, which surprised me a little since I was the new Dante on the block. I set my jaw.

"We should do what we do best," I said, and caught the faintest hint of a smile pinch the corners of his lips.

"I was hoping you'd say that."

As one, we turned toward the trees and the fiery eyes

hovering deep within ink black hoods in the cloudy darkness, then stepped forward.

"Ringleader at twelve-o-clock is a Reaper," Jordan said, voice low as we approached. "Can't tell whether the rest—"

"The rest," I interrupted, "are dead demons walking." And I meant it. My vision tunneled, focus sharpened to match the edge of the blade which would be the last thing these demons would ever see. Reapers or not, none of them would be leaving the forest as anything other than a pile of ash. Malum had cursed my sister, and as far as I was concerned, every single one of the demons brooding ahead in the darkness was Malum, and every single one of them was about to meet the same fate he did, and by the same sword.

I raised the blade, pointed it directly at the Reaper's chest, and charged. Jordan matched my pace. He swung his hatchet high. The Reaper growled and blocked Jordan's blow just as I slid low and to one side, past the demon's rustling black robes, ripping my pants and knees across hard dirt and sharp rocks. By the time the Reaper realized what had happened, it was too late. I stood and turned to see a bright, golden ribbon of light escape from a thin line that spread across the demon's waist.

"Goodbye," I said through a wry smile. "And good riddance."

The thin golden line burst into a roaring flame that engulfed the Reaper's robes. Then, in a brilliant flash, it burst into a million orbs of light, each orb crackling as it reached the earth. I turned, double-gripped my sword, and glared into the other remaining eyes hanging in the darkness ahead of me.

"Who's next?"

I didn't bother waiting for an answer and bolted to the closest set of eyes—another Reaper. In one hand, it raised a dark blade. Its other hand was directed toward my chest, skeletal fingers splayed open, shaking with the desire to reach into me and petrify me by gripping the fear inside.

But there was no fear inside. Only hot anger.

The demon slashed its blade downward. My razor focus plunged each move into slow motion. I blocked blow from above, gritted my teeth and landed a devastating front kick to the monster's chest. Our blades slid apart with a high-pitched squeal as I spun fully around to my left. Like a discus thrower, the high-speed spin gave me momentum, power. The Reaper's eyes widened just before I took its head off in one, clean slash. The resulting golden explosion illuminated the forest around me just long enough to spot two pairs of eyes attached to two black-robed bodies making the fatal mistake of snaking through the trees toward me.

Neither had a weapon that I could see. I smiled, licked my teeth realizing Tweedledee and Tweedledum here were lowly Phantoms. No wonder they'd held back—they were hoping their Reaper overlords would've given us Dantes a run for our money first. They were dead wrong.

Another burst of golden light exploded behind them— Jordan, taking care of business. As the forest lit up, I bolted toward the two Phantoms. Like the complete idiots they were, they stretched forth their hands to take hold of me. I shot for the tree that stood a few feet to their left and took three large, vertical steps up the cracking bark. My last step was a spring-board off the trunk. Sword cocked overhead, I launched toward them. One wide, arcing slash cut through the air and both of the demons' necks. I landed hard, and the shower of golden embers that followed illuminated a small, sharp blade out of the corner of my eye. Spinning, I shot to my feet, slashed, but was blocked.

"Whoa there, tiger." Jordan's hatchet held my blade a few inches back from his shoulder. "I saw two coming at you and thought maybe you'd need some help. That was some move."

I pulled my sword back. Normally, a compliment like that would've reddened my cheeks, but I hardly heard it. My body was an electric wire, buzzing, crackling. Blood pounded in my ears as I peered past Jordan into the trees, searching—almost begging—to find more eyes, more hoods, more flowing black robes to drive my sword into. Instead, all I saw was darkness. Jordan placed a hand on my shoulder.

"They're gone," he said. "But there will always be more."

I didn't know whether to smile or sulk at that. At that moment, I felt like I could take on Hell's entire demon army, and honestly wished I could. I wished I could take them all out in one fell swoop, one epic battle, and never see another demon ever again for as long as I lived. Even more, I wished I could've killed them all right then so Em would never have to see another demon again for as long as *she* lived. I glanced through the trees toward the cabin and found her rooted to the spot where I'd told her to wait.

With one heaving exhale, I attempted to settle my nerves. But just as I made to shrug Jordan's hand off my shoulder, he squeezed. Hard. I had never seen so much of the whites of his eyes. His pupils were fixed like lasers on something in the distant forest behind me.

"What is that?" he whispered.

Creeping, icy dread formed a knot in my stomach as I turned slowly, narrowed my vision and peered through the thicket of trees.

Eyes. But not the thin, burning, yellow slits belonging to a demon. No, these were large—*huge*—ovals, glowing green like a big cat's in the dark. They floated seven or eight feet off the ground, which meant that whatever they were attached to had to be absolutely massive. After what seemed like an eternal stare, the thing's eyes floated closer, smooth, stalking.

"Back to Em," I said. But Jordan stood stock still. By the looks of it, he hadn't blinked since spotting those green eyes in the distance. If I didn't know better, I'd say he was letting fear get the better of him, which was the worst possible scenario.

I slapped his face.

He blinked, looked at me.

"Come on."

Slow and methodical, we stepped out of the forest, into the

moonlight bathing the patch of open dirt riddled with pine needles behind the Camp's main cabin until we reached Em. The eyes followed but seemed to keep consistent distance away from us. Whatever it was, maybe it had more reason to be scared of us than we did of it. Perhaps the moon's reflection glinting off the razor edge of my sword held its attention and kept it at bay.

Or maybe it was waiting for the right opportunity...

"Keep your eyes on it," I told Jordan—not that I needed to. The look I saw on Em's face when I turned to her confirmed my dreadful suspicion: She could definitely see the green eyes, too. Was it because I had pulled my sword? Could she see into the Gray when I was inside of it and close to her? It might've made sense, except for that fact that she'd spotted those demons in the dark woods before I'd entered the Gray...

So many questions pinged off the inside of my skull.

"Hey," I said, rubbing her shoulder as we reached Em. Her wide eyes met mine. "I don't know what's going on, but we've got to get you out of—"

"Excuse me."

A low, unfamiliar voice came from behind me, electrocuting my nerves. But when I turned toward the woods, I couldn't see the voice's owner.

"Two o' clock," Jordan whispered.

Sure enough, there, leaning on a cord of firewood was a tall, wiry man in flannel and blue jeans flicking what looked like a toothpick between his bony fingers. A trucker hat cast a dark shadow over his face. In a swift whisper, Jordan confirmed my first thought.

"Vessel," he said. And he had to be right. A dark, fuzzy shadow served as an aura, monopolizing the air around him like a swarm of a trillion microscopic flies. The man tipped the brim of his trucker hat back, allowing the moonlight to cast over his striking features—sharp jaw, five-day stubble, high cheeks and, as I suspected, black-as-onyx eyes.

"Mister Riggs," Em said softly. "He's the Camp Director."

Slowly, she slid behind my back and I had to remind myself that even though she didn't have a weapon to pull her into the Gray like I did, she could probably see everything I could see. She knew something was very, very wrong with him.

A 'Vessel,' I had recently learned, was a person completely possessed by a demon or, more commonly, multiple demons, and not typically your average Phantom or Reaper, either. The power it takes to overtake and control a human body... let's just say it was a safe bet that whatever was inside Mister Riggs could probably dole out some serious damage. And if Crew and Sloane were right, there really wasn't a way to destroy the demon or demons inside of a person without destroying the whole person. Worse: by allowing the person to carry on living, it would only make the demons inside stronger. It's a catch twenty-two. To destroy the demon means to kill the innocent person they've possessed, but to allow the person to keep on living means putting countless others' lives in danger.

If Mister Riggs had become possessed to the point of becoming a Vessel, what else was out in those woods with all of the other campers and counselors? My heart wrenched once I remembered in a flash that Scarlett was still out there, somewhere.

Mister Riggs pushed off of the wall and stood up straight, legs wide like a gunslinger ready to draw, and I heard Jordan pull in a deep breath. "You're supposed to call the number on the paper in front if you need some help," Mister Riggs said. His voice was gravel, low and breathy. He took a heavy step forward, a malicious smile spreading across his thin lips. "Do you need some help? I can help you..."

This wasn't my first run-in with a Vessel, even though I hadn't known what a Vessel was when the lady laid pipe across the back of my car, or when that hospital security guard shot at me. At that thought, I remembered the vial of graveyard dirt in my car's center console, the effect it had on the security guard when I threw it in his face. Panic had clouded my judgment, and

I hadn't even thought to grab it. Now, it was too far for me to get to.

"That's close enough," Jordan said. He seemed calm, steady, which fortified me since only a few seconds ago he had seemed fearful. That reminded me... what happened to those green eyes? I scanned the dark woods ahead, but they were gone, now. Disappeared.

Mister Riggs—or, I should say, the body of Mister Riggs—took one more step, then halted. That was when I noticed the long axe in his right hand, and the snake-like trail of dirt he'd made by dragging its heavy blade behind him.

"I'm speaking to the entities inside of Mister Riggs," Jordan said. "If you knew who you were dealing with, I doubt you'd take another step forward."

Mister Riggs took another step forward. "And if you knew who *you* were dealing with, Dante," Mister Riggs growled, "I doubt you'd speak to us in that tone."

'Us.'

I squeezed my sword hilt, my knuckles turning whiter with every step Mister Riggs took, dragging the heavy axe head behind him. Jordan, to his credit, remained cool.

"I don't want to have to kill the body you're occupying, demons," he said, voice level. "But I will. And I will not hesitate."

Mister Riggs stopped about ten feet from us, stood straight, pulled the axe to his side and leaned on it like a cane. The wicked smile never faded from his lips. In fact, the thin line spread wider, curling into a snarl like something invisible sliced the edges of his mouth with a knife. The moon reflected like a diamond in contrast to his onyx-black eyes.

"It's not this body you need to worry about, Dante," Mister Riggs said. "No, no, but there is something here you should worry about."

Something sounded from the darkness in the woods just beyond where my eyes could see. It sounded thick, low.

"You see," Mister Riggs continued, "changes are coming. Changes like the world has never seen before. The animals are out of their cages."

Another snapping noise, this time a little closer. Afraid to take my eyes off Mister Riggs for too long, I only glanced to my left where I thought the noises came from. My gaze snapped back to Mister Riggs as soon as I heard the earthy scraping sound of his axe being dragged through the dirt as he took another step forward.

"Yes, the animals," he sneered. "Out of their cages and hungry. Ready to eat." He was stepping to his right, his dragging axe forming a crescent around our position. "Do you like animals?" he asked Em.

"Don't talk to her," I spat. Mister Riggs chuckled, ignored my command and spoke again to Em.

"Cats, maybe? Every little girl likes cats..."

Just then, rustling sounds came from the dark woods immediately behind Mister Riggs. My heart became a block of ice the moment those two large, green eyes appeared again at the forest's edge, that thin line where darkness met moonlight. Beneath the green eyes appeared a jagged outline of orange fire, like the mouth of a jack-o'-lantern. But unlike a jack-o'-lantern, this mouth moved. Slowly, deliberately, the thing attached to the eyes and mouth inched out of the darkness and into the silvery moonlight. I swallowed the knot of fear that had formed in my throat and forced in a breath before the demons occupying Mister Riggs could grab ahold of it.

"Em," I said, reaching behind me and grabbing a fistful of her jacket, "listen to me. Whatever you do, don't be scared. I know it's hard. But I'm going to need you to be brave right now. Do you understand?"

Em didn't answer. I could feel her bones rattling through her jacket. The monster in the woods had revealed its full face now. Jet black fur rippled in the breeze. The space inside its mouth behind its black fangs was dragon fire. Above its green eyes were two long, pointed ears. It looked like…

"A hellcat," Jordan finished my thought. He spat the word out as if it were laced with poison, and the look in his eyes told me this wasn't his first up-close encounter.

The hellcat slipped into the moonlight, stalking the forest's perimeter, never removing its laser-like glare from where the three of us stood rooted to the ground. It was then that I noticed the massive, gray claws connected to massive, black paws that moved noiselessly across the earth. Its tail swayed above its head like a cobra played out of a wicker basket. As it released a low, guttural growl, the flames licking the top of its mouth radiated bright orange.

"How…," I began, but Jordan cut me off before I could formulate the question.

"I don't know."

'…the animals… out of their cages… hungry…'

Mister Riggs leaned against his axe again, licking his teeth. "It obeys us," he said. "The only reason you're not dead is because we haven't told it to kill you. Yet."

Every muscle in my body tightened to the point of tearing. "Any ideas here, Jordan?" I whispered through the corner of my mouth. The only sound coming back from him was an audible swallow. Meanwhile, the hellcat stalked the forest's perimeter, inching closer, visibly eager to bolt for us at the word of its masters. I looked from the hellcat to Mister Riggs and set my jaw.

"Why not? What's stopping you from siccing your stupid cat on us?"

The hellcat hissed. Tendrils of black smoke curled around the corners of its mouth. Mister Riggs sighed.

"I enjoy scaring you is all. But yes, it seems the time for fun and games is up."

Just then, I felt a sharp tug on my wrist. Em twisted out of my grip, then bolted for the edge of the cabin behind us.

"Em! No!" My voice cracked with desperation.

Mister Riggs shouted something in some hellish language I couldn't understand, but that didn't matter. I knew what it meant.

The hellcat wailed, lowered itself down on its hind legs like a compressed spring. It's massive, muscular legs pressed the earth down in a giant leap. I turned back toward the cabin, toward my fleeing sister and ran hard. Time slowed with each step. I didn't know where Jordan was, or Mister Riggs. Only Em and the hellcat, and that if I didn't move fast, the monster would leap right over me and there would be nothing standing between its flaming jaws and my sister's neck.

The earth shook when the hellcat landed just behind me. I whipped around, slashing my blade through the air between us. The hellcat flinched, if only just a little. "Keep running, Em!" I screamed.

I turned, glaring straight into those poison-colored cat eyes. The monster hissed, brought itself low until its face was level with mine. The furnace inside its maw sizzled.

The hellcat let out a tiger-like roar. By the time I noticed that it had pulled back its paw, it was too late. I couldn't move quickly enough to dodge the oncoming swipe. Eyes shut, I braced myself for the blow.

Thwack!

The hellcat roared again, this time a high-pitched whine. My eyelids shot open to find Jordan's hatchet buried deep in the cat's paw.

"No!" Mister Riggs yelled.

The cat staggered backward, pawing the ground, releasing heavy huffs that caused the dust to plume around it as it tried to dislodge Jordan's hatchet blade. I took a five-step drop.

"Jordan!" I screamed as I took my first running step.

Jordan turned his attention away from the hellcat to find me rushing directly toward him, sword gripped firmly in fist. "Boost!"

Seemingly on instinct, Jordan leaned down, stretched his arms outward, and weaved his fingers together to create a single, solid foothold. In stride, I leaped to him, pressed one foot into his waiting palms and felt his strong arms launch me into the air like a trapeze artist. The force, the timing; everything was perfect. At the apex, I double-fisted my sword's hilt, and with one primal scream I landed hard on the hellcat's mangy black back and slashed the blade down hard across the hellcat's neck.

Something beneath my blade cracked, then snapped like a giant rubber band. Thick liquid oozed and bubbled with each of the hellcat's pathetic sputters. It struggled for breath, dropped to its knees. I freed my blade from its spinal cord just as the green light of its eyes flickered out forever.

Any sense of triumph was short-lived. Hot hellcat blood cascaded off the point of my blade when I cast my eyes toward Jordan. Mister Riggs was flying toward him, axe raised high above his head, but Jordan was fixated on me, oblivious.

"Jordan, duck!"

Like when I'd called for a boost, Jordan trusted me unquestionably and dropped to the ground at the exact millisecond I launched my sword through the air like a boomerang. The blade sang over Jordan's head. The pointed end hit with a sickening, low *thunk*.

Mister Riggs dropped his axe, then fell to his knees only a few feet from Jordan. My sword protruded out of his chest directly where the ribcage protects the heart, wobbling back and forth like I'd hit a bullseye in a tree trunk.

Mister Riggs' eyes grew wide. The already bloody blade became newly soaked in dark liquid—the same that began dribbling from the corners of his open mouth.

Electrified, I made my way from the hellcat over to Jordan. Mister Riggs sucked air, then fell in a heap to his side. The blackness from his eyes faded like black dye disappearing in white milk. His mouth opened wide—wider than seemed possible—and in the next instant, a swarm of dark particles rushed out of it. The tornado of demon entities escaping Mister Riggs' body intensified, like they were being sucked into the sky by a supernatural vacuum for what felt like an entire minute. Then, as suddenly as it began, the blackened blast dried up. Like a swarm of black hornets, the entities—there had to be hundreds—flew into the forest in the direction from where the hellcat had come.

Mister Riggs lay there, his lifeless eyes unfocused, staring into the beyond. I realized that I'd been holding my breath. My lungs burned. When I finally breathed, it came in hitching waves. With one trembling hand, I pulled my sword from his chest.

There's a difference between slaying a beast from hell and slaying a perfectly innocent human being. A huge difference. Mister Riggs the man didn't deserve it. He didn't deserve to have his body overrun by demons, and he didn't deserve to lose what was left of his life for it.

I was in trouble. Here, behind Camp Sego Lily's main cabin, lay Mister Riggs, Camp Director. Dead. Stabbed in the heart. How could I ever explain myself in a way normal people could understand? I am not a murderer.

Am I...?

My thoughts turned briefly to the man in the suit I'd faced in the Borderlands during my second trial. The one who had a daughter my age. The one who I fought, left behind to fade away in the darkness. Survival was a messy, dark thing. Something like barbed wire tightened around my heart.

In a blast of illogical panic, I scanned along the cabin's eaves and corners, looking for security cameras. If—when—the police were inevitably called, all it would take is one glance at the security footage and I'd be labeled wanted for murder.

Murder.

What have I done?

I felt Jordan's arms wrap around my shoulders. "Hey," he said, "you had no choice. He was going to kill me. You saved my life."

Somewhere deep down, I knew that was true. But that knowledge didn't soften the sharp, painful guilt wrapping itself around my insides. Behind us, the hellcat disintegrated into ash, blown away by the strengthening wind. I sheathed my sword, entered the dark real world where Mister Riggs somehow seemed worse, deader, than he did in the Gray.

"We need to get to higher ground," Jordan continued. "Come on, let's grab your sister."

That sent a spark directly into my brain. "Em... Em!"

"She's fine," Jordan said, "I saw her squat behind the car. She's still there."

I made a run for the dusty parking lot. Sure enough, Em was curled up in a ball against the back tire staring straight ahead as if she'd seen... well, a ghost. I pressed the hair back from her face and pulled her to me, shushing her even though she was perfectly silent. Every inch of her vibrated with fear. In a sense, I was glad she took off running. The things the demons inside Mister Riggs could've done to her if they'd gotten ahold of her fear...

I forced that thought away. That part was over now. The demons were gone. The hellcat was dead.

"Over here," Jordan called. I found him climbing the cabin's front porch railing. He was just tall enough to stand and reach the roof's overhang. "I'll boost you up," he said.

I stood. "What?"

"We need to get on the roof," he said matter-of-factly. When he saw the confusion mask my face, he added, "I have an idea of what's going on here. I need a better view, but I'm not about to leave you both down here while I'm up there. Who knows what else is out here watching us...?"

A shiver ran down my spine as I glanced behind and around me, into the blanket of darkness just beyond the trees, and considered what types of invisible things could be lurking there. Invisible to me, anyways. I glanced down, reached out for Em, but she was a stone, unmoving.

"I need you to stay with me right now," I said softly. "I'll try to explain everything soon, I promise."

Finally, her tepid eyes met mine. I pulled her up by the arm, and with a hand around her waist, walked over to the porch's edge where Jordan stood waiting.

"Her first," I said, then turned again to Em. "Jordan's going to lift you, but you need to pull yourself over the edge and onto the roof."

"Why are we going on the roof?" she asked, voice rattling.

"I don't really know," I answered honestly. "But Jordan thinks we should, and I trust him."

Em glanced from me to Jordan, breathed, then stepped toward him.

"'Atta girl," he said, then lifted her by the waist until she grasped the rain gutter, then pulled herself up and over the edge. "You next," he said, then formed a basket with his hands exactly like he'd done to send me flying through the air and onto the hellcat's back. I placed my hands on his shoulders, stepped, gripped the rain gutter as he hoisted me above his head, then pulled myself up next to Em. I thought to offer Jordan a hand up, but he was already up and over the roof's edge by the time I turned.

Gray, mottled clouds drifted lazily across the sky, blanketing the stars above. The full moon silhouetted each cloud with a silver lining. The breeze had picked up enough that I really started to miss my jacket. Strange weather for summer.

"Okay, Jordan," I said, "what are we on the roof for?"

Jordan stood, transferred the dust from his palms to his jeans, then took in his surroundings. With a head nod, he directed us to follow him up the roof's pitch. We straddled the peak, then sat silently for a few seconds, waiting for Jordan to reveal his reasoning. At least, that's what I was doing. Em was still shaken, staring off into space, processing the horrors she'd seen like an ancient laptop trying to download a massive media file. I pressed a hand against her leg.

Jordan pulled his hatchet, and I followed his lead. In the Gray, he let out a heavy sigh. "That's what I thought," he said, somber.

"What is it?"

Jordan pointed the butt-end of his hatchet toward the forest behind the cabin. From up here, I got a better sense of the forest's size and density. The terrain was rough, rocky, covered in dense patches of trees and boulders. A mile or so out, maybe less, the trees ran into a sharp rock cliff on one side. It rose a few hundred feet in the air. The bright moonlight fractured against the mountain's back end, casting a long, craggy shadow across the forest toward the cabin. And there, near the base of the cliff…

"What *is* that?" I asked.

"That would explain how a hellcat found its way into our world," he said. "We need to get Crew on the phone. Seems we've finally found the portal to Hell."

16

E m and I sat in silence for a few moments after Jordan climbed off the roof to fetch his phone from the car. Distantly, I heard him speaking with Crew, but that wasn't where my attention was focused.

Em was a rattling autumn leaf in a windstorm, and not because it had suddenly become chilly. I wrapped my arms around her and brought her head to rest on my chest, yet she still seemed distant.

"I have a lot to tell you. A lot I should've told you a long time ago, Em. And I'm sorry. I shouldn't have kept everything from you for so long."

Em remained silent, her chest fluttering like she couldn't quite pull in enough air. I held her out to me, forcing myself into her line of sight.

"Em. Talk to me. Tell me what you're seeing."

She winced, like my words were darts.

"Do you see… more of them? Like the ones in the forest? With yellow—"

"Eyes," she said, then dropped her gaze to the ground. "Yes."

"Look at me, Em."

Reluctantly, she brought her eyes, brimming with wetness, to meet mine. "What is wrong with me, Hannah? Why am I seeing monsters?"

My chest tightened. How in the world would I be able to explain everything to her?

From the beginning, Hannah…

After a heavy breath, I asked, "Do you remember last fall? When you were in the hospital?"

"Yeah."

"Well, you were about to die, Em. The tumor… it was in a really bad spot. They said you only had a few days left…"

Em watched as a flood of emotion rushed to my face. I cleared my throat, tried to choke it down.

"I… I had to do something. I couldn't lose you. Not after losing mom and dad."

Em wiped a trundling tear from my cheek with her thumb, and I gripped her hand, holding it tight against my hot cheek.

"Adam. He told me… well, I asked him if…," but I couldn't finish. I couldn't find the words.

Just tell her, Hannah. Keep it simple.

"Those monsters with the yellow eyes… those are demons, Em. I sold my soul to one of those demons, in exchange for your life."

The words floated in the air between us like they were made of feathers, softly trundling through in the breeze toward Em. Once they landed, though, they physically knocked Em back.

"You… you what?"

"I sold my soul so that you'd live. And Em," I said, gripping her hands in mine, "it worked. The doctors and surgeons couldn't explain it when your tumor suddenly moved and became operable. They kept calling it a miracle, but I knew better. When I made my deal with Malum, I—"

"Malum?" Em's eyes were saucers.

"Yes, the… the demon that I sold my soul to in exchange for your life. His name was Malum."

Em blinked.

"And I didn't understand it at the time… gosh, I don't know if I even understand it now. I think when I sold my soul to him, he moved your tumor, or did… something… to save your life. But when he did that, I think it affected you somehow."

Em blinked again, and the stone expression on her face didn't budge. I had no idea whether or not she was comprehending anything I was saying, but it almost didn't matter. The fact that I was saying it, that I was finally telling her *everything* that I'd so carefully kept hidden from her, locked away in my deepest inner vault… It was a boulder rising from my shoulders.

"I talked to Adam about it," I continued. "What he said made sense to me. You were touched by a demon, Em. And you can't expect to be touched by a demon without any consequences."

A stiff breeze climbed the cabin rooftop and swept between us, but I don't think it was the breeze that caused Em to shiver. Jordan must've finished his call to Crew, because I could hear him struggling to climb back onto the roof.

"So," she finally managed after a few painfully long, silent seconds, "you sold your soul? Does that mean that you're… that you'll end up—"

"In Hell? Luckily, no. At least not for that reason." I tried to wink, lighten the mood, but Em didn't catch it. "That's where Adam came into the picture. He helped me get my soul back."

"Get it back? How?"

"Well… I went down there and took it back from the demon I'd traded it to."

Em's brow wrinkled. "Down there?"

"Down to Hell. Well, the Borderlands of Hell, anyways. I realized that I hadn't really read all the fine print when it came to selling my soul, and that demon I'd traded with—Malum—was making my life a literal living Hell. What's worse was, because he owned my soul, he was actually able to drag me down to Hell any time he wanted to, leaving you behind with no memories and no family." I slid a stray strand of hair behind Em's ear.

"Adam did a lot to get me through those Dark Trials. I owe him everything, really."

Whether Em looked terrified or impressed, it was hard to tell in the dark. Jordan reached the roof's peak and squatted down a ways behind me, respectful of our conversation.

"Where is Adam?" Em asked, glancing around.

My stomach curled in on itself. I gazed across the swaying, pointed tips of the trees ahead, to the base of the cliff where Jordan had pointed out the portal.

"I think he's close," I said, then glanced back toward Jordan. He nodded seriously. I shifted sideways so I could look comfortably between him and Em. "Em, this is my friend. You haven't been properly introduced yet. His name is Jordan."

"Hi," Jordan said with a wave. Em gave a limp wave back.

"He's like me," I said, "as I'm sure you've probably already figured out. He can see things, too."

"And kill them," Em said matter-of-factly. "I saw both of you in the woods killing the things with the yellow eyes. That was pretty cool."

I chuckled, tousling her hair.

I could've told Em everything about why Jordan and I were together, about how we belonged to a secret, exclusive group of demon hunters called the Dantes, and that Adam had been kidnapped by a different organization and handed over to demons to be tortured or worse. But she'd seen enough, tonight. She'd heard enough.

A blast of wind rushed through the trees, making them creak and groan. Beneath them, creatures and demons lurked unseen.

We have to find Adam and get that portal closed soon.

"Crew should be here soon," Jordan said. "Until then… I'm happy hanging out up here."

"Yeah." I cleared my throat, pulled Em close. "Me too."

17

I t didn't take Crew long to get to Camp Sego Lily, but during that time, the world devolved to chaos. Em became jumpier, more nervous, and I couldn't blame her. Every few minutes, I pulled my sword and peered into the Gray. Every time, the woods became more alive. Slitted yellow eyes darted between the dark spaces. Unnatural screeches pierced the air. Then there were the sharp spoons hollowing out my insides like a pumpkin being prepped for carving.

It was the same pain I'd felt before, just more pointed; more intense. The pain came on in an instant, without warning, as if all of the adrenaline that flooded my veins minutes before had been replaced by searing hot wires. Em placed an arm on my shoulder as I gripped my sides and struggled for breath.

"What is it?" She asked softly. I heard Jordan scoot across the roof's shingles toward me.

"I don't... I'm not sure I can explain it right now," I managed. Which was true. *Anima circulo*, or the 'soul circle' that linked mine and Adam's together, was difficult enough for me to understand even despite my experience with the Dark Trials— something I still hadn't explained fully to Em. The pain was vicious, deep. Yet, somewhere deeper, I was relieved to feel it. It meant he was alive, feeling, albeit terrible pain. We were closer now.

Closer to Adam.

The second I thought it, I knew it was true. This pain was similar, yet different—intense, like a game of hot or cold. The closer we got, the hotter the pain...

"Crew's here," Jordan said. He slid down the scratchy tiles and climbed off the roof to meet him. In my periphery, I saw dim orange fog lights pull into the dirt parking lot. The Jeep was slow, careful, like Jordan had given him a warning. *'Careful, Bro. There are... things... out here.'*

"Are you sick?" Em asked. One glance told me that she didn't mean the flu. Her eyes were wide, dry yet cloudy with the remnants of tears, her cheeks flushed. I forced in a heavy breath and held it, focused my mind, regulated my heartbeat until the sharp pain began to dissipate.

"No," I said after what felt like a full, awkward minute of silence. "I don't think so."

"Hey Hannah," Jordan whisper-screamed from below. "Come on down, we need to talk."

I looked deep into Em's eyes for a moment. "Adam is in trouble, and we're going to go find him," I explained.

"In trouble? What kind of trouble? Where *is* he?"

Another deep breath, but I fought the urge to let my eyes fall. With a nod toward the woods and what lay beyond, I said, "I think he's out there."

I didn't think Em's eyes could have opened any wider, but somehow they grew as they shot from me to the woods, then back to me. Her bottom lip quavered as she struggled to formulate words. It was all too much.

"But we're going to get him, Em. He's going to be okay. And then I'll be okay."

Her breath quickened. Standing, I offered her a hand up. "Come on. Let's go talk to the guys."

After a few seconds' hesitation, Em wordlessly reached for

my hand, and we descended the roof together. Jordan helped Em to the ground gently, then me.

"You okay?" Crew asked.

I nodded. "He's close," I said. He and Jordan exchanged a glance, nodded.

"You're...," Crew began.

"In pain. Yes. A lot." I choked down another wave as I could feel it rising through my guts. "Which means that he's in even more pain and we need to get to him fast."

Crew looked to Jordan. Em shot silent, questioning glances between all of us.

"Soul circle," Jordan said, answering Crew's unasked question.

Crew flexed his jaw, apparently thinking for a few seconds before his gaze landed on Em. His stony face softened a bit when his glance landed on Em. "You are clearly Hannah's sister," he said. "The resemblance is uncanny."

"This is Crew," I told her. "He's like me and Jordan, and he's going to help us find Adam." Em nodded, her hands busy crumpling up each side of my shirt.

"What's with the rope?" I asked. Crew palmed a wrap of thick rope that hung over his shoulder and across his chest.

"Jordan mentioned the portal was near a cliff," he said. "Figured I'd come prepared. So, what else are we dealing with here?" Crew asked no one directly, and while I waited for Jordan to answer, he apparently was waiting for me.

"There's an army out there," I said as a shiver snaked down my spine. "Reapers, Phantoms, Vessels—we've already had run-ins with all of them. Not to mention the hellcat."

A collective swallow, then Crew said softly, "Jordan mentioned. So that means the portal's close by, and worse, things are finding their way out."

"Like we thought," Jordan said. "It explains the huge uptick in activity around."

"Hellcats, though?" I asked. I didn't mean for my voice to

quaver in a panic, but it was out of my control. I pulled Em close to me. "I mean... what does that even mean? Are hellhounds next?" The shiver that snaked down my spine solidified into a sharp icicle threatening to puncture my lungs at the thought of running into another hellhound, and without trees with poisonous sap around to soak my blade first.

"I'll admit," Crew said, "this is uncharted territory for all of us. I called the Ring before coming to you, explaining what I knew. They're on their way with some backup."

"We can't wait for backup," I said as another swell of hot pain rose into my lungs. "Who knows how many of them are close enough to get here soon or how long they'll take to get here at all. He doesn't have time, Crew." I gripped and scraped along the edges of my ribs, which again began to feel like someone had doused them in kerosene and set them aflame one-by-one.

Crew turned and gripped the back of his head with both hands, then stepped away from us. As the de-facto leader of our little gang of demon hunters and Hell portal-seekers, Crew was finding himself in an impossible situation: Either risk our lives by heading through forest and into the portal, or wait for a little backup, but every second that ticked by was another second Adam drifted toward irreparable damage or death. Luckily for Crew, I didn't really feel the need to wait around for orders from anybody, including him.

"I'm going now," I said. "Come if you want. Or don't."

Jordan was nodding his head like he'd already made his choice too, the edges of his lips pinching together in slight grin. Crew turned back to us, to me, stone-faced. Wordlessly, he nodded in Em's direction. His silent question was the same I'd been wrestling with ever since Jordan found the portal.

The soul circle meant a lot of different things. Sometimes I could feel Adam's pain. Other times we shared memories, maybe even thoughts. Altogether, I was the best chance Adam had at rescue. I knew it, and Jordan and Crew knew it. But that would mean leaving Em behind, because there was absolutely no way I'd risk bringing her through the portal with me. That thought was unimaginable.

"Jordan?" I said. "Stay with her for a sec?"

Jordan nodded. I gripped Em, told her everything was okay, and Crew and I stepped away toward the cabin. Crew made to pull his haladie, but I waved it off. "Doesn't matter," I said. "She can see into the Gray."

Crew's eyebrows arched. "That's an interesting development."

I sighed. "I don't understand it all yet either. Look," I whispered once out of Em and Jordan's earshot, "you won't find him without me. But I... I can't just leave her here."

Crew nodded, contemplating. "She sees demons?"

"Yes. And she says they see her. That's why we came up here in the first place."

"Were there any demons near where you found her?"

I wasn't sure what exactly he was getting at. "No," I answered. "Well, I can't be sure. We didn't see any at first, but we weren't in the Gray, plus I wasn't really looking for any signs. I would've noticed if they were waiting around the shed where we found her, though."

Crew let that information sink in for a few seconds, sucking on his teeth. Seconds ticked by, each one longer than the last.

"What do you think?" I finally asked.

After a long exhale, Crew finally left his thoughts and focused on me. "The Dark is attracted to us. They're aware of us, our presence. I don't think that's true for your sister, even if she's aware of it; of them."

"Why do you think that?"

"The demons you saw didn't show up until after you arrived. They weren't lurking, looking for her, attracted by her. Right?"

My turn to digest. I traveled back in my memories. Had I been so frantic that I wouldn't have noticed the tell-tale signs of demons haunting the spaces around the cabin while we searched for Em?

No. I would've noticed any anomaly, any fuzzy dark matter, any icy change in temperature. Jordan would've noticed, too.

"You're right."

"With us in there," Crew said, pointing toward the woods behind the cabin, "I'm pretty sure any and all focus will be trained on us. If she stays hidden, she stays safe."

I swallowed. That was easy for him to say—Em wasn't his sister. At the same time, what he said made logical sense. My guts started boiling again as I peered beyond the cabin, into the woods.

"Plus," Crew pulled out his phone, "I can call the Ring, let them know to post someone wherever you decide it's best to hide her." He swiped, unlocked the home screen. I grabbed his hand.

"No," I said. Crew looked perplexed, so I added, "I know you trust them. But I don't. I don't trust anyone outside of this parking lot. Her hiding place stays between us."

Crew allowed a reluctant nod. "Your call."

"Why aren't they here now?" I asked. "If the Dark is attracted to us, why isn't this spot teeming with demons?"

"They know full well we're here," he said. "They know why, too. And they're waiting."

I pulled my sword. From ground level, Crew was right. There were no yellow eyes, no Hellish sounds floating from the trees nearby. I peered sharply into the woods on the other side of the parking lot, behind where Jordan stood with Em. There, only thick darkness. I sheathed my sword and we made our way back to them.

Reaching Em, I leaned down. "Em, I know this is hard. I have to help these guys get Adam back. I don't think they can do it without me. But... I'm going to need you to stay behind."

I shouldn't have been surprised, but when Em met my eyes and put on her brave face, I was. Especially considering everything she'd seen and heard. "You'll bring Adam back?"

I nodded slowly. "Yes."

Em lifted her chin, straightened her shoulders. "Where should I hide?"

I smiled despite my heart twisting like a wrung sponge. "I have a blanket on the floor of the car's back seat," I said. "You can hide under it and I'll lock you in." I pulled her face to within inches of mine, then spoke slow and clear. "No matter what, don't pop your head up, don't look out the window, especially if you hear something outside."

Em swallowed, tightened her jaw. A sudden rush of anxiety ripped through me.

What am I thinking? I can't leave her here, under a blanket in a car in the woods with every conceivable demon or monster roaming around freely. I can't—

"It's okay, Hannah," Em said quietly, apparently reading the thoughts as they scrolled across my face in various screwed-up expressions. "You're the only one who can save him. You have to go."

If there was one person in the world who loved Adam as much as I did, it was Em. And if there was one person who needed him back as much as I did, it was her. With one deep breath, I tried my best to mirror Em's brave face, to match her stoicism, to pull from her the last ounce of courage I'd need to enter the woods and face whatever lay within them. When I wrapped my arms around my little sister, I realized she was no longer a rattling leaf. She was still, solid, brave.

"You're amazing," I whispered.

She squeezed my waist. "Please bring him back," she managed.

"I will." I released her and held her shoulders at arms-length, gazing into her green eyes. Dad's eyes. "I promise."

18

"You'll know when I'm back," I'd said as we'd walked toward the car, arms wrapped around each other.

"How?"

"Secret knock. I'll tap three times on the window, wait three seconds, then tap three more times. Got it?"

"Got it."

"Don't move, and don't look out the window unless you hear my signal."

"I won't."

"I don't know how long I'll be. It probably won't seem very long to you, but..."

I realized that I didn't actually know whether that was true. Usually, the people around me froze in time when I entered into the Gray unless they were a fellow Dante. But there was still so much I didn't know about Em and her abilities. Given everything that had happened over the last couple hours, though, I knew the time barrier that affected regular people when someone near them crossed the invisible veil into the Gray didn't affect Em in the same way. She was fully aware of everything that happened when Jordan and I rushed into the woods to take on those Reapers. She saw Mister Riggs for what he was—

possessed—and obviously the hellcat. Hell, I was the one who had to enter the Gray in order to see what *she* was seeing in the woods as we sat on the cabin's roof. Something deep inside told me that the curse Malum had left with Em meant that she had drifted into living between both worlds ever since last fall, slowly becoming fully conscious of both worlds and all the horrors that lived within them.

The thought ripped at my heart. At least I had some mode of escape from the other side. I could always sheath my sword and plunge back into reality—or, at least, the semblance of reality. Sure, I could still make out those fuzzy dark shadows—Phantoms or Reapers—that followed people around, trying their damndest to latch onto their souls, or the translucent cloud of black hornets that loomed over the rare Vessel. But Em? She was stuck, one foot in each world with no sword to protect herself with, and no sheath allowing her to escape, fully aware of the demons and monsters that haunt the shadows.

"I love you," I told her.

"I love you too."

I kissed Em's forehead before tucking the blanket behind her head, triple checked that all the doors were locked, all the windows shut tight, locked her inside, then popped open the vial of graveyard dirt I'd pulled from the car's center console. Carefully, I spread the dirt in a thin line around the car.

A DARK BREEZE whirled through the pines, wrapping itself around Jordan, Crew and myself as we stood, weapons drawn at the edge of the woods. I already felt too far from Em, but I choked the emotion down and focused.

The woods, which had been filled with howls and the awful sounds of undead life while Em and I were perched on the cabin's roof suddenly became eerily quiet. I didn't like that.

Whatever was in there knew we were coming. They lay in wait. I could almost feel them.

Crew's haladie sang as he spun it, splitting the dense air. Next to me, a soft, wooden *tap... tap... tap...*as Jordan rapped his hatchet's handle against his open palm. I spun my sword in a tight circle because, well, I wanted to look as cool as they did. I nearly dropped it. That made Crew smile.

"You good?" he asked. I cleared my throat, collected myself, tightened my grip on the handle.

"Yeah, I'm good." Which was true. Any fear of what might lay in the woods, or worse, of what came from leaving my sister behind in a locked car, had been locked away somewhere deep. Heading into demon and monster-infested woods with fear in your heart is far worse than heading in unarmed. Fear was their weapon—one that they could use to grab ahold of and end you in seconds—and I wasn't about to enter the woods as a flashing neon target.

Crew lifted his chin toward Jordan, who nodded back with angry eyes.

"Let's go get our guy, then."

TREES SWAYED IN THE WIND, their jagged branches threatening to reach out and grab us as we padded softly but quickly across the ground made soft by a layer of leaves and pine needles. We had decided to spread out a little. Ten feet or so separated me from each of them on my right and left. Occasionally we caught each other's glances between gaps in the trees, but for the most part, it was eyes ahead. This place—the woods, the warm wind— reminded me way too much of the Borderlands.

A full three or four minutes passed away as we made our way closer to the cliff base. The woods stayed quiet, muffled. Too quiet for my comfort. And then, finally, an unnatural sound from my right.

Laughter.

But not the high-pitched, tinny laughter the flying creatures in the Borderlands made. No, this was deep, ominous, and completely human.

A blade sliced through the air, followed by a soft explosion of bright, golden particles. Crew let out another laugh, and I couldn't help but smile myself.

"That's one for me. Pretty sure that puts me in the lead." We continued walking until I finally caught a glimpse of Crews eyes flashing back at me in the darkness.

"No way," I said. "Me and Jordan already took care of a few each before you even got here. Not to mention the hellcat and the Vessel. The hellcat counts as like five I'm pretty sure."

"True story," Jordan called from the dark distance.

"Whiners," Crew said. "Fine, you get a head start."

We had to be about halfway to the cliffside when an unholy howl split the air. Crew howled back. To my left, branches and shrubs began cracking under the weight of Jordan's rapidly increasing speed.

"Bring it!" he yelled, and in that moment, warmth bloomed in my chest. If there was anyone in the world I could've asked to storm the hillside covered in hordes of demons and underworldly beasts, it would be the guys to my left and right.

And Adam.

The blooming warmth turned hot. I matched Jordan's pace footfall for footfall. As the ground beneath us shifted to a gradual incline, I saw them—hordes of fiery yellow slitted eyes bobbing in the darkness beyond, nearly hidden beneath jet-black hoods. Vision tunneling, I white-knuckled my sword and ran harder.

Bring it.

The first few demons unlucky enough to meet the edge of my blade were Phantoms. It was almost funny, the way they tried to scare me by shrieking as they drifted across the forest floor toward me, skeletal arms outstretched like bad Halloween lawn decorations. Yet it was no less satisfying to see each of them burst into a million shards of crackling golden light the moment I sliced through them.

Demons are cowards. They act tough, but in the end, they suffer from the very thing they prey on: fear. I know this, because they placed their weakest on the front lines to face us first, to size us up, to determine whether we were actually serious about charging the hill. They learned very quickly that, yes, we were. Soon, the hill's initial slope was covered in flashes of sparkling dust, all that remained of the first wave of Phantom demons.

"Sixteen!" Crew grunted out numbers. "Seventeen!"

Don't get me wrong; seventeen was an impressive number. And maybe I should've been keeping track of my numbers, too. But it's not like there was a prize at the end for the highest number of demons sent back to Hell. For that reason, I decided my ultimate number was going to be Crew's ultimate number plus one.

The look on his face when I tell him...

Ahead, two pairs of yellow eyes appeared. Silvery moonlight silhouetted their flowing black robes. Then something else materialized in the distance beyond them. An outcropping jutted out from the cliffside's base, leading into what seemed to be a small cave. The inside of the small cave was illuminated in a soft glow, as if a single candle flickered inside. But it was no candle.

It was the open portal.

Like the ones who came before them, both demons ahead of me stretched out their arms in a futile attempt to grasp the fear inside me, to control me. It was like reaching for a cookie only to find the jar empty. When that didn't work, long jagged spikes jutted out from their sleeves.

Reapers.

"Finally." I smiled.

'Don't ever try to take on a Reaper on your own,' Sloane told me

the day we met. But that was the old, pre-Dante version of me. And besides, these two were in my way.

I sprinted up the hill. The Reaper on my left stepped forward to meet me, spike readied at its side like a joust. I slowed, realizing that pure adrenaline could only carry me so far up the hill before I ran out of breath. Feet away, I found myself in a very small clearing encircled by swaying trees, like an octagon encircling cage fighters.

I circled the first Reaper, blade outstretched, careful not to turn my back to the other. The first Reaper lunged forward, its spike missing my sleeve by centimeters.

I countered with a slash, but the Reaper was just out of reach. Its eyes grew hotter. Mine matched them.

In sync, both of us lunged. My blade crashed against the edge of its spike, slowly sliding down its length with a Hellish screech like nails scraping down a chalkboard.

I released, ducked, spun, anticipating the Reaper's block. When it came, I counter spun, slashing the air with all my momentum toward the Reaper's unguarded midsection and then...

Contact.

But not with the Reaper. With a spike.

But not the first Reaper's spike.

The second Reaper loomed over me, standing sentinel next to the first. If I could see into the eternal black space beneath its hood, I would've bet money right then that it was smiling wryly at me. *Not so fast little girl.*

The move was meant to scare me. I knew that right away, because instead of driving its spike down on me while I was in a vulnerable position, the first Reaper stretched out its robed arm.

Still no cookies.

I scraped my blade backward along the length of the second Reaper's spike, whipped it over my shoulder and down on the first Reaper, driving it deep into the space where I knew no heart resided. In the resulting explosion of light, I had just enough time to duck beneath the second Reaper's driving attempt to skewer me. With a heavy *crack*, its spike drilled deep into the tree trunk behind me. I matched the wry smile I had imagined on the Reaper's face when it had blocked my blade. Double-fisting the hilt, I swung my blade straight through the Reaper's midsection like Bryce Harper cracking off a homer.

Fireworks.

When the light twinkled away, I made out Crew who at some point had entered the octagon of trees. He offered a golf clap, and I responded with a curtsy.

"How many is that for you?"

"Hmm." I pretended to count on my fingers. "How many you got?"

"Twenty-three," he said ruefully.

I pointed in the direction where the two Reapers had been standing moments before I exploded them, pretending to count. "Twenty-four, for me."

Crew's smile turned upside-down. I would've chuckled if it weren't for the return of that ear-splitting howl we'd heard before. It was close—too close. This time, Crew didn't howl back.

"I know what that is," I said, doing my best to secure the rattling inner-padlock that caged my fear.

"Yeah," Crew said, "I think I do, too."

"Hellhound?" Jordan had entered the octagon behind me. He drifted over, hung his arm casually on my shoulder. "You good?"

"I'm good."

"Same here," Crew said, "thanks for asking."

Jordan stuck out a pouty bottom lip toward Crew.

"And no," Crew said, leaning against a tree, "that's not a hellhound."

I nodded toward him in confirmation. I had heard that unique howl once before, in a memory that was not my own.

"Manticore."

Crew nodded back.

The woods seemed emptier than they had before. The floating, yellow eye-slits had disappeared.

"Where did they go?" I asked.

"Seems they've retreated back to the portal," Crew said. His smirk returned.

"Cowards," Jordan said, mirroring my thoughts.

Crew stepped toward us, lowering his voice. "There's one thing you need to know about Manticores," Crew began, addressing both of us like a battlefield General. "Not going to lie, they're pretty scary."

"Okay thanks for the pep talk," Jordan quipped. Crew shot him an impatient glance before carrying on.

"They've got one weakness. I think the three of us should be able to exploit it if we work together. We have to go for—"

"The telson," I interrupted. "More commonly known as the scorpion's stinger. Separating the Manticore from its stinger is like driving an arrow through Achilles's heel." I made a slashing motion across my throat.

Crew deflated. I mean, he really, *really* wanted to impart the knowledge about a Manticore's weakness so badly. I almost felt bad for taking that from him.

Almost.

"Yeah," he said. "That."

"So, we stick close?" Jordan asked.

"Probably a good idea." I said. Crew nodded in agreement. With a collective deep breath, we turned toward the faint golden light shimmering within the outcropping. We were close, now—maybe half the length of a football field or so.

We didn't make it more than three steps before I was on the ground heaving and fighting for consciousness.

19

Light became dark, flickered into fuzzy grays. Searing pain leeched onto the inside of my skull like a red-hot cattle brand. A vision, a memory—not mine—materialized in my mind: a rust-red banner of cloth fluttering against an ash-gray building.

Someone said something.

Someone grabbed my arm.

Everything was dull fuzz. Everything but the pain, which was sharper than a razor's edge.

Palm pressed against my forehead, nails digging into my hairline, digging at the hurt, digging it out, digging...

I screamed. Dull gray became bright, became searing white, became pitch black.

"HANNAH," a voice said. It was a deep voice. Far away.

My eyelids were vices, my heart a thundering drum. But the pain was nearly gone. All that remained was a warm, dull remnant, a hot brand doused in water.

"I think she's coming to."

I stretched my fingers. My nails scraped against dirt, my palms poked by the sharp ends of pine needles.

Pressure on my shoulder. "Hannah," the deep voice came. "Let me know you can hear me."

I imagined responding to the deep voice, telling it that I was okay, that I must've blacked out for a minute, that the pain in my head made me want to die but it was gone now, that this was all a mistake, that I should go back to Em, that I need my sister, that my sister is all alone, that I'm going back, that—

"Holy sh—"

The pressure on my shoulder disappeared. The deep voice was saying something, yelling something, but it was drifting farther away from me.

Crashing sounds, like trees cracking in half.

A roar that sounded like thunder, but not the normal kind. More like what thunder would sound like if you were somehow suspended in the middle of the thundercloud.

Yelling.

I need to see.

Hand trembling, I reached for my face, felt my hot, wet cheeks, then realized in horror that my eyelids were not in fact vices. My eyes were open. Yet all I could see was pitch dark.

Something massive hit the ground near me, like a boulder dropping from the sky.

"Get away from her!"

"This way you ugly—"

A thunderous roar tore through the woods. Realization was a two-by-four slamming into my stomach.

The manticore.

Breath quickening, I uncurled from the fetal position and propped myself on hands and knees, sweeping the ground with desperate hands for my sword. It had to be close. Unless it wasn't.

I can't see!

Something heavy *whooshed* over my head, sending down a jet of air.

"Watch it!"

"Get behind it!"

Feeling, searching, the pine needles made it feel like raking my palms across a pin cushion until…

Something solid. Metallic. Sharp.

I felt down the length of my blade until I reached the hilt, a wave of relief settling over me if only for a millisecond.

A sound like dynamite exploding rattled through me.

"Hannah!" the deep voice shouted. "Move!"

Move. Move Hannah. I can't see. Move where? I can't see. I can't—

Something in front of me shook the world.

In front of me.

I turned and, dragging my blade, crawled on hands and knees away from where the crashing and quaking and yelling and howling was coming from. Every foot or so I stretched out my hand to make sure the way was clear until it hit something solid, rough.

A tree trunk.

I felt my way around to the opposite side of the trunk and pressed my back against it. The yelling turned to screaming. The roars became impossibly louder.

Are they dying? Is the manticore… killing them? Crew… Jordan…

I have to help them.

Another roar, and I felt hot tears running in rivulets down my cheeks. I raked the back of my arm against my eyelids, pressing hard against my open eyes, again and again…

See. *See*!

The pure black remained, except for the tiniest flicker of gray in the furthest corner of my periphery. I focused on that flicker harder than I've ever focused on anything in my life. Was it there before? Had I just not noticed it? Or was it new?

It was new. I knew that because it expanded ever so slightly.

Something gigantic rammed against the tree I was leaning against. Pine needles fell like tiny blades all around me, poking at my hands and covering my hair. The tree trunk leaned, roots snapping, pressing me forward. Someone yelled something, followed by the loudest, sky-splitting roar I had heard yet. Then, heavy breathing laced with high-pitched whines, like the manticore was trying to breathe through a seashell.

Silence fell over the woods.

The fight was over. But who won? The manticore or the boys?

I tried to swallow, but my mouth was pure cotton.

I screamed when a hand rested on my shoulder. Then, realizing it had to be one of the boys, I grasped it, wrapped my hand around his pulsing arm, and said a silent prayer of thanks to whomever was listening.

"Hannah," his voice came softly. "Are you okay?" It was Jordan.

"I...," I began, but formulating words was a struggle, not to mention my throat felt like sandpaper that had been set on fire. "I can't see," I finally managed. "Where's Crew?"

My question was answered with a few seconds of unbearable silence.

"Jordan. Where is Crew?" My head whipped from side to side out of natural muscle memory. My vision was still mostly black.

Mostly. The jet-black night that covered my eyes dulled a little, giving way to the slightest, darkest shade of gray as if the sun was rising behind the horizon but hadn't yet crested.

I sat bolt upright, heart pounding. "Jordan, where is Crew?"

"Right here, Hannah." A rustling against the forest floor, dirt and needles and leaves, then a second hand cupped my arm. A fresh wave of warm emotion, some mixture of relief and anger and desperation rose from my chest and manifested as soft sobs.

"It's all right," Crew said. "We killed it. What happened with you?"

"She says she can't see," Jordan offered. A long moment of silence lingered between the three of us as the wind picked up strength, whipping through the canopy above.

"I think it's coming back," I said. "Slowly." I focused on what was now the wall of gray, which had lightened a few shades during the last few, eternal seconds.

"You passed out," Crew said. "Screaming, grabbing your head. Is it him?"

Is it him...

It had to be. It had to mean we were closer to Adam. And it had to mean that Adam was drowning in the same excruciating pain I had felt. The same pain that stole my consciousness and my eyesight. A pain I wouldn't wish on anyone other than the people who took Adam from me and the demon who touched my sister, leaving her cursed to see what dark things linger on the other side of the veil.

"It's coming back," I said, trying desperately to regulate my breathing. The pinprick of light at the corner of my periphery expanded like a window covering slowly being peeled back. The metal-like curtain of gray gave way to static fuzz until I could finally make out shapes. Fuzzy blobs of nothing at first. Then, slowly, they began sharpening into focus.

I didn't like that the guys had seen me cry. But if I'd had more tears to shed, I would've let them fly right then. Of all the things I'd taken for granted my entire life, my eyesight might be the one thing I took for granted most. The dark woods slowly came back into focus, and it was one of the most beautiful sights I'd ever seen.

"Help," I said, reaching my hands out. Each hand found one of the guys'. They pulled me gingerly to my feet. I blinked hard and fast, eyes still adjusting, fading in and out of focus like a twisting camera lens.

"You good?" Crew asked. Jordan, though, only looked at me with soft, sympathetic eyes filled with obvious concern. I appreciated that.

"I'm good," I answered, even though I felt like I'd overdosed on a cocktail of pure terror mixed with high-octane adrenaline. I only hoped my face didn't belie my words. I turned, cleared my throat. "Sorry for leaving you guys hanging."

"Not going to lie," Jordan said, "we could've used your help. But we took care of big beastie over there." We curled around the tree in the direction Jordan was pointing his hatchet and, sure enough, there lay the massive manticore, mouth agape, tongue outstretched. All the light had drained from its eyes. Dark liquid pooled on the forest floor near its neck. Its stinger lay a few feet away, separated messily from the rest of its tail as if it took multiple chops to tear it off. Like the hellcat before, the manticore had already started to disintegrate into ash. The breeze began breaking pieces off, blowing them into the trees.

"Guys," I said. "I'm sorry—"

"Don't apologize," Jordan interrupted with a smile. "You were in a bad spot."

"I'm just glad we distracted it enough that it mostly left you alone while you were blind," Crew said.

"Mostly?"

They shared a wide-eyed look.

"That stinger was hovering above you for a couple seconds, and…"

"We thought it was lights out for you," Jordan finished Crew's trailing thought. "So to speak."

The mental image of the manticore's stinger dangling over top of me was a bucket of ice water dumped down my neck.

"I need a reset," I said. I slid my sword into its sheath and stepped out of the Gray. Jordan and Crew both stepped out with me. The dark woods swayed. I was grateful to see detail in the real world and with my own eyes; the craggy bark along the tree trunks, the leaves and sharp needles nesting on the forest floor. Seemed that my eyesight had finally, fully returned. At least, I hoped so. Otherwise, I'd have a really hard time explaining what I had just seen appear from behind a tree ahead of me.

"Crew," I said. "Behind you." With measured calm, Crew and Jordan turned.

A man stood in the middle of two tall trees about fifteen feet away. He was at least six feet tall, dressed in black clothing. It was impossible to make out other features, because his face was entirely covered in a clean, white mask. The middle of the forehead portion was engraved with the image of a snake consuming its own tail.

The same masks Adam's kidnappers wore when they shoved him in the back of a van.

Rage filled me. Fists clenched tight, I stepped toward the man in the trees, but Jordan caught me and held my arms tight.

"You," I spat. "Where is Adam!"

Only the man's eyes were visible behind the mask, and only barely. He chuckled watching me struggle to escape from Jordan's grasp.

"Go ahead," the man said. His voice was muffled like he was speaking through a thin wall. "Let her go. Let's see what happens."

Jordan's grip remained tight.

Crew took one step toward the man, fists clenched. "You heard her," he said. "Where is he?"

"Oh, come on. You know exactly where he is." The man spread his hands and appeared to take in the height of the trees around him. "Otherwise, what would you be doing here in the middle of the woods?"

A twig snapped to our left, then another to our right. More white masks appeared, three or four on each side, surrounding us. I stopped struggling as the reality of our situation began to settle heavy in my stomach.

"You see," the man continued, "you've fought valiantly. Really, it's impressive. But we have a deal with... well... the ones in there." He motioned toward the outcropping ahead which, in the real world outside of the Gray, was now devoid of the golden light indicating a portal to Hell existed. "We can't let you get any closer. Sorry."

Each of the white-masked people took a collective step forward as if they were all connected to the same brainwave. When I looked closer, I noticed that each of them was dressed head-to-toe in black garb—black pants, a long-sleeve black shirt, black shoes. Thin black hoods covered their heads. One, I noticed, held a hammer. Another, a rung of rebar.

My guts clenched. I fell back a step, ran into Jordan. When I glanced up at him, he didn't glance back. He was too busy sizing up each Order of the Snake member as they slowly and deliberately closed in.

We need a strategy. We need to enter the Gray. They can't follow us there. We need to—

A sickening, dull *crack* split the air. Before I could register what happened, Crew pooled to the ground unconscious. A fist-sized stone lay on the ground next to his head.

"Crew!" I shouted, but when I started to go to him, one of the white-masked Order members stepped between us—the one with the hammer.

Behind me, where Jordan had been standing, something hit the ground with a heavy *thud*. I whirled to see another body on the ground. The white mask attached to it stared blankly up into the night sky. Jordan loomed, arms flexed, fists clenched, daring whoever was behind the mask to get back up and catch more hands.

My fight response kicked into overdrive, and with every single ounce of momentum I could muster, I whipped around and smashed a left hook directly into hammer-guy's earhole, dropping him to the ground next to Crew. In a flash I saw rebar swinging toward my face. I ducked; it whistled over my head. I drove myself upward with all the power in my legs and hammered an uppercut directly under the attacker's mask, sending it flying into the air. Their hood flew backwards the second they landed hard. When I saw their face staring dumbfounded up at me, a burst of shock hit my nerves.

It was a girl, not much older than I was. She was thin with short black hair. Her eyes began welling up with tears as she held a hand to cover her face in a *please-don't-hit-me* motion, crab-sliding away from me, slinking back into the cover of the trees.

Crew began regaining consciousness near my feet. He groaned, reached a hand to the back of his head to massage his skull where the rock had hit. I didn't have time to help him up, though, because two more white-masked Snakes were tearing through the trees directly for me. A millisecond of focused listening told me Jordan apparently had things under control on his side, but I didn't know exactly how many Snakes there were, and he'd probably need help soon.

Or I would.

Luckily, neither of the two approaching Snakes had weapons that I could see, and one of them seemed to cower slightly behind the other, waiting for the other to make the first move—a courtesy that I wasn't about to grant. Strangely, I thought I heard the one hanging back say something like, "Don't hurt her too bad." Whatever was said apparently mystified the Snake in front enough to distract them. I seized the opportunity and lunged forward, whipping a heavy kick that landed with a *snap* on the first person's thigh. It was a guy, based on the low groan he emit-ted. His knee buckled inward, sending him slightly off-balance. Just as advertised, his arms dropped from their defensive posi-tion in a natural response to try and re-balance himself.

I wound my right leg back one more time and sprung another kick, this time up high. He tried to raise his hands again but wasn't quick enough. The top of my foot landed squarely where his jawbone met his ear, and I heard a low *crack* just before he pooled to the ground.

The second Snake backed up. Besides seeing his friend lying unconscious on the ground, there was no doubt he could see the fire in my eyes as I stalked forward into the trees toward him. He was tall, well-built, but so was his newly-unconscious buddy who now lay in a weird pretzel shape on the pine needles. He raised his hands, stepping backward into the trees.

"Hold up," he said. "I don't want to hurt you."

"Funny," I said, my words rattling with rage. "I'd believe you if you weren't literally a Snake in the grass." I matched his strides, stalking forward, a lioness stalking a wildebeest. My fists tightened, nails digging into my palms. A mirthful smile stretched my closed lips the second before the coward in front of me smacked into an unseen tree trunk. The unexpected blow dropped his hands, and I raised mine, wound back a fist with bad intentions, and—

"Hannah," he said, low and soft.

I knew that voice. The mask muffled it, but... could it be?

No.

"Hannah, I need you to listen to me," he said. He pressed himself away from the tree trunk, hands low, completely vulnerable. If there was ever a perfect time to strike, it was now, but...

"There's a lot happening right now. A lot of things you probably wouldn't understand. But I can explain, if you'll let me."

I swallowed, refusing to believe my ears. Slowly, he showed me the whites of his palms in surrender. Then, with one hand, he pulled the black hood off the top of his head and reached for the bottom of his mask, sliding it up, revealing his face.

My shoulders slacked, arms dropped. The utter rage I'd felt was quickly replaced by a blend of shock and confusion.

"I have a lot to tell you," Ryan said.

20

"How… what…," I began, but words escaped me.

"I know," he answered and reached a hand toward my shoulder. I bristled and knocked it away. He reached into his pocket for something and, thinking it could be for a weapon— would Ryan ever use a weapon?—I grabbed his arm and tried to trap it.

"Hannah," Ryan said coolly. "I'm going to need you to trust me for a second." His words were a whip against my steaming brain.

"Trust you… Trust you! You… you're…," but before I could muster the words to tell him just how untrustworthy he turned out to be, that he was a traitor, a horrible, evil person palling around with the most horrible and evil miscreants who took Adam from me, my thoughts briefly dove into memory— Michael sitting across from me at Clark's, showing me the video of Adam being dragged across the dirt and into the waiting van by a group of thugs in white masks.

'How did you get this video?' I had asked.

'We have moles within many organizations that provide us intel,' Michael had answered.

I released Ryan's arm and stepped backward. Ryan produced his smartphone from his pocket.

"You're the mole," I said, more to myself than to him.

He fired up his phone and lit the flashlight, dousing us in a small circle of uncomfortable white light. My eyes had adjusted to the darkness long ago, and the bright light was harsh, but at least now I could see his face, the whites of his eyes. He gave the slightest of nods, confirming my suspicions. I didn't know whether to hug him or punch him in the face for keeping this from me, and soon my mind became overwhelmed with unanswered and probably unanswerable questions, like how in the world he became a mole for the Ring and installed within the Order of the Snake. How long had he been steeped in the world of the supernatural? He knew about demons, Hell beasts? And more importantly...

What, exactly, did he know about me, and how long had he known it?

All the shock, the unasked and unanswered questions, the obvious betrayal, the confusion all wound itself into a knotted ball manifesting in a closed fist. Before I could formulate another thought, I hammered it against Ryan's unguarded chest. The blow must've landed harder than I'd intended, because Ryan wheezed and dropped his phone to the needled ground. I reached for it.

"No," he managed. "Wait."

The home screen was open to the Photos app. An array of photos filled the screen, each a tiny rectangle. Most of them were of me.

None of them were of me looking at the camera.

There were pictures of me talking to Crew and Adam at the gym, of me getting into my car, of my apartment, of Adam, his motorcycle and license plate, of Crew dropping me off at my place, Crew's jeep...

These weren't merely random photos. These were surveillance.

Hot anger re-settled in my lungs and cheeks as the truth began to wrap itself around my mind.

Ryan stepped toward me. "Hannah, listen."

I leveled him with a fiery glare.

"Those aren't… it's not what it looks like."

My jaw was a vice. I sucked on my teeth wordlessly as I scrolled through picture after picture.

"You knew what I was this whole time?" I managed.

Ryan stared blankly.

"And Adam, too?"

Still, Ryan gave no visible cues. Ryan, the sandy-haired boy who made me feel for the first time like I belonged, who introduced me to his friends, who kissed me in the soupy darkness that filled the tunnels under the High School and countless other places since. And yet…

I don't even know him. Not like he knows me.

He held out one hand, reaching for his phone. That's when I noticed the mark on his forearm, illuminated by the phone's flashlight. Yesterday, his arm was covered in a bandage. *'A cut,'* he'd explained. But it wasn't a cut. That was a lie just like everything else. Black ink formed a symbol I had come to know and hate all too well—the symbol of a coiled snake eating its own tail.

Another body hit the ground in the distance. I whirled to see Crew on his feet, but only barely. A white-masked Snake charged, ran shoulder-first into his stomach and drove his back hard against a tree trunk, sending flakes and chunks of bark flying. I made to run to him, but Ryan reached out and gripped my wrist and yanked me backward, then used his momentum to whirl me around and pinned me against a tree. He pressed his body close to mine, cancelling out any space necessary to throw a knee. I pulled, yanked, tried to twist.

"Hannah, stop struggling."

"Ryan! Let me go!"

"Always so stubborn." He whispered snake-like into my ear.

"Always missing the forest for the trees. I want you with me, Hannah. Think of all the great things we could do together."

His words were pointed icicles. "The hell are you talking about?"

Ryan sighed, the way a parent sighs when trying to exercise patience with a small child. "The world is chaos," he said. "Humanity craves it. Thrives on it, even. Without it, the universe becomes unbalanced. The world needs the right people in power to keep it balanced."

Rage flowed hot through my veins with every single word Ryan uttered. Rage, and complete, utter disbelief, to the point where it seemed my body couldn't contain it any longer. Trembling, I managed to whisper back, "And let me guess; you're one of those 'right people?' What did you do, Ryan, make a deal with the Devil? Because I can tell you from first-hand experience that that's a mistake."

"You don't understand—"

"Oh, I understand. You're a coward and a traitor."

"I care about you—"

"You used me!" My head pounded, mind reeled as the fact of *why* he'd used me crystalized. "You used me... to get to Adam. By turning him over to the demons, you killed two birds—you got your deal in exchange for whatever you made a deal for, and you got him out of the picture. You know I love him. You saw him as a threat. You're jealous."

Ryan snapped his head back to look at me. An expression of pure ire replaced the white mask that had been there moments before. "I'm not—"

I smashed my forehead into his nose before he could articulate the word, 'jealous.' The blow landed with a wet-sounding *pop*. Ryan howled, released my wrists and cupped his nose, which was quickly turning into a faucet. I pushed him back. He lost his balance and fell, still cupping his face.

I turned and was happy to find that Crew had turned the tables as well. The Snake who'd had him up against a tree was now the one up against the tree, being used as a human punching bag. I was about to heave Ryan's phone into the woods and join the others when I noticed something peculiar.

The final photo in the mosaic of photos wasn't a photo at all. The small, white triangle in the thumbnail's center indicated it was a video. The first frame showed red brake lights cascaded across gravel and weeds. As if...

I held my breath, pressed the play button and turned up the volume. Tinny sounds of commotion and mirthful laughter escaped the phone's small speakers.

"Okay, okay, ready?" One voice said, apparently behind the phone camera. The picture became fuzzy, out of focus, like someone had just placed their finger in front of the lens. The voice behind the camera was the same one I'd heard behind the mask.

Ryan.

"Places everybody," he said. Those around him responded with chuckles. "Especially you, Cassie. Get behind me."

"Yeah, yeah," came a female voice that I assumed belonged to the aforementioned Cassie. "Watch yourself. Boss me around too much and you'll end up like him."

Another round of laughter.

"All right," Ryan called. "Here we... Robbie, you idiot. You don't even have your mask on."

"Oh. My bad." A swell of groans and epithets. "There!" Robbie said, his voice slightly more muffled. "It's on. Calm down."

"We good?" Ryan asked the group that I had yet to see on camera.

"Just press record already," someone called.

"All right. And....—" Ryan removed his finger, so it was no longer blocking the camera lens—"action."

The video struggled to find focus in the low light. A fuzzy cloud of reds and browns floated around amorphous, black shapes until...

My heart stopped. My hand flew to my mouth.

The small screen filled with red brake lights from a white van, illuminating a group of black-clad, white-masked people. They stood in a crude semi-circle around Adam, who was on his knees, hands bound with heavy duty zip ties. Dust swirled around him every time one of the Snakes took a heavy step. Adam coughed, spat something dark onto the ground.

The tallest Snake approached Adam from the side. He chuckled once, said something I couldn't quite make out, then landed a vicious kick to Adam's unprotected ribcage. Adam dropped, pooling in a heap on the ground.

Another Snake approached, grabbed Adam by the collar and lifted his head off the ground. It lolled back and forth like someone who couldn't wake from a deep sleep. Adam's arms remained splayed outward, unmoving, his hands brushing the ground. With his free hand, the Snake cocked a fist, smashed it against Adam's cheek, then dropped him against the dirt and gravel.

Adam's body went completely limp.

The screen in my hand began to shake, and I realized I hadn't breathed.

One of the Snakes leaned over Adam. "You want some more?" Adam managed to rise again to his knees. The others surrounding him laughed. The Snake who spoke crouched to Adam's level. "Trust me," he said, "you don't want some more."

Adam spat a thick dark streak of blood across the Snake's white mask. The Snake reciprocated with a vicious right hook. The others joined in. Adam became enveloped in a cloud of dust as each took their turns landing kicks against his exposed ribs, stomach, shoulders.

The phone's camera operator—Ryan—took a slow step back, and then another, until another one of their crew came into view from the side—A girl with pixie-style black hair, dressed in a black leather jacket and black leather pants, her hand resting at her side. Like before, her hand was missing Sloane's arrow tattoo.

"You know," she said, just like I knew she'd say, "your bosses won't be too happy with you if you bring them a dead Dante."

The beatings ceased. Each white mask turned toward the girl. "Something tells me you'd all try to pin it on me if this one didn't make it down to Hell alive. And we all know I wouldn't let that slide," she said. "Well, load him up and do whatever you're going to do with him. And someone punch me in the face a couple times for good measure."

Three Snakes lifted Adam's nearly lifeless body into the back of the waiting van, then slammed the doors.

The first and only other time I'd seen this video—at Clark's with Michael—it cut to black after Adam's assailants threw him into the van, but this version of the video kept rolling. It must've been the original, the one they used to cut the other, shorter version.

"Nice, Cassie," Ryan said from behind the camera. "You sound just like her. And you look just like her from behind."

"Stop looking at my ass," the girl named Cassie said, then turned. "Or don't." She winked.

Ryan was right, that at least in the dark, this girl—Cassie—looked nearly identical to Sloane from the back. That wasn't accidental. They did it on purpose. From the front, the pixie cut that had seemed so telling looked unnatural. Her face was much paler than Sloane's, her eyes more almond-shaped, her jaw line not nearly as sharp and defined as Sloane's.

I'd seen her face before, and only a few minutes ago. It belonged to the girl who's mask I'd punched off. The one who crab-crawled away, slinking into the woods like a coward.

Everything inside of me was consumed in a raging bonfire. If I clenched my jaw any harder, I'd shatter teeth. Seconds before the video came to an abrupt end, the camera panned to the right. What I saw set my blood to boiling. It was slightly out of focus, sure, but I didn't need 4K resolution to see the real Sloane splayed out across the ground in the weeds near the fence line, clearly unconscious.

I threw Ryan's phone to the ground and stomped toward him, determined to give each of his ribs the same treatment I'd given his nose. "You're a mole all right," I spat, looming over him. "Just for the wrong side. You used me. To get to Adam. And all for power."

Ryan's eyes widened as I wound up for a kick. But before I could launch it into his ribs, someone grabbed me around the throat from behind, then grasped my wrist and levered my right arm painfully behind my back. They whispered a high-pitched, clicking noise into my ear and backed me away a few steps from Ryan.

"Can't have you doing that," the voice said. "Not to our newest recruit."

The voice behind my ear was the same voice who told the white-masked thugs to load Adam into the back of the van. The fake. The imposter.

Cassie.

When I struggled, she forced my wrist upward along my spine sending spikes of pain through my arm and shoulder—the same shoulder I'd broken last fall when I was thrown from Adam's speeding motorcycle. Re-breaking it wouldn't take all that much effort, especially in the compromised position she held me in.

"I, for one, think you'd make a great trade," she said. "What do you think Ry? Throw her into the pit with her boyfriend?"

Ryan had finally managed to pull himself to a crouching position. His hands looked like he'd submerged them in dark red paint. He held his chin up high in a failing attempt to control the bleeding, then shot Cassie a silent glare.

"Oh, that's right," Cassie spat, "you don't want us to hurt this one." Cassie forced my wrist half an inch higher along my spine and I winced. My arm felt like a creaking tree branch in a hurricane. Everything inside me tightened like a winding wire realizing that if she applied any more pressure, my shoulder would explode like glass into shards.

"Good thing you're not the one in charge around here," she said to Ryan, but in a whisper that only I could hear. Ryan's eyes widened. Then, Cassie pulled in a sharp inhale and her breath froze.

"Let go," a calm, measured voice said from behind both of us.

Cassie released my wrist. Ryan shot to his feet and began to back away.

"Please," Cassie said, voice trembling. "Don't shoot me."

I turned, found Cassie locked in the same position she'd been holding me in only seconds before, her arm cranked uncomfortably behind her back. The person leveraging Cassie's arm was wearing a black hood that cast a dark shadow across their face, making it impossible to make out. They weren't much taller than Cassie, and with their free hand they held something metallic against Cassie's temple.

Behind them, in the clearing, Crew helped Jordan to his feet. Others—some with their masks still on, others not—lay unconscious or semiconscious on the ground or awkwardly against tree trunks. Crew turned toward me. The sight sent Ryan crashing into the dark woods.

"Please," Cassie begged, voice trembling like a dead leaf. "Don't shoot me."

The person holding Cassie released a mirthful chuckle. My heart raced at the sound of it. I knew that laugh, because usually it came at my expense.

Suddenly, the person released Cassie's arm and Cassie fell forward in wobbling steps toward me.

"You know," the familiar voice said, "from the back, I would've probably fell for the fakery too. Have you been doing squats?"

The hood dropped, allowing the moonlight to accentuate her beautifully sharp features.

Cassie raised her head slightly, meeting my gaze with panic-

eyes. She was trapped between the two of us. I grinned, licked my teeth. Cassie turned.

"Hi. You already know me. The real Sloane. Good to meet ya."

"I—" Cassie began, but Sloane's lightning-fast right hook landed square on Cassie's jaw. Her lights twinkled out, then Cassie fell in a heap to the ground.

"Been there," Sloane mused. "Doesn't feel good, does it girlie? Oh!"

Sloane took two reeling steps backward, surprised that I'd thrown my arms around her neck.

"Sloane, I am so sorry," I said. "I didn't... I wasn't..."

"Hey, it's okay," she said. "I get it. Water under the dock or whatever."

I released her. "How did you know to come here?"

"Crew left me a long voicemail," she said. "Told me we'd been played, gave me the rough coordinates."

I grinned. "Is that a gun?"

Sloane laughed and held out her hand. "Hammer. I found it on the ground by that tree over there. She didn't have to know that, though," she said, gesturing toward Cassie's limp body.

Crew arrived and stood behind Sloane. "You okay?" Crew asked me, but before I could answer, Sloane reeled on him.

"Oh, don't pretend I didn't save your ass, too."

Crew couldn't hold back a tongue-in-cheek, uneven smile and rolled his eyes. "You had good timing," he said, then motioned toward the clearing. "Come on."

"Wait," I said, glancing into the woods behind me. "Ry— another Snake was here. He got away."

"Lucky him," Crew chimed, taking in Cassie's unconscious state.

"Yeah," I said, "It's just that... that..."

"It's her ex-boyfriend," Sloan interjected, then turned sharply to me. "At least, he'd better be your ex after all of this. Stay with him and I'll give you the Cassie treatment."

Crew's eyebrows stitched together. At first, I wondered how Sloane could've known about Ryan until I remembered that moment when she saved me from the Reaper in the road. Ryan had walked me to work that morning. She must've had eyes on me.

"I had no idea, guys." The weight of it, what it all meant, started pressing down on my shoulders. "He... he used me. I don't know for how long. If I'd had any clue..."

In truth, I felt dirty. Violated. Blindsided. Broken in a way that only comes with shattered trust.

Crew pressed a light hand on my shoulder. "We're all surprised, Hannah," he said. "What's done is done. We'll find him." A sliver of silver moonlight twinkled in his sympathetic eyes. "But right now, it feels like we're running out of time."

He was right. If it was true that most of the demons retreated back into the portal after we entered the woods, it probably wouldn't take long for word to pass that we were on our way. Crew nodded toward the clearing.

I followed him and Sloane through the trees to the spot where the Order of the Snake jumped us. A couple bodies still sporting white masks lay groaning on the ground, returning slowly to the land of consciousness. Jordan was there, on top of another. The Snake lay face down in the dirt. Jordan held his twisted wrist high, drilling a sharp knee into the middle of his spine.

"Let him up," Crew said. Jordan released the Snake's wrist, stood, then pulled him up by the neck. "I'm guessing you saw this going a different way," Crew told him.

It was their leader, the one who'd appeared first in the clearing.

"What are we going to do with him?" Jordan asked. The Snake was clearly outnumbered and didn't put up a struggle.

Crew seemed to ponder the question for a few long seconds before Sloane chimed in.

"We could end him right here and now." She sauntered

toward the masked man, hammer in hand. "You know that's what he'd do to any one of us."

"We're worth more to them alive than dead," Crew said. "And besides, we're not killers." Crew's words, though, didn't diminish the hateful flames dancing in Sloane's eyes. Other than Adam, she'd been hit the hardest by the Order of the Snake in the last couple days, and revenge was clearly on her mind.

"Fine, then. What?" she said.

"I called the Ring before we entered the woods. They're on their way." He patted the thick cord of rope wrapped over his shoulder. "We'll lash him to a tree and let them know where to find him."

Laughter shot from behind the man's white mask, startling me.

"You think that's funny?" Jordan said.

"Yes," the man said in a muffled voice between laughing fits. "Yes, I do. So easily played, all of you. Like puppets on a string."

"We don't have time to wait for the Ring to show up," I said. "We've got to get through the portal now."

"I can stay behind," Sloane offered with a way-too-happy grin. "Me and Snakey here can have some fun for a while before our friends at the Ring show up…"

"You're right," Crew told me, ignoring Sloane. "But we can't let him get away, either. He needs to pay for what he's done."

Sloane sighed. "Don't you think maybe we should talk about this in private and not in front of our hostage? You guys are bad at this."

Crew opened his mouth to answer, then closed it again.

"She's got a point," I said, tossing her a nod. She grinned back. "Gray."

Me, Crew and Sloane each drew our Borderland weapons. Jordan soon followed, apparently able to get to his hatchet and pull it without releasing the Snake leader. I wasn't too worried about the Snake leader scampering off, given that time essentially stops outside of the Gray for non-Dantes.

"All right," Jordan said, "what's the plan?"

"I don't know how long it'll take the Ring to get here, but we obviously can't just let him go free," Crew said.

"How long to tie him up?" I asked.

"Couple minutes," Crew said. "If the Ring doesn't find him, we'll carry him out of the woods ourselves on the way back."

The rest of us nodded.

"Also," Sloane said, "let the record show that I am very much against leaving him conscious."

"Noted," Crew said.

"Sorry to be the bearer of bad news, but I'm afraid that plan just doesn't work for me," a low voice said. The speaker stood in the Gray behind Jordan with a short sword drawn, the blade reflecting his white masked face.

Jordan reeled, stepped back.

"You're… a Dante…," I managed. The mask laughed back.

Crew shoved his way between me and Sloane. "Explain yourself."

A long pause, and then the man we thought was the Order of the Snake's leader brought his free hand toward his chin, reached beneath the mask, and slowly pulled it away.

The triumphant look on his familiar face electrocuted me.

21

"Michael?" I said. "You're... the mole?"

He narrowed his eyes and smirked. "Such a stupid girl."

"Damien," Crew said.

Damien?

While Crew and I leveled the man in front of us with questioning glares, Jordan and Sloane exchanged confused glances.

"What do you mean, 'Damien?'" I asked Crew without looking away from Michael. One corner of Michael's mouth curled into a smile.

"This is my contact within the Ring," Crew said, teeth clenched tight. "He's the person I called when Adam went missing, and the one I reached out to for backup on my way here." I could almost hear Crew's knuckles tighten and whiten on the grip of his haladie.

The man named Damien, whom I knew as Michael, shook his head and laughed. "About that," he said, voice thick with mirth. "Yeah, no backup is coming tonight."

"You're a traitor, then," I said. "'Michael,' or 'Damien'—it doesn't matter what your name is. You're a traitor."

He looked down on me with big eyes full of false sympathy, the way someone looks down on a lost puppy.

"Let me guess, Hannah," Crew offered. "This is the guy you met with? The one who poisoned your head with the idea that Sloane had double-crossed us and turned Adam over to the Order of the Snake?"

My entire body rattled. Seething, I could only manage a terse, "Yes."

"Well," Sloane chimed in, stepping forward, hammer tapping in against her open palm. "Whoever this is, I still see four of us and only one of him." Jordan began closing in as well.

"A lot of things make sense now, Damien," Crew said. "The Portal, the Order of the Snake's presence, the Dante kidnapping and offering... it was all you."

"Took you long enough to figure out," he spat back. "How the Ring decided to promote you to de-facto leader of your own regional faction, what with your super brain and all, beats me."

"The Ring will hear about this, Damien," Crew said, "and I have a feeling it'll be worse for you than any Vessel."

Suddenly, from one millisecond to the next, Damien lashed out with a silent strike toward Crew who only barely stepped back enough to dodge the sharp edge of Damien's slashing blade, but not far enough to avoid his heavy fist that followed. The direct hit on Crew's temple dropped him.

Before anyone else could react, Damien whirled, landing a spinning heel kick with a leathery *thud* directly on the side of Sloane's head. Jordan jumped forward, slashed his hatchet through the air, but Damien was too quick. He side-stepped, allowing all of Jordan's heavy momentum to carry him forward, then landed a heavy-handed punch directly into Jordan's exposed sternum.

Nearly blinded by red rage, I double-fisted my sword and sent the blade singing through the air directly toward Damien's neck. My wrists buzzed when our blades collided instead. Damien, who stood at least half a foot taller than me, glared hatefully into my eyes. But no matter the amount of hate he felt for me in that moment, it was a drop of water compared to the boiling ocean raging inside of me.

I shouted, spun, slashed toward his thigh, but he was fast. Our blades clashed, then again when I pulled back and stabbed hard at his chest. My vision became a dark black tunnel when I threw a side kick, which he blocked with a lifted leg. Control became a foreign concept as all of my anger, my shock, my raw sense of betrayal by Ryan and now the man I'd come to know as Michael utterly possessed every fiber of me which, in the world of technical fighting, wasn't a good thing.

I threw fists, kicks, and slashing blades, but nothing landed clean. Each were met with growing laughter which only enraged me more. Finally, done playing around, Damien caught my right hook by the wrist, gripped my forearm hard, then sent me flying back-first into the large tree trunk behind him.

I had expended nearly all of my breath, but when I smashed into the trunk, whatever meager amount was left in the gas tank flew out on impact. I dropped helplessly to the ground. When my vision finally cleared enough to look up, the only thing I saw were three other Dantes groaning on the ground, trying and failing to rise to their hands and knees. Then I spotted Damien, now a few yards away, the smirk never having left his narrow face. He nodded, shot me a sarcastic salute, then turned, left the Gray and disappeared into the woods.

My lungs were fire, but I finally forced myself to settle down enough to re-fill them with air.

Sloane rose, one eye clamped shut in a wince as she gingerly rubbed her Jaw. Crew stood behind her, chest heaving. His face was stone, but his sharp, hateful eyes told all. His nose twitched slightly, like it was the only thing holding the rest of him back from absolutely exploding in rage.

"I'm sorry," I offered. "I... I couldn't stop him."

"None of us could," Jordan said, reaching an arm around me and resting his hand on my back.

Sloane spat blood. Between all of our heavy breaths, Crew finally spoke.

"He'll pay," he said sharply. "But right now, we have to stay focused on the mission at hand. Get through the portal and bring Adam out. Then we'll contact the Ring and use every resource to bring Damien down."

"Contact the Ring…," I said. "How can you trust them? You trusted Damien." I didn't mean for my words to land like an insult, but based on the way Crew winced, they did. "And what did you mean when you told him that a lot of things make sense now?"

Crew didn't answer. Instead, he trudged past me toward the cliff face, the outcropping ahead, glowing golden in the Gray.

"It means," Jordan whispered as we fell into line, "we now know who's been behind the recent mayhem. In order to open a portal from this side, it takes someone who can travel between worlds—between reality and this." He gestured to the Gray world around us.

"Like a Dante," I said as the truth dawned on me like the first rays of a rising sun. "Mich… Damien. He's the one who opened the portal."

Jordan nodded. "And he's got to be the one who recruited all the new Order of the Snake members."

I thought of Ryan, how Damien caught hold of his mind like a fly in a web.

"And worst of all," Jordan continued, "he's the one who orchestrated the most valuable sacrifice to the Dark he could make."

"He offered them a living Dante in exchange for power," I said, my mind filling with the picture of Adam unconscious on the highway's shoulder being shoved into a van.

Jordan nodded again. "He tried to sew distrust, break the rest of us apart with a fake video, make us think one of our own was the traitor when it was him all along."

I couldn't help but glance toward Sloane. Raw guilt settled in my guts, tightened around my stomach. I had fallen for Damien's trap and nearly ripped the Dantes apart when I flew into HQ intent on beating the truth out of her. But she'd been telling the truth the whole time.

Sloane glanced back, smiled, nodded.

"Time's ticking," Crew called from the trees ahead. "Let's move."

We marched forward, silently swimming in our thoughts. Up ahead, the portal's golden glow grew brighter, and I realized gratefully that we probably wouldn't need Crew's rope after all. We trudged through a thicket and climbed a small incline to reach the cliff base. The portal rested inside a rock cavity, maybe twenty feet deep. Each of us stopped short of its entrance.

The portal wasn't a doorway, like I'd half-expected. More like a crude tear in the rock as if someone had ripped open a gray ship sail with a dull knife. It pulsed as if it carried a heartbeat. Smoky vapors danced around it, reached out like bright solar flares.

Black burn marks crept along the stone wall, curling around the portal's opening. A small ring full of ash rested at the foot of the portal. Next to it sat a small collection of what looked like small animal bones along with bits of sage and other plants—the makings of some kind of ritual, I guessed.

"Remember," Crew said, "we're exchanging one reality for another. What we call the Gray in this world is the reality in the one beyond this portal. Stay sharp, and remember—"

"If you die down there, you die forever." I hadn't meant to interject, or even to speak out loud. The portal pulsed, snapped, crackled like the end of a live electric wire. Adam lay waiting somewhere beyond it. Something deep in the recesses of my mind ticked like a racing clock, reminding me that every second spent waiting was precious time wasted.

Sword in hand, I stepped through the portal's amber glow.

22

Blinding white light dissolved into terrible reds and charred black. My breath caught, clung to the walls of my throat as if it didn't want to be released in this world and honestly, I couldn't blame it. Gnashing teeth, green bubbles of noxious sap, and black water overtook my mind in a brief flash of post-traumatic horror.

Breathe, Hannah.

I stepped forward, stood tall, straightened my shoulders and, finally, pulled a breath into my burning lungs. The portal glowed behind me, although not the same bright amber color. Here, the portal was a dull gray, only slightly brighter than its surroundings. I turned, forcing myself to face my new reality.

The Borderlands of Hell was exactly how I remembered it, and exactly how it appeared almost nightly in my nightmares. The angry red sky pulsed with electric lightning, rumbled with rolling thunder. The portal opened up on a hill surrounded by charred woods. In the far distance to my left, the volcanic mountain bled hot orange lava. My mind traveled backward to Adam gripping my hand as we rushed, sprinted to escape certain and eternal death while Malum, hand outstretched, pulled the earth away in crumbling chunks, sending it crashing down to the pool of lava below. I could feel the heat licking my heels, Malum's laughter crawling along the inside of my skull like spiders. Instinctively, I raked the sky with my eyes, searching for any sign of the giant black crow that had nearly ended me the second-to-last time I'd traveled through these woods. The mad sky was empty. In a thought that seemed simultaneously obvious yet incomprehensible, I knew I wouldn't see that bird. It was tied somehow to Malum, and Malum met his fate at the fiery bottom of the distant volcano.

A low tearing sound, like someone ripping cardboard, pulled me back to the present. Jordan stepped through the gray portal, and for an instant I could tell he experienced the same visceral reaction as I did as he took in the Borderlands for the first time in what I imagined was a long time. I realized then that I didn't know very much about the guy who helped free my sister, who killed a hellcat with me, and who eviscerated countless demons in the woods. What were his Dark Trials like? When were they?

Like mine, they were wretchedly awful. I knew that much by the look on his face as he took in his familiar surroundings.

"Hey," I said, stepping aside to give him and the others who'd follow some room to land. "Something tells me you don't need me to give you a tour of the place." He grinned at that.

"Nah," he said. "I'm pretty familiar." His eyes reflected the oozing volcano in the distance.

I traced a line from the volcano to the edge of the woods that ringed a woodless patch of craggy desert—the Circle. A black door jutted like a gravestone exactly in the Circle's middle. From up here, the door was about the size of my thumbnail.

Another tearing sound. Sloane stepped through. The sight of the Borderlands seemed to anger her more than anything else.

"I hate this damned place," she spat, then visibly shivered even though it was quite literally hotter than Hades down here. Thick, warm wind rushed through the trees to greet us the moment Crew tore through the portal. His demeanor was all business. I noticed the thick wrap of rope around his shoulder and chest. I guess that was the difference between literally dying to get here and passing through an open portal—in the latter scenario, you can take some things with you. Crew stepped to us, and we formed a small huddle, heads close, voices low.

"I obviously don't need to tell any of you how dangerous this place is," Crew said. "Let's move quickly but quietly, even though I'm pretty sure all of Hell already knows we're here."

Jordan turned to me. "How are you feeling?" he asked, and at first I felt a little offended, like he was implying that I was some kind of weak link amongst the three of them, as if I hadn't been through and beaten the same Dark Trials they had to become what they are. But then, my sense caught up to my emotions.

"It hurts a little," I said, focusing momentarily on the warm pain blooming inside my chest. "But that's a good thing, right?"

"We're close," Crew said.

"Where do we go?" I asked, remembering just how vast the Borderlands were. Unlike during the Dark Trials, it wasn't like we had a tornadic pillar of light leading us to Adam.

"Isn't it obvious?" Sloane interjected. But to me, nothing in this scenario was obvious. Adam could be near the lake, or somewhere—anywhere—within the unending, noxious woods, or atop the molten mountain in the distance. Anxiety began wrapping its wiry fingers around my pulsing heart.

"He's not here," Crew said. Each of them looked to me expectantly as if I were the last one to understand some obvious bit of information, and apparently, I was.

"What do you mean?"

But none of them answered. They simply stared, eyebrows raised.

Adam had been turned over to some powerful demon, or demons, in an exchange with the Order of the Snake. Where would they have taken him?

The answer crept into my brain slowly. They would've

brought him through the portal, yes. But the portal wasn't simply a portal to the Borderlands of Hell.

It was a portal to Hell, of which the Borderlands were merely that—a border.

I stood straight and slowly shifted my gaze down the hill to the desert Circle below, resting on the single black door that somehow seemed larger than it had before. I swallowed hard.

"Do we know how to get through?" I asked.

"We've all opened it before," Crew said.

I pictured the black wooden door. On one side, directly in the middle and just above my head, a demon's gnarled face held a heavy metal knocker in its fanged mouth. Three taps made its eyes glow red before the door swung slow and wide. Black tendrils of smoke snaked down what I remembered as a set of bottomless steps before meeting Malum's fiery yellow eyes.

Through the black door. Down the black steps. Something in the back of my brain told me the Borderlands were tame compared to the actual Hell that awaited us at the bottom.

But first, to the door.

The rest of the Dantes apparently read the realization as it dawned on my face. Each of them sheathed their weapons— down here, that didn't take us out of the Gray like it did in our world. There was no escaping this side of the veil once we'd crossed through the portal. I sheathed my sword also, just as Crew spoke again.

"Obviously the quickest path is straight. Point A to Point B."

"They would be expecting that," Sloane said.

They…

I imagined the hoard of demons we'd seen in the woods of Camp Sego Lily pouring back through the portal we'd just come through and regrouping in the blackened woods ahead of us— their home turf. Not to mention the Hell beasts they'd brought along with them.

"I don't think we can afford to take an alternate route," I said.

"Plus, it could be that that they've all retreated through the black door."

"Good point," Jordan said. I appreciated the back up.

"Straight line, then," Sloane agreed.

"Straight line."

We wasted no more time. We, the Dantes, descended from the portal and into the forest, eyes sharp, hands on hilts, listening hard for any noises that haunted the spaces between the rustling trees.

WE SPREAD OUT IN FORMATION, boys on the right, girls on the left, and moved swiftly yet quietly down the hill. The forest became thicker. The familiar soupy fog that blanketed the forest floor curled itself around our ankles. Each step left a wake of fog rippling behind us. As we descended the hill, the black forest canopy above us became thicker until only razor slashes of red skylight pierced through, as if the sky above was black with burning red stars. I was acutely aware of the canopy. I knew all too well what was hidden up there.

And I wasn't the only one.

Sloane had an arrow nocked and pointed upward as she walked, scanning every tree branch. Crew was doing the same. Only Jordan kept his eyes down and forward as the slope toward the Circle began to level out.

A collective wave of dread washed over us when we heard it. The laughter. The fluttering of invisible wings attached to small, lanky bodies with mouths full of razorblades.

"Keep moving," Crew whispered just loud enough for each of us to hear.

I kept moving, but only because that's what the others did, and I didn't want to be left behind with the flying creatures. I'd faced them alone before and would really like to never do that ever again.

Every step we took triggered new rustlings. The canopy creaked and cracked. They were following us, and by the sound of it, there were a lot of them.

Sloane jerked her fully-pulled bow in every direction. Her eyes, normally narrow and cool, were wide ovals. I moved closer to her, nodded when she finally glanced my way, lifted my sword.

I've got you.

She released a heavy breath. Her footsteps returned to regular, soft intervals.

"Whoa!" one of the boys cried out to our right. It startled both of us so badly that Sloane almost lost her arrow.

We rushed toward the sound to find Jordan frozen, rooted to the spot, staring straight ahead at a flying creature.

"Watch your back," Crew and I said in unison, then formed an outward facing circle along with Sloane.

"Get away and take your friends with you," I told the flying creature, which I couldn't see but could hear its leathery wings flapping behind me.

"Four of you," the creature hissed, its voice high-pitched, gravelly. "How interesting."

"We're not here for the Dark Trials," Jordan said. "We're on business that doesn't concern you. Or your friends," he added after an audible gulp.

On cue, the flying creature's friends descended from the canopy from all sides amidst a hail of high-pitched laughter and clicking jaws. There had to be a dozen or more, not counting the ones still hiding out within the canopy's darkness.

"We do not care why you are here," the creature hovering ahead of Jordan said, sneering. "We do not care where you are going. We only care that…"

But the creature trailed off. It's urine-colored eyes darted left, right, then upward. Its ears rotated rapidly back and forth like a radar dish scanning for… for what? The others surrounding us became skittish, hovering backward. A couple flapped hard and shot into the trees for cover from... something.

"What is it?" I asked, turning to face the leader. "What are you afraid of?"

Its lips peeled back revealing a pointed, razor blade smile. "Oh, you'll see soon enough, I believe." It cackled, then joined the rest above.

"I don't hear anything," Jordan said.

"Shhhh," Sloane hissed. "We won't hear anything if you're talking."

A hellhound was the first thing that came to my mind. My first trip down to the Borderlands, the flying creatures had been deathly afraid of one in particular. They sent me on a quest to kill it for them, and in exchange, they graciously agreed not to eat me, not that they intended to keep their end of the bargain.

But no, if it were a hellhound, I'd be able to hear its Earth-shaking footsteps approaching. Whatever the flying creatures were afraid of now had to be something else.

"No use waiting around," Crew said after a few tense, silent beats. "Keep heading toward the door."

We did, slowly. I listened hard, but couldn't make out any sounds other than hot wind rushing through the canopy. Seemed like the flying creatures thought it best to stay in place, stay quiet. Maybe we should've done the same...

Halfway to the Circle, the forest opened into a clearing. Lightning rent the red sky, splaying into pieces. The sky roared.

We entered the clearing cautiously. I felt somewhat relieved by the fact that the flying creatures—or anything else—couldn't drop on us from the trees. But once we were halfway across the clearing, Jordan stopped.

"What's up?" Crew said. Jordan didn't reply. Instead, his eyes focused like lasers on one spot in the sky. Each of us traced the line of his gaze with our own.

"What is it, Jordan?"

Jordan held up one finger to his lips without looking at me.

For a few beats, silence. And then…

"What's that sound?" Sloane asked.

I heard the sound the second after she asked the question, like black sails on heavy seas. Every muscle tensed as I dared a glance upward.

Two small, thin figures materialized against the red sky. They were so high, it was difficult to make out their shape other than the two large, bat-like wings and long, trailing tails.

"Let's move," Crew whispered. "Quietly."

The moment we stepped forward, the flapping sound ceased. I looked up, could still see the two figures in the sky, but it was like something had cut off their wings. Now, they were two thin lines, growing gradually longer, larger with each passing heartbeat.

"What the…," Jordan said as he slowly raised his hatchet. But by the time I figured out exactly what was happening, it was too late.

"They're diving!"

My scream was followed by a severe rush of wind as both creatures re-extened their wings. We dove to the ground as one flew low, rushing overhead, claws extended like an eagle plucking fish from the water.

These things were massive. Their black wingspan had to extend twelve feet. Their bodies were long, thin, trailed by a scaly tail that ended in a spaded, sharp point. Their heads made me do a double take. They were shaped like a horse's head, thick and elongated, but with long, curling fangs. The second of them dove, its jaws snapped as it barely missed Crew, then rose to join its companion fifty feet above. Together, they released an ear-splitting screech so horrible, I clapped my palms against my ears.

Each of us rushed to our feet and bolted for the tree line. We didn't make it more than a few steps before one of them dive-bombed, this time directly for Sloane. I dove sideways and tackled her only a second before the creature clamped its claws tight where she'd been standing. We hit the ground hard, blasting the wind from my lungs.

"Thanks," Sloane said.

I meant to say something like, "Don't mention it," but garbled wheezes were the only sound my lungs allowed.

We were pinned down in the middle of a clearing, fully exposed, and the second we'd stand to make a break for the forest's cover, the dragon-like creatures would snatch us for lunch.

"Any great ideas?" Jordan called to nobody in particular, but it was enough to grab one of the creature's attention. It dove right for him, narrowly missing as Jordan rolled out of the way.

"Crew!" Sloane yelled. The beasts circled above, and Crew broke for us, slid down next to Sloane. "I've got an idea," she said, out of breath. "But I need your rope."

Without question, Crew pulled the wrap of rope off his shoulder and handed it over. Sloane rose to one knee and turned to me.

"I need a distraction," she said, soft enough so that only I could hear it. With one eye on the sky, she furiously unraveled the rope and drew the arrow from her quiver.

"What... what are—"

"Just run as fast as you can to Jordan, and don't stop until you get to him."

I stared wide-eyed at the terrors circling in the sky. "But..."

"Now!"

The time for questions was over. Now it was time for trust, and after everything that had happened between me and Sloane in the last two days, I owed her that. I swallowed, rose quickly to my feet. One of the circling beasts above snapped its head in my direction. I pulled the sword from my sheath, lowered my head and ran hard.

Jordan screamed at me, held his hands out, motioned for me to drop. I didn't. I only focused on my feet pounding against the ground in even intervals. One of the beasts screeched. I fought every single instinct to splay myself against the ground. My leg muscles tightened, threatened to seize up as some form of mindless effort at self-preservation, but I wouldn't allow it.

Giant wings flapped above me, behind me, rocketing toward me like an Apache attack helicopter but with claws and jaws. Legs churning, I winced, waiting to be enveloped by blackness.

But the blackness didn't come.

Instead, I heard a quick *thrum* of Sloan's bowstring like a low-tuned harp note, followed by the worst sound I had ever heard in my entire life.

I dove for Jordan just as the creature released a truly blood-curdling scream—high pitched and loud enough to vibrate my skull. When I rolled to my back and saw why, every single nerve in my body went numb with shock.

Sloane's arrow had pierced clean through one of its wings. The arrow's fletched end was tied with Crew's rope and lodged itself on the high side of the wing like a grappling hook. The other end of Crew's rope was tied... to Sloane.

She harpooned it.

Sloane dropped her bow and leaned back hard, yanking at the rope and digging in her heels. The thing tried to rush away, but with only one fully functional wing, it jerked sideways instead. Still, it was strong enough to drag Sloane forward, her heels carving two straight lines in the ground.

"Guys!" she yelled. "A little help!"

Jordan left me, rushed to Sloane's side, and grasped the Sloane-end of the rope just before the creature could lift her into the sky. Both of them pulled hard. The creature screamed, struggled, but slowly Jordan and Sloane gathered fistfuls of rope as they reeled the creature in like a deadly, fanged kite.

Worst kite ever.

"Now, Crew!"

But Crew was already on his feet, rushing toward the struggling creature, which was becoming more erratic and desperate by the second. With one more hard yank, its harpooned wing hit the ground followed by the rest of its body.

The animal was trapped, cornered, and more dangerous than it had ever been in the sky. Its eyes became fire. It released a loud huff of air, then turned its ire toward its captors, Sloane and Jordan. Claws gripping the ground, it rose awkwardly like it wasn't used to walking. Then it opened its jaws, spittle dripping from the ends of each fang, and screamed again.

The scream only lasted a second or two before its head—mouth and eyes wide open—hit the ground with a thud. The thing had been so laser focused on Sloane and Jordan, it never saw Crew rush toward it, fly through the air while spinning his haladie, then slice through its thick neck. The rest of its body seemed to need a few extra seconds to compute what had happened before it collapsed to the ground, heavy and lifeless.

I stood, barely registering what I'd just seen with my own eyes, numb with shock. That is, until I heard the second creature flapping above.

It was circling. Watching. Hesitating?

"Come on!" Jordan yelled, waving me over.

I rushed toward them, watching Crew cut Sloane's rope to free the arrow that brought the animal down. He slid down the beast's back, shot toward us, wordlessly handed Sloane her arrow just as she finished re-wrapping the rope. We bolted for the forest and slipped through the trees. When the canopy was finally thick enough to conceal us from anything circling in red sky above, we stopped, chests heaving. My lungs were fire, begging for breath.

"Holy crap, Sloane," I managed. "That was… that was—"

"Awesome!" Jordan said.

"Well," I said to Jordan, "you weren't the bait."

"Good job, bait," Sloane told me. Sarcastic, like usual, but I could tell she meant it.

"You too."

"Ready to do it again?"

I hesitated, trying to read her face. Yeah, she was still serious. I sighed, hung my head. "What are those things, anyway?"

Jordan chimed in again. "Not sure what they're called exactly, but I'm pretty sure one escaped from an open portal a couple hundred years ago and took up residence in New Jersey."

"Okay," Sloane said, "on my signal."

I gulped.

We stared at the sky, waiting for the second and hopefully last devil to appear. The term "devil" made sense after Jordan's comment about New Jersey. Actually, a lot of those old monster myths were beginning to make more sense, now.

"I see it," Crew whispered.

We were crouched exactly at the tree line where the dark forest met the Circle. The door wasn't far now, which meant Adam wasn't far, not that I needed to see the door to realize that. Tamping down hot pain through intense concentration was a constant struggle. I studied the sky, but couldn't make out the devil's ominous shape—dark, leathery wings, long tail...

"Where?" I asked.

Crew glanced at me, pointed just over ninety degrees upward, then shifted his finger slightly as he listened. I had a difficult time making out the sound of the devil's flapping wings over the wind, not to mention my pulse thrumming through my ears like a constant, beating bass drum. Crew's finger shifted forward. I traced its invisible line into the sky and, sure enough, there was the devil, circling a couple hundred feet in the air and probably not happy we'd just killed the only other devil in the Borderlands. At least, I hoped it was the only other devil...

"Show time," Sloane whispered. Like before, in the clearing, she'd knotted Crew's rope around the end of her arrow, nocked it, then stretched back the bow string. "Three...," she said, "two..., one..."

My body tensed, like some sort of reverse fight or flight response had kicked in. My tingling brain screamed. Don't move. Do not move.

My legs became cement, my feet cinder blocks.

"Go!" Sloane whisper-shouted.

I locked my eyes on the black door like a laser beam and forced my legs to move. The first few steps were like wading through thick, muddy water until my brain realized that, now that I was in the Circle and outside the cover of the forest's canopy, moving slowly was probably much worse than not moving at all. The nerve endings in my body tingled to life, and I flew.

The devil screeched its eardrum-piercing screech. I made the mistake of glancing up as it folded its wings behind its back and dove, a heat-seeking missile rocketing straight toward me with fangs bared.

I gripped my sword and dashed. Halfway to the door, the devil leveled out somewhere behind me, opened its leathery wings and cruised toward me like a fighter jet, engines roaring.

Now, Sloane! Shoot it now!

The devil was close. Too close. I dove, hit the mudracked dirt about twenty feet from the door. The devil's claws snapped as it blasted past me, a hawk just missing the field mouse and rising for another pass. It rose upward, rotated backward in a loop, then began another descent. Its eyes were murderous, and I was debilitated on my butt with absolutely nowhere to escape.

"Shoot!" I screamed.

The devil landed hard on the ground, taking no chances at a fly-by this time. It stalked toward me, jaws clapping, fangs dripping. Fifteen feet... ten...

Struggling backward, I heard the snap of Sloane's bowstring, the whistle the arrow made through the air...

... and the *thunk* when it speared into the dirt a couple feet short of the devil's open wing. Quickly, Sloane yanked the rope, freeing the arrow, and began reeling it back for another shot. The arrow skittered across the desert, but I knew there was no way she'd have enough time to ready another arrow before the devil had its way.

My lungs deflated. My heart sank. I crab walked backward, the devil matched my pace, never unlocking its hot gaze from mine. I hit the back of my head hard on what had to be a corner of the black door. Stars exploded in my vision.

The devil stepped forward, sniffed the nearly nonexistent space of air between us, then huffed like a horse. Its breath was hot, rancid, rotten. Thick globules of bubbly saliva dripped from its fangs, pooled on the dirt. Like a winding snake before a strike, it rose to its full height and spread its wings to their full length. The red sky exploded in lightning, and I knew only one thing: This view was the last I'd ever see.

My heart stopped. I shut my eyes and thought of Em waiting for me under a blanket in the back of the car; of Adam being tortured in Hell with no hope of rescue.

Lightning and thunder ripped the sky apart. Without vision, the rest of my senses heightened. I sensed the air around me shift as if all of the molecules and atoms that I'd always knew were there but could never see or feel suddenly became solid. As the devil moved in for the kill, each molecule and atom rippled like small waves in the ether.

Thunder rumbled.

The entire world rattled.

A lifespan of time passed. Followed by another.

I risked lifting one eyelid. The world was a blur. I realized my eyes were full to the brim with warm, wet tears. With one dirty hand, I wiped them away, then opened both eyes slowly.

The devil remained in front of me. Its horse-like head lay between my open legs. Its eyes were open, but no longer staring at me. They weren't staring at anything in particular. They were just... open. Lifeless.

A hatchet's handle stuck out from the top of the devil's skull like a car's antenna.

The devil's body shook, spasmed. Jordan materialized on top of the devil's back, his silhouette striking against the blood-red sky. With one strong pull, he reclaimed the hatchet from the devil's skull, then wiped the blood and matter off the blade onto one of its lifeless wings. Somehow, he was smiling.

"Close one, huh?"

He hopped off the devil's back and reached for my hand, but I couldn't move it. I couldn't move anything. My brain hadn't caught up to the impossible reality that I was not, in fact, being digested at the moment. I pulled in a hitching breath. The thick, hot Borderlands air actually tasted sweet as I drew it deep into my lungs.

Sloane and Crew rushed around each side of the dead devil. Sloane looked as panicked as I'd ever seen her. An invisible weight visibly lifted from her shoulders the second she saw me prostrated against the door, impossibly alive. A hand rushed to her chest.

"I am so sorry," she said.

I grabbed Jordan's waiting hand and let him pull me up on trembling legs. "Can I not be the bait next time?" I managed, voice shaking.

Sloane approached and, to my complete surprise and the apparent surprise of the guys, she... hugged me.

"Deal," she said. "No more bait."

I hugged her back, realized she was trembling every bit as much as I was. After a few moments, she pulled away, cleared her throat.

"Okay, now that that's over...," she said, scanning the sky one last time for good measure.

"Want to do the honors?" Crew asked. A couple silent seconds passed before I realized he was speaking to me. He must've noticed the confusion masking my face, because he gestured toward the door behind me. I turned, saw the large knocker held tight in a black demon's jaws.

It was time to knock three times. Time to pass through the

door, into the darkness below, into unknown territory. I forced my trembling hands still, reached outward, gripped the knocker.

Tap.

Tap.

Tap.

Like the first time I'd journeyed to the Borderlands, the demon-knocker's eyes suddenly glowed red. A sharp sound emanated from behind the door, like bolts unlatching. The door moved.

Tendrils of hot black smoke drifted out from behind the door as it slowly turned open. Each of us took tentative steps backward, enraptured, white-knuckling our weapons. The door drifted lazily open. When the smoke cleared, we stepped forward.

The faintest outline of descending stairs disappeared into a sea of blackness below. There were no glowing yellow demon eyes ascending like there were the first time I'd seen these stairs —Malum's eyes, just before I demanded the Dark Trials. But something deep inside my guts told me there were things far more terrible, unimagined, waiting for us in the depths.

But so was Adam.

I placed my foot on the first step. Then the second.

The other Dantes followed.

23

Step by blind step, we left the Borderlands' red sky behind and plunged deeper into the abyss. The soupy air was weighed down by a visceral sense of dread and foreboding. 'Dark' doesn't even begin to describe the blackness we were traveling through. We were surrounded by the blackest black I'd ever experienced. I couldn't imagine the same deep level of dark existing in the world we came from, not even in the darkest cave beneath the deepest ocean.

I knew Crew, Sloane, and Jordan followed behind me, but only because I could feel Jordan's hand on my shoulder and hear Sloane mumbling something. Despite that, though, I felt entirely and completely alone, knowing that if I lost physical contact with the others, I'd lose them forever, swallowed by the Dark.

And then I heard the door slam shut behind us.

I hadn't realized what a comfort it was knowing the door at the top of the steps was open, leading to the horrible yet at least familiar Borderlands.

How would we open it again?

One thing at a time, Hannah.

One step. One slide of my fingers against the ragged stone that walled the staircase.

I pointed my sword forward in case something we couldn't see decided to sneak up directly in front of me. Not that it would help. It was impossible to know what could be in front of us, or directly behind us, watching, staring, breathing, planning; impossible to know what underworldly creatures, uninhibited by thick darkness, lay in wait. I forced myself to compartmentalize the thought and step, step, step until the only sound was that of our soft footfalls, shoe soles dragging on stone in perfect sync like a procession of invisible ghosts.

"I hate this," Sloane said, finally breaking the silence. She'd whispered, but her words bounced hard and sharp off the walls as if she'd shouted.

I hate this too, I wanted to say, but didn't. The abdominal pain was returning, searing my insides like a cattle brand. It was all I could do to keep a steady pace and wait for it to pass.

And then I heard something.

Something soft. Skittering along the walls. The ghost of an echo from somewhere far off.

I halted, causing a reverse domino effect as Jordan crashed into me, Sloane into him, followed by Crew.

"What the hell?" Sloane said. I shushed her.

"I heard something."

We stood still, listening.

There it came again, the same sound—a low pitched echo curling up the staircase toward us.

"Heard that," Jordan whispered. Someone else behind me swallowed hard.

"Want me to take the lead?" Crew said. But I didn't need to stand behind anyone. I took another step forward, re-extending the Dante accordion.

Soon, the sound became louder, clearer, though I couldn't put a finger on what was making it. It still sounded like an echo of something made miles away, but who could really tell?

More sounds. Clicking noises. Low-fi buzzes.

Suddenly, I could make out the faintest outline of my hand to my right as I dragged it along the rough wall. I slowed, turned my head. "Light."

Each step became slightly brighter as whatever light lay beyond reflected up the stairs and along the walls. The light was a soupy, dingy grayish green. It swirled, the way light that reflects off water shifts and shimmers on walls and ceilings.

The staircase took a sharp turn. When we curled around it, the walls to the sides of us fanned away from the staircase. When I peeled my eyes off the stairs and gazed into the distance, I lost my breath. Jordan's hand fell away from my shoulder. Looking back, I saw the same grayish-green light dancing like flickering flames in his wide eyes. I turned and took in the impossible view ahead of us, unable to wrap my mind around it.

I'm not sure what I expected to see when we reached Hell, but it was not this.

Not a city.

I physically rubbed the backs of my hands against my eyes, took in a sharp breath, and re-opened them. The city was still there, massive, sprawling... and horrifying.

For miles in every direction, crumbling buildings that looked like they belonged in a post-apocalyptic nightmare jutted up from the ground like huge gravestones that had been weathered over a thousand years. Black smoke rose from orange-red flames that haunted the spaces between them. The smoke rose, curled, and settled like the darkest thunderclouds imaginable beneath the rocky underground ceiling hundreds of feet above. The ceiling itself was smoldering, like someone had doused it with kerosene a thousand years ago and was still burning.

Flying things left wake trails through the smoke as they circled the city like vultures.

The crumbling city was caged within a massive wall that, from here, appeared to be made of black iron. Spikes of varying sizes lined the top of the wall, some of them straight, some of them curved; some thick, others razor thin. I couldn't be sure whether they were meant to keep things out, or keep them in...

A moat lined the outside of the iron wall. No, not a moat—a flowing river. And not just any river.

This river was somehow neon green, the color of poison. As it flowed, large bubbles formed and popped along the river's surface, releasing jet streams of thick, noxious vapor.

The sights were awful enough, but that's to say nothing of the sounds.

The gigantic, miles-long cavern that enveloped the city reflected moans, screams, crumbling stones as decaying buildings fell apart, crackling fire, cackling creatures—a cacophony of noise that words couldn't do justice in describing.

"Pandemonium," someone behind me said. One of the guys. I couldn't peel my eyes away long enough to pay him attention.

"What's that, Jordan?" Sloane said, her voice slurred as if the very act of speaking would somehow dull what she was seeing.

Jordan cleared his throat, brushed past me and stood facing us on the steps.

"I've read about this," he said. "Pandemonium. Hell's city of the dead and damned."

The moment he said it, a high-pitched scream was followed by a deadly screech, and somehow I knew the sounds were connected to each other—hunter and prey.

"Pandemonium," Crew said. "I've heard that word before, but not in that context."

"That's because we use it sometimes to describe when a big group of people act chaotic and panic. Like on Black Friday when hordes of people rush like an overflowing river through a dam and trample other people to get the newest PlayStation. They kick and yell and it's... well, it's pandemonium."

I nodded, still unable to speak. The heavy thumping of my heart began filling my ears and drowning out any other noise. I wanted to turn away. The overwhelming, cold, soaking blanket of dread wrapped itself around me and all I wanted at that moment was to flee back up the dark staircase and through the door to the Borderlands' red sky.

From down here, the Borderlands actually felt *safe*. And we weren't even within the city walls, yet. The city of Pandemonium.

"How do we even get in?" Sloane asked.

"Good question," Jordan said.

I gazed ahead, where the winding staircase opened onto rocky ground. Further on, the poison green river was split by a thin, black line that connected the rocky ground to the iron wall.

"There," I said, pointing. "A bridge." Calling it a bridge was a bit of a stretch—more like a balance beam made of who-knows-what, dangling precariously above a toxic river that I didn't want any part of.

None of the others responded. I didn't blame them, because it would mean acknowledging that there was, in fact, a way across the river when our psyches—if the others' were anything like mine—were searching desperately for a reason to climb back up the steps.

"All right," Crew said, "let's not waste any more time then." He stepped past Sloane and Jordan, past me, and continued down the steps toward the rocky bottom without beckoning us to follow. I set my jaw, steeled my nerves, and followed Crew toward the thin black bridge and the city of nightmares that lay beyond.

WHAT I'D thought was a mostly flat but rocky surface as viewed from the steps above actually turned out to be a small slot canyon. Ten-foot walls of onyx stone funneled us toward the river, toward the bridge. The bubbling river became louder as we approached. The sound of each popping bubble reminded me of smashing pumpkins—not the band—they're horrible—but actual, smashing pumpkins when you raise them high above your head and smash them on the pavement. And the smell... I had to focus on breathing slowly, in and out, and set my mind on something—*anything*—else, or risk puking.

The slot canyon walls fanned outward when we reached the narrow bridge. The bridge was maybe three feet wide, narrower in some places. It stretched a couple hundred feet in an uneven rainbow shape across the neon water. On the other side, a gate, out of which escaped a thin ray of flickering, fiery light. I'd expected the bridge into Pandemonium to be guarded by someone, or some*thing*, but the thick, dark space surrounding us was empty.

I guess they're not all that keen on security around here. Then again, I don't think they have many uninvited visitors trying to break into Hell's city of the dead and damned…

A six-foot high spike stood erect a dozen or so feet ahead of us where the rocks met the bridge. What looked like a small sign hung crooked from its top. Crude letters were scrawled across it in strange handwriting, but the letters didn't form any word that I was aware of.

AAHYWEH.

"Aw-way?" Sloane said, approaching it. "What does that mean?"

"It's not a word," Jordan said.

"Yeah, no kidding," Sloane snapped back.

"No, I mean it's an acronym," Jordan said, then looked at each of us expectantly for a few unanswered seconds before rolling his eyes. "Honestly, you guys need to read more."

"Enlighten us," Crew said.

"Okay then, an acronym is—"

"We know what an acronym is," Sloane said. "Just tell us what it *means*, Smarty McSmartypants."

A tight smile crept across Jordan's lips. "If I had to guess, I think it comes from that one poem written by our namesake."

"The Divine Comedy," Crew said. Jordan nodded in agreement, then continued.

"Dante's Inferno, to be exact."

The rest of us nodded collectively, waiting for the punch line.

"Anyways," Jordan said, "seems like what Uncle Dante described in his famous poem wasn't pure fiction." He nodded toward the sign, the letters.

AAHYWEH.

"Get on with it," Sloane said.

"A-A-H-Y-W-E-H," Jordan said. "Abandon All Hope Ye Who Enter Here. Dante Alighieri allegedly saw the same sign before he descended into Hell."

The blazing ceiling above seemed to brighten at Jordan's words. Something entirely non-human wailed in the distance. The poison-green river churned. My guts twisted, tied themselves in knots. Suddenly, the narrow bridge leading to the black wall and the entrance to Pandemonium seemed to shrink even narrower, extend even longer.

"Cool story, bro," Sloane said with a scoff. She took a step onto the bridge and waited, listened. No traps were triggered, no alarms sounded. Yet, I couldn't shake the feeling that it just couldn't be this simple. That familiar feeling began leaking its way into my insides, my mind—that internal warning that triggers your instinct to run from the thing in the dark you know is there but can't see.

That feeling was fear, and down here, in a city filled to the brim with demons that could smell fear like great white sharks smell blood in the water, it was lethal.

I turned, gripped my temples, shut my eyes. I needed to center myself. I needed to suppress the fear, to release it. Slowly, deliberately, I exhaled in intervals until the fear subsided. But when I opened my eyes again, the feeling came screaming back and petrified my bones.

There, in the darkness ahead of me, were two eyes. They were only four or five feet off the ground, but they were narrow, angry, the same shade of red as the Borderlands' sky. The shape attached to those eyes seemed to materialize wholly out of the onyx rock behind it.

"Guys," I think I said, shaking.

No one heard me.

The creature peeled back its lips in a murderous snarl revealing neon white fangs beneath those red eyes. The river's green glow reflected off the walls yet did nothing to illuminate the beast in front of me. Whatever it was, it was created from darkness incarnate.

I tried to shout again, to get the others' attention, but any attempt at words died in the back of my throat and became ash. Rushing blood filled my ears. My vision dimmed and lit with the beat of my pulse.

My legs became numb, but somehow I managed to step backward, then stepped again until I finally made contact with someone—I didn't know who and I didn't care.

They said something I couldn't make out. I stepped back again, stumbling. The person caught me before I fell. My eyes never left the hot gaze of hateful red staring back at me.

The person said something again. Then another person shouted—Crew, I think. He stepped in front of me, between me and the blood-red eyes and neon-white teeth.

That's good. That means he sees it too.

A growling sound reverberated off the stone walls. It got louder.

Crew pulled his haladie and spun it in his hand, crouched in a fighter's stance. The beast approached slowly, methodically, strategically.

He's going to need help. Crew needs help.

The thoughts came, but the fear batted them away. It was as if all of the fear I'd compartmentalized ever since I'd returned from the Borderlands with my soul—months and months' worth of suppressed terror—broke out of its cage and wreaked havoc on my mind.

Get ahold of yourself, Hannah.

Get a grip.

I sucked in a breath. The tightness in my chest began subsiding. Feeling returned to my legs. Chaotic sounds slowly replaced the pounding pulse that had monopolized my ears. Time rushed me forward until it slammed me into reality.

"Back!" Crew shouted

Sloane rushed between us, climbed up to a small outcrop, nocked an arrow, pulled back her bow string and took aim.

The person holding me up—it had to be Jordan—let me go. Their support fell away, and I nearly fell away with it. Crew was shouting, slashing at the Hellish beast in front of him and I expected to see Jordan rush to his aid, but he didn't. I turned to find him facing away from me. Like Crew, he'd assumed a fighter's stance, hatchet outstretched.

"We've got another one!"

Another one.

My blood threatened to freeze in my veins, but I wouldn't allow it. I gripped my sword and rushed to Jordan's side. That was the first time I got a good look at the entire creature outside the shadows of the black, rocky wall—The shadow from which it created itself.

Beyond the red eyes and bright fangs, the creature reminded me of a hellhound, but smaller, crouched low on four legs, tail swaying behind its body. Every inch of it was tar pitch black and covered in wiry fur. At its greatest height, its eyes were level with mine.

It was a wolf unlike any wolf I'd ever seen. A shadow wolf, created from the darkness surrounding us. The shadow wolf was to the hellhound what a Velociraptor was to the Tyrannosaurus Rex—smaller, leaner, meaner, deadlier.

I backed away, stood next to Jordan. The shadow wolf snarled, growled, then barked. The sound reverberated off the stone walls and seemed to rise all the way up to the smoldering ceiling. Not good. If we didn't shut these wolves up and soon, who knows what kind of unwanted attention they'd bring out from inside Pandemonium's iron walls.

"Spread out," I told Jordan. "You go left, I'll go right."

We split the wolf's attention left to right, surrounding it on each side, which seemed to be a great idea at first—it couldn't stare at both of us simultaneously—until we realized a second too late that all we had done was open up a human door way directly to Crew's back.

The wolf snarled, set itself back on its hind legs like a spring-board, then lunged.

"No!"

I jumped, slashed my blade through the air wildly, but only managed to nick the backside of one leg. If the shadow wolf noticed, it didn't show it. I landed hard on my shoulder and winced. The wolf landed next to me, clawing the stony ground desperately a few feet from Crew's exposed back. Its claws scratched and scraped against the ground, but the wolf didn't advance. Rising quickly, I found why.

Jordan had it by the tail. Teeth clenched, eyes wide, every vein in Jordan's muscle-strapped arms pulsed as he used every ounce of effort to hold the beast back. It was a sick game of tug-of-war and if Jordan lost, Crew would meet his final fate at the end of its wet, dripping fangs.

There was not enough time for thoughts to formulate. The shadow wolf's ribs expanded and contracted in front of me as it struggled mightily to free itself from Jordan's grasp. I plunged my blade deep in between two of them. The sensation sent ice up my spine. It felt like... nothing. Other than its outer layer of mangy fur, it felt like I'd driven my sword through vapor. The shadow wolf stopped moving, stopped struggling, but not because I'd injured it.

I'd angered it.

Snarling, it turned on me just as I'd managed to pull my sword free. Its blood-red eyes brightened, narrowed on mine. Two paces backward, my back flattened against a stone wall—nowhere to go. I swung my blade again, this time for its neck. But once I'd pierced its skin, the blade passed though like I'd slashed at smoke.

Every single nerve inside of me tightened and crackled. The beast lunged for my face, barking, its jaws open wide, fangs dripping. Warm, putrid breath blanketed my face and blew out my hair. Jordan groaned, straining against the shadow wolf's mighty power.

"Eyes!" Sloane called from somewhere nearby. But before my brain registered what she'd meant, the shadow wolf released a horrible howl that forced my eyes shut and nearly deafened me. My eardrums pulsed, reverberated, rang at a nearly inaudible, piercing high whine.

Suddenly, as if someone flipped a volume switch, the wolf's howl ceased.

I looked. Sloane's arrow jutted out from the exact middle of its right eye, which no longer shone glowing red. Sloane's shot was ice water over fire. The wolf pawed at Sloane's arrow the way an injured dog would paw at a porcupine's needles.

'Eyes!'

I pulled my sword back like a jouster and stepped forward. Jordan, hatchet in hand, materialized on my right. Even Crew and Sloane, who must've taken down their shadow wolf, appeared to my left. I stepped forward, aware that it still had one good eye; it could still put up a fight.

It growled low and turned its one good eye toward me. I was glad. A clear target was all I could've asked for.

I sunk my blade deep into the fire of its one remaining eye like a blacksmith plunges a blade into the forge. With two hands, I pulled both my blade and Sloane's arrow free from each eye which had faded to black. The animal backed away, head bowed low.

It opened its dripping fangs to release one final howl. Instead, it whined as I landed a kick hard against the side of its jaw, sending it reeling. Blind, it staggered backward huffing, struggling for breath. Apparently, it wasn't deaf, though, as each one of my heavy footfalls herded the beast toward the edge.

Toward the river.

One paw slipped, then another.

I launched one final kick into its mangy ribs. The shadow wolf splashed with a pathetic bark into the neon-green river below. Hot green flames sprang from the river's surface, wrapped themselves around the wolf's smoke-black body until, finally, the wolf disintegrated. The river released a large bubble where it had swallowed the wolf, like a hearty burp after a hefty meal.

"Hey guys," Jordan said, "let's not fall in there."

"Good idea, genius," Sloane said, chuckling. I turned toward her.

"Thanks. That's two I owe you."

"Don't thank me," Sloane said. "It was Jordan there who held the thing back long enough for me to even get a shot off. Otherwise, you'd be a dead Dante."

I turned, saw Jordan. I could tell by the hint of smile across his lips that he'd heard what Sloane said, but he kept his eyes down, brushing non-existent blood and dirt off the edge of his hatchet.

The other shadow wolf—the first one I'd seen—lay on the ground near the rock wall where it had materialized. Its eyes were black holes. Crew turned his attention back to it too, just to see it break into particles like a charred log and blow away in an invisible, unfelt wind.

"And here I was thinking the bridge was unguarded," I told him.

Crew smirked. "Is anything ever that easy?"

24

We crossed the precarious bridge and formed a tight huddle when we reached the iron gate leading into Pandemonium. It stood partially ajar, leaking flickers of orange and yellow light from flames that danced in the city. Creatures flapped high above our heads near the cavern's ceiling like vultures. Either they hadn't seen us crossing the bridge, or they did and, realizing we weren't yet cold corpses, didn't bother.

I was the first to venture a look into Pandemonium through the gate's open crack. I stared in for a second, maybe two, before sharp needles of pain stabbed the backs of my eyeballs. In a rush of blinding white, my mind flashed, filled with a colorless memory that was not my own. Vision cut in and out like I was watching through the worlds slowest strobe. I saw the gate. I saw the cavern's smoldering ceiling from narrow alleyways far below, between crumbling buildings illuminated by crackling fires. A crude, ripped, rust-colored banner hung pathetically from the side of one building—the same one I'd envisioned while I was blinded in the woods. Another building nearby seemed taller than the others surrounding it. A Reaper stood sentry on its rooftop. The body that was not mine was dragged through crude streets toward that taller building, pulled roughly inside…

Blinding white faded to ink before my vision returned. Hot pain settled behind my eyeballs.

"What is it?" Crew asked.

I blinked hard, pressed my palms against my eyes and temples as the pain slowly faded. "I… I saw where they took him."

"Do you know where to go?"

I didn't. But at least I had a landmark. "I have a rough idea," I said, still wincing.

Nobody liked that answer, but each of them understood it. It's not like I could crawl into Adam's memories any time I wanted and map our route. The rust-colored fabric banner fluttering near the tall building was more than nothing, but just barely.

We re-huddled, and Crew spoke quietly.

"Gut check time. We all know what waits for us in there. This would be the worst possible time and place to harbor any fear. Don't let them smell it on you. Give them nothing to grab ahold of."

Each of us pulled in a deep breath, exhaled slowly. Impatience, angst, the knowledge that we were *so* close to pulling Adam from the depths of this place filled me to the brim. No room for fear. Only resolve.

And yet, busting through the gate with guns blazing, so to speak, was not the play.

"Stealth," Crew continued as if reading my thoughts. "If at all possible, we must get in and out without drawing attention to ourselves. Each of you are badass demon slayers, but none of that matters if we bring the entire City of the Damned down on our heads."

We nodded.

"We'll follow Hannah."

Each of the Dantes turned to me, and I met each of their gazes in turn.

I will not let you down.

"All right," Crew said, clapping me on the shoulder. "Let's go."

PANDEMONIUM WAS A LABYRINTH, and we were mice in a maze. The buildings were less like actual buildings and more like giant termite nests made of decaying, weathered stone. Wails and shouts and screams reverberated from inside many as we passed between them, backs to the walls. The whole city seemed blanketed by a thin, smoky haze. Flakes of smoldering ash floated down like fiery snowflakes from cavern's high ceiling, singeing our exposed skin. Sharp, acrid air stung my nose. Despite the crumbling city being nestled within a gigantic cavern, a hot breeze snaked between the buildings.

We agreed on certain non-verbal cues—hand signals we'd use to navigate ourselves through the city without being detected like a rag-tag, wannabe crew of Navy Seals. I poked my head around the corner of one building, surveyed the open space, then signaled the Dantes to cross to the next building with two fingers. Each of them crossed quickly and silently, but as soon as I made to join them, Jordan held out his hand.

Stop.

Slowly, he lifted one finger, pointing toward the sky, then brought that finger to his lips.

I glanced upward. A demon materialized on the corner edge of the building's roof, black robes flapping in the hot breeze. It stood there a moment, still, without breathing.

Move, demon.

The demon moved. I kept my eyes on Jordan until he motioned me across. I patted him twice on the arm.

Thank you.

We were getting closer. I could feel it, though I couldn't explain it. None of the crumbling buildings or cracking streets looked familiar—none of the one's I'd seen so far appeared in Adam's flashing memory. Yet, we advanced forward because it was the right way to go, as if my body and mind had been here before, even if my eyes hadn't.

I reached the next corner. Back to wall, I peered around it.

Shocking yellow eyes stared back at me, through my eyes and directly into my soul.

I yanked my sword from its sheath and, one-handed, drove it hard into the demon's chest before it could make any sound other than the soft sucking, popping sound all of their bodies made before bursting into particles. I scanned the streets, the rooftops, the dilapidated windows to be sure the exploding demon didn't attract any unwanted attention. For a few long heartbeats, nothing else appeared—only the vulturous creatures circling the city high above. For some reason, it seemed they didn't want anything to do with the city and things dwelling in it below, and I couldn't blame them.

Something yelped nearby. Eerie moans and cracks and thuds floated like wispy smoke between the crumbling buildings, and it was impossible to determine from which direction any of it came. It would be so easy to go completely mad down here. I blinked, shook my head, trying to clear the noises which seemed to form spiderwebs around my brain and pull it toward every direction at once.

A tap on my shoulder.

"Where to, boss?" Crew whispered. His eyes were wide, but not alarmed. Focused. He gripped his haladie, but his shoulders were relaxed. Here, in the City of the Damned, he placed his fate in my hands, and did so with confidence. Jordan and Sloane, too. Each of them looked to me expectantly, but without a hint of panic or misgiving. Each of them nodded, waiting for my answer.

I drew from their energy and galvanized myself.

"This way."

We slid through the narrow space between two buildings, then slipped around a corner.

Something strange was happening here. Something I couldn't explain. Noise surrounded us—awful, horrible sounds—a cacophony of dark, grieving wails, crackling fires, chunks of rocky wall crumbling to the ground. Yet, the "streets," the spaces between buildings, the uneven rooftops—all of them were empty, save for the one Phantom I'd driven my sword into.

No, check that. Not empty. There, a few buildings ahead of our position, a familiar black robe fluttered as it slipped around a corner and out of sight.

"Seven o' clock," Sloane whispered.

Simultaneously, the rest of us turned our heads to see another pair of yellow eyes glancing out of a hole in the side of a building. It made no moves toward us, sounded no alarms. Just... watched.

If they know we're here, why haven't they swarmed us?

The demon in the building suddenly disappeared behind a sullied, decaying cloth. The whole scene could've been taken from any old western movie, with dust and tumbleweeds skittering across the barren ground as the village folk locked their doors and shuttered their windows before a gunfight.

I didn't like that thought once it settled.

What are they hiding from?

Us, was my first thought. But no, that didn't feel right.

One glance back told me the others were wrestling with the same thoughts, realizations.

Sharp pain stabbed my ribs from the inside, and I winced.

No time to ask questions. Only time to move.

"Come on," I said. "Let's keep going."

Stealthily, quickly, we moved between buildings, through narrow gaps in walls, over crumbled, steaming stones until we reached a wide road—three times wider than any of the other streets or alleyways we'd come across so far. The road curved, bent, like a river flowing through Pandemonium for miles in both directions. Like everywhere else, it was inexplicably devoid of demons, creatures. Ominously, a pile of bones lay scattered across the middle of the dusty road—a warning for any who'd attempt to cross.

"Too quiet," Jordan said. "I don't like it."

When I turned to him, my nerves jolted with sudden elation. Out of the corner of my eye, I finally saw something familiar—something from Adam's shared memory. Less than a football field's length away, a crude, rust-colored banner of fabric fluttered against a tall building in the hot breeze on the other side of the wide road.

"What's up?" Sloane asked.

I pointed toward the banner. "We're going the right way."

We slid between buildings, constantly checking rooftops and peering around corners. Finally, we faced the fabric banner directly across the wide road. I focused, scanned for something familiar, waiting-hoping—for synapses to snap.

Then, there it was.

A city block or so beyond the building with the banner rose a narrow, taller building—the building Adam was dragged into. Hot fire flickered inside my chest, blooming. Adam was there, deep in the tall building's bowels being held, tortured. Close, yet a million miles from here.

Before I could think, my legs began moving. If it wasn't for Crew's firm hand on my shoulder, I would've bolted across the wide road to the tall building, vision tunneled, ready to burn the damned thing down if that's what I had to do to free Adam. Ready to burn the entire city down, to drop a bomb on it, to raze all of Hell if that's what it took.

Crew chuffed in my ear, then pointed one end of his haladie toward the tall building, tracing an invisible line to the rooftop. There, like in my memory—Adam's memory—stood the sentinel, a demon with black robes fluttering like a flag in the wind. A Reaper, and not just any Reaper—the archetypical grim

Reaper, razor-sharp scythe in hand. The Reaper's black hood seemed tethered to one direction. It peered far down the wide winding road that split Pandemonium in half.

"Solo mission," Crew said, still pointing a sharp end of his haladie toward the rooftop Reaper. "No need to draw attention to all of us at once. I'll climb up, take care of Sparky there, then the rest of you follow."

"He's in that building," I said.

Crew's eyes widened. Jordan and Sloane leaned in close.

"Adam? That building?" Sloane asked.

"Yes." I turned, glaring, like if I stared hard enough, the building would crumble to the ground. "That building."

She smiled, nodded, and I couldn't tell if that meant she was impressed or whether she hoped there'd finally be some action inside. Something told me it was the latter. "Let me handle Sparky," she told Crew. "It'll be easy. One shot and Sparky's toast."

"That would be easy," Crew said, "but something else is going on here. There's something keeping all the other things down here, with us, at bay. I want to get up there and get a lay of the land to maybe see if I can figure out what that is. I'd hate to find that out too late and end up buried in demons in the basement with no way out."

Disappointment masked Sloane's face. Suddenly, she ran two light fingers along the sharp bottom of Crew's chin, grabbed it, then planted a, uh, not-soft kiss on his lips—the kind that makes kids cover their eyes at the movies. Jordan shot a surprised look at me. I shot an equally surprised look at him, then shrugged. Surprise quickly turned to awkward discomfort as the sounds of lips and tongues doing battle seemed to overcome all other sound in Pandemonium,

A few beats later, Sloane released Crew, but not before whispering something into his ear that made his face light up like a red candle.

Jordan cleared his throat, cutting the awkward tension. "Careful, man," he said. "For real."

Crew nodded, bumped his haladie against his chest. He looked absolutely invigorated. With one last glance toward Sloane, he turned and stepped forward, a gladiator entering a stadium to face a lion.

There was no cover under which Crew could sneak across the wide expanse. He crouched low, moved swiftly, quietly, yet totally exposed. I finally exhaled the breath I didn't know I'd been holding once he reached the banner building on the other side. He disappeared from view as he curled behind it and moved toward the taller building. The grim Reaper hadn't moved. Not even a flinch. A quick flash of golden light illuminated a narrow corridor behind the tall building. Sloane nearly bolted past me. She would've shot across the wide road if it weren't for Jordan's firm hand gripping her forearm.

"There are more demons over there," she said, struggling to free herself from Jordan's grasp. He didn't give an inch.

"If he needs our help, he'll let us know," he whispered sharply. "Blowing his cover is bad for everyone."

Sloane's chest heaved, face twisted before she finally nodded in agreement. We looked on, studying the view for any sign of Crew. I tried to swallow, but my throat was a cracked desert.

A few eternal seconds later, Crew materialized. Slowly, deliberately, he scaled the jagged edges where pieces of the tall building had broken away. He was climbing the side opposite from where the Reaper was still gazing. It hadn't moved. If it weren't for its black robes whipping in the hot wind, the Reaper could've passed for a statue.

An overhang blocked the way between Crew and the top of the building. He slipped the handle of his haladie between his teeth like a pirate scaling a merchant ship and reached. One hand found purchase, then the other. Sloane and I both gasped when his feet swung outward.

Crew dangled precariously off the lower edge of the overhang, climbing with his hands alone. Even from here, we could see his substantial forearms and biceps flexing, straining. We could only hope that part of the building wouldn't crumble away under the strain, sending Crew to his certain death a hundred feet below.

Crew reached the precipice, hooked the edge with his fore-arm, and simply hung there for a few seconds, catching his breath while the rest of us collectively caught ours.

The Reaper stood still.

The high wind pasted Crew's long hair to his face. He whipped it back, looked down at us, blade in mouth and gave us a thumb's-up with his free hand.

"Hell yeah," Sloane whispered.

Crew pulled himself quietly up and over the edge. Crouched low, he freed the haladie from his teeth. Crew crab-walked slowly in the Reaper's direction, an assassin, a lion in the grass stalking its unsuspecting prey.

Except the prey was not as unsuspecting as we'd thought.

In a flash, the Reaper whipped around and swung its scythe in a wide arc. Crew dropped, rolled. The scythe sliced through the air exactly where his neck had been only a millisecond before.

The Reaper wasted no time. It stepped forward, raising the curved scythe blade high over its head, then brought it down hard. The blade must've cleaved the rooftop between Crew's legs, because Crew scrambled backward as the Reaper struggled to free its blade.

Sloane was halfway across the wide road before I even real-ized she'd left. But suddenly, she slid to a halt, frozen. What froze her was the same thing that drove every demon in Pande-monium into hiding, what the rooftop Reaper was watching for. One heartbeat later, it released a roar that made buildings tremble and stones fall away.

High above Sloane, Crew got to his feet spinning his haladie. The Reaper freed its scythe. They circled each other, fighters in a ring, but instead of ropes or a cage, the ring was lined by sharp, rocky edges. One bad move and it was a long, long way down. Eyes on the Reaper, Crew pointed in the direction the roar came from yelled something like, "Help her!"

Help Sloane.

Frozen in place, Sloane pulled the bow from her back, freed the only arrow from her quiver, nocked it and aimed in the same direction the Reaper had been facing.

The ground rumbled.

Jordan and I raced toward the middle of the road, toward Sloane, but slid to a stop before reaching her.

Dread, horror, and disbelief swirled together in a terrible cocktail that shot through my veins as I traced the invisible line where the end of Sloane's arrow was aimed. There, in the exact middle of the road a few buildings' lengths away, something made from nightmares stood.

No, not something

Some*things*.

"Jordan," I managed. "Wh... what are those?"

"It's one creature," he answered. His voice was impossibly steady, calm, but not in a confident way. More like how you'd tell someone you love them while you're both standing on a beach watching a two-hundred-foot tidal wave rush toward you and you've resigned yourself to your fate kind of way. "Three heads; one creature."

I looked again. Jordan was right. Four powerful, muscle-bound legs covered in patches of brown fur held the creature's massive body. Scaled wings lined its back, folded neatly in on themselves. Its long, wrecking-ball of a tail was thicker than a tree trunk, swaying back and forth. One whip could collapse a building.

Six eyes glared forward, two on each head, one head for each Dante on the ground. The two eyes trained on me belonged to the head on the creature's right. Black as marble, they sank deep beneath crimson-colored, scaled hoods. Two twisted horns curled atop its head. It's long, scaled snout split horizontally, revealing rows of black, pointed teeth. The teeth separated as the creature opened its maw. Bright orange flame danced in the back of its throat. Smoke rose in tendrils out of its nostrils, curled around the edges of its mouth.

A dragon.

The wings on the beast's back matched the dragon head's scaly texture and crimson color. Its eyes narrowed, taking in my puny body, my pathetic, shivering sword.

To its left, the middle head was even larger than the dragon's. Its eyes were as bright and piercing as lasers and seemed to change color between burnt orange and bright, citrine yellow. Its face was covered in short, sand-colored fur framed by a mangy dark mane.

A lion. The source of the roar that shook Pandemonium.

Most of the beast's body belonged to the lion, or at least seemed to match. As weird as it might sound, the lion head seemed to be the head in charge. The other two followed its lead.

The third and final head seemed completely out of place. Two large horns curled around the sides of its head ending in sharp, deadly points. Its eyes were same dark purple you'd see if you place a black light over a black light poster. Dark black, scruffy fur covered its face, ending a crudely pointed beard at the bottom of its chin.

A ram. And it looked extremely angry.

"What is it, Jordan?" I asked through thin, unmoving lips. He released a weighty sigh.

"One of the most feared beasts in all of Hell."

"Of course it is."

"Chimera." Jordan's voice dropped into a lower register when he said the word. A light went on somewhere in the back of my brain. I'd heard of a chimera somewhere before—in a book, or on some obscure online forum. None of that vague recognition sparked any idea on how to kill it, though. All three of the chimera's heads huffed simultaneously, the dragon releasing a thick puff of smoke.

A shout reverberated off the buildings from high above. Each of us turned our gaze to the top of the tall building. Crew was still locked in a battle with the Reaper and, to my horror, seemed to be getting tired. Reapers, though, don't get tired.

The chimera took another step forward. Pandemonium shook.

Sloane drew back her bowstring, but jerked the arrow point indecisively between the chimera and the grim Reaper. One shot could end the Reaper before the Reaper ended Crew, but then gone would be her arrow. Without a weapon, Sloane could only serve as a useful distraction against the chimera. Jordan and I would have to manage the heavy lifting. And even with Sloane as a distraction, I wasn't sure how we could outsmart it. The chimera had three brains, after all.

Crew grunted low when he blocked a heavy blow from the Reaper's scythe. He was pinned down on the corner of the rooftop, no longer making any offensive advances. It was only a matter of time...

"Sloane!" I yelled. "Shoot it!"

She didn't need to be told twice. A heartbeat later, Sloane loosed her bowstring and sent her arrow whistling toward the rooftop, carrying with it Crew's last and only chance at survival.

The chimera's roar stopped time. The soundwave smacked me like a wall, nearly knocking me off my feet. Oven-like heat singed my arms, my eyebrows, the ends of my hair. Thick pillars of smoke poured from the dragon's mouth as a new flame began forming in the back of its black throat. The ram lowered its deadly horns. One of the chimera's paws scraped against the ground like a bull about to charge.

And then it did.

The ram head aimed directly for Sloan while she watched Crew's fate sail through the air toward the Reaper. There was no time for me to warn her, say her name, release a single breath.

The dragon's jaws snapped open before everything went silent other than the pulse pounding drum in my head.

Jordan dove sideways toward the wide road's middle. I dove opposite, back toward the buildings from where we'd broken cover.

The dragon's onyx eyes drilled me as the chimera's body charged forward, kicking up a world's worth of dirt and stone and ash. I struggled against the ground, unable to gain traction, sliding inch by inch, watching the dragon's mouth transform from black to orange to yellow like the sun rising over a mountain. I gripped the crumbling corner of one building and pulled myself around it just as the dragon released a tidal wave of hot fire. I felt the wall heat up against my back as the dragon's fire threatened to melt it down, turn the stone into fine grain, into glass before shattering through it and ending me. Flames licked the building's corner, reaching like long fingers toward my arm and leg. My skin turned an angry shade of red. A hundred years later, as the chimera rumbled past the building, the flames finally went out.

The others were somewhere across the ocean that was Pandemonium's center road. Thick clouds of smoke cut off my view. I had no idea whether the others survived the chimera's charge. If they did, they probably thought the dragon had done me in.

It nearly had.

The earth trembled again. Small pebbles broke away from the building's edge and rained down on my head. Time sped back up with a heart-pounding jolt. I dared one glance around the building's corner to find the chimera turning, slowly. But not a deliberate kind of slow. A lumbering, struggling kind of slow, like it's three heads couldn't quite make up their minds as to which way to turn or whether to turn at all. That's when I realized something.

The chimera was most dangerous when its prey was directly in front of its three heads. When that was the case, it moved swiftly and with one purpose. But now that we were spread out, it struggled to focus on more than one target.

"Hey!" someone shouted. It was Sloane. She shot out from between two buildings and darted into the middle of the road. "Hey, you stupid bastard!" Arrowless, she planted herself in the road, arms hanging wide like a gunslinger.

Arrowless.

I shifted my gaze upward, but the chimera's body blocked the tall building from view.

"Yeah, that's right," Sloane said as the chimera turned to face her, pawing at the ground again, readying itself for another charge. "Come to momma." This time, I didn't have to worry as much about dragon fire—I was on the side of the ram's head.

Sloane shifted her attention from the chimera to me, my back against the wall, sword clutched against my heaving chest. Realization dawned during the half-second that our eyes locked. I sheathed my sword, pressed myself up and off the wall, and positioned my feet as if in starting blocks.

Sloane turned, ran, kicking up a wake of dust for the chimera to follow.

With all six eyes laser focused on one piece of running meat, the chimera launched itself forward the exact same second I launched myself around the smoking building's wall. Four swift steps and a giant leap, I gripped the ram's long, mangy fur and pulled myself up one fistful at a time until I reached the base of its horns. I wrapped my hands around them and heaved myself into a sitting position.

Sloane ran straight with nowhere to go, nowhere to hide. The chimera gained.

I pulled my sword, raised it upside down with two hands above my head, then plunged the blade hard and deep through the ram's skull. The lion roared. The whole chimera listed to the left, then dropped to its front knees as if the lion and dragon could feel the ram's pain, which would make sense—they were all connected somehow. The ram's head drooped, lulled, became listless. It was my only chance to get to safety. I heaved my blade from the ram's skull, slid down its fur, found Sloane getting to her feet only a yard or two in front of the dragon head which, for the moment, seemed disoriented.

"Come on!" I yelled. She ran toward me and we made for the edge of the road to a narrow alleyway to catch our breath. Sloane held out one fist. I bumped it.

"Where's Jordan?" I asked. "Is he okay?"

"Take a look," she said, then motioned around the building's corner.

I looked just in time to see Jordan sneak up behind the chimera and raise his hatchet high above his head. He brought it down hard on the beast's massive tail. The second the hatchet hit, I knew it was a bad idea.

The lion head released something between a roar and a howl that nearly burst my eardrums. The chimera whipped its huge tail away from Jordan, jarring the hatchet handle loose from his hands. The tail recoiled, whipped back, smacked Jordan right in the chest before he had time to realize what was happening.

Jordan flew through the air, arms and legs flailing. He slammed hard into the side of a small, deteriorating building. His body was a wrecking ball. Stones, dirt, dust, debris collapsed around him, on top of him, until he disappeared from sight.

Numbing, icy shock pierced my heart.

"Jor—"

But Sloane wrapped her palm quickly around my mouth before I could finish screaming his name.

"He can't hear you," Sloane whispered in my ear. "And there's nothing we can do for him right now except kill that thing."

Her palm tasted like salty dirt. We locked wide eyes, I nodded, and Sloane slowly lowered her palm from my lips.

"Any bright ideas on how we might do that?" I asked.

The chimera let out another roar, swishing its tail in an arc across the dirt, slapping it on the ground. Jordan's hatchet, still embedded deep, clearly bothered it.

Sloan's arrow was gone. Whether it hit its mark was impossible to see from where we stood. If she missed, Crew could very well be hurt or dead. Jordan lay under piles of rubble. I was the only one between the two of us who still had her weapon. So yeah, if Sloane had any bright ideas on how we could kill the lion and dragon thirds of a chimera without getting eaten, burned, or smashed, I was all ears.

"Yeah," she said. A wry smile crept across her lips. "I've got an idea."

25

W hy is it that whenever Sloane hatches a plan, I'm always the bait? Pretty soon I'll start taking that personally.

I made my way through narrow, smokey alleyways. The chimera twisted, turned, brushed and smashed its tail on the ground trying to dislodge Jordan's hatchet. All that movement created a cloud of dust just thick enough to allow me to pass through it and cross the wide road without attracting the chimera's attention.

If only I could've reached the now-collapsed building that buried Jordan. But the chimera's dragon head was too close and looking in that direction. If it spotted me on the rubble, it would either light the whole thing on fire or smash it. I could only hope Jordan was somewhere in there, breathing, awake, alive.

I crossed, entered a tight space between two buildings and found exactly what Sloane had thought she'd spotted there—a strip of ancient-looking fabric that stuck out of a pile of gray rocks.

"This better work," I mumbled. I plucked the dusty fabric from the rocks, backed myself against a wall, then waved the fabric in the direction I'd come from. Sloane responded with a thumbs up. "This is insane," I continued mumbling to nobody in particular as I wrapped the fabric tightly around the blade of my sword, secured it at the bottom with a knot, then tested its tightness a few times and exhaled through a pin hole.

I hate fire. But here goes nothing.

I rolled away from the wall and into the open.

"Hey!" I yelled. "Hey you stupid lizard!"

The chimera stopped banging its tail against the ground. The dragon head snapped to attention. Its black marble eyes narrowed, focused. Its mouth revealed teeth, then glowing orange and yellow flames dancing in the back of its throat.

I waved my cloth-covered sword in its direction. In my mind, I was making myself look as threatening as possible, but I probably looked as threatening as a capering circus clown with one juggling pin.

I growled at it.

The dragon hesitated. Either it wasn't threatened by me in the slightest or it suspected something was up, or both. The chimera had underestimated the tiny humans with their puny weapons once, and lost a head for it. Sure enough, even though the dragon was trained on me, the lion was looking elsewhere. If our plan was going to work, I'd need the chimera's full attention.

I reached down, palmed a rock from the ground. It was surprisingly warm to the touch. With one heave, I threw it as hard as I could. It thudded off the lion's right temple. Bullseye.

The lion shook, then turn its attention toward me in an angry huff.

The chimera took one earth-shaking step toward me. Dust and grime shook free of rattling buildings. Tendrils of black smoke wrapped around the dragon's snout as it huffed and puffed. Its eyes narrowed further. The flames shimmering in the back of its throat became brighter.

Steady, Hannah. This is it.

The dragon pulled its head back. The lion roared at the exact moment the dragon released a heavy stream of flame, which singed the back of my neck and legs the second I dove behind the building's edge. Hot fire roared past me. I had exactly one chance at this…

I stuck my fabric-wrapped blade directly into the roaring furnace. The intense heat singed my hands and arms. I forced myself to hold steady, forced my eyes to remain open despite the sensation of staring directly into the sun. After counting to three-Mississippi, I pulled the sword back and backed up. The dragon's flames ceased, leaving behind a dense cloud of heavy black smoke. My sword, though, was a pillar of fire.

"Holy crap," I said, chest heaving. "It worked."

Hurry, Hannah.

I held my breath and curled around the corner of the building again. Under cover of thick smoke, I could just make out the chimera, the dragon and lion head still trained in my direction. The dragon's mouth opened again, its inner furnace burning yellow and orange and angry.

I heaved the flaming sword end over end like a boomerang over the chimera, beyond the ram's head.

Sloane, you'd better be there…

"Missed me, you overgrown gecko!" I yelled, maintaining the chimera's attention as the flaming sword spun through the air. The dragon released another stream of hot fire and I dove behind the building. I stood, back against the wall. Then all at once, the flames stopped.

The lion released a pulse pounding howl that iced my nerves. I fled through the remnant black smoke to find Sloane postured in front of the lion's head, the sword—still on fire—embedded deep into its right eye.

"Sloane! Watch out for—"

But I was too late, and she hadn't heard my warning.

The chimera raised one of its massive, clawed paws and slammed it down on top of her, pinning her to the dirt. My first thought; Sloane was dead, crushed under the chimera's weight. But Sloane growled, yelped, struggled to wriggle herself free from between its claws. The chimera had her trapped, a mouse under an elephant.

"Hey!"

The chimera didn't notice me. It was fully focused on the meal beneath its substantial paw.

I ran without a plan toward Sloane just as both the lion and the dragon lowered their heads, jaws wide open and dripping.

Sloane screamed. I screamed. I'd never reach her in time.

Then another scream, this one lower, came from the chimera's direction. I slid to a stop in the road and cleared the dust from my eyes.

Crew stood tall on top of the lion's mane.

"Here!" Crew tossed Sloane's arrow down to her. In one swift motion, she caught it and drove the arrowhead down hard into the chimera's paw. The beast roared, pulled back, releasing her. She slid backward across the dusty ground. I ran, reached her and pulled her backward by the arms. Crew's voice came again from on top of the lion's head.

"You son of a...." In one hand, he gripped his haladie, while in the other, Jordan's hatchet—he must've managed to pry it loose when he climbed up the chimera from behind. He brought both down fast and hard.

One of the haladie's sharp points slid wetly into the lion's left eye. The hatchet embedded deep into the lion's forehead. Either one of the blows should've counted as lethal, but instead of dying, the lion roared louder than it had ever roared before and threw its head backward. Crew fisted its mane, struggled to maintain balance. He reached for my sword jutting from the lion's right eye, pulled at the hilt, but just as the sword came free, the chimera raised its front paws and bucked forward.

The sword landed in a cloud of dust near my feet. Crew hung one-handed in front of the lion's snapping jaws. The chimera's paws thundered to the ground, missing Sloane by mere inches. She struggled to move, no matter how hard she tried. She was hurt.

I gripped her wrists, pulled her across the dirt as she hissed in pain. There was no way to tell just how injured she was, or whether I was exacerbating her injuries—all I knew was that I had to get her as far away from under the chimera's deadly, stomping, clawed paws as fast as I could. Once she was at a safer distance, I released her and rushed toward my sword.

The fabric I'd wrapped around the blade had burned away. The blade glowed an angry shade of red hot. I gripped the hilt, took a step toward Crew and the chimera, then froze.

For the first time, the chimera spread its wings with a single, leathery *snap*. Each had to be twenty feet in length, covered in the same dark red scales that covered the dragon's head. The hot breeze ruffled them like ship sails on the ocean.

The chimera flapped its wings once. The wind they created was a solid wall that sent me reeling backward.

Another flap, and its massive body left the ground.

"Crew!" Sloane yelled from behind me, but it was too late. He clung to the lion's mane as it forced itself to deadly heights.

Every creature that hovered high above Pandemonium scattered, some of them releasing a terrified, high screech as the chimera rose hundreds of feet to the smoldering ceiling. That was when I first realized something was very wrong with it.

The chimera's body twitched, almost as if it couldn't control both of its giant wings at the same time. One would flap, sending it careening sideways until the other flapped, like a massive, out-of-control kite flying through a thunderstorm. It listed to one side, then another, slowly but steadily losing its ability to maintain its altitude. From way down below, I could see the lion's head begin to lull, raise, cry out, then drop.

The lion was dying. The chimera was about to fall, and Crew with it. The same second that realization crossed my mind, the chimera ceased flapping its wings and began cruising down-ward like a lightning-struck airplane. The dragon released flames in spurts and sputters as the rest of the chimera lost control.

And then, another realization…

"Where are you going?" Sloane yelled, still lying across the ground gripping her injured midsection. I didn't have time to answer her. I was already running, sword gripped tightly in hand, shifting glances between the building I'd scouted ahead of me and the chimera, falling like a plane on fire, cruising down-ward at an unsurvivable rate of speed toward the city below.

Stay on that trajectory. Please, stay on that trajectory.

I hop-skipped up a pile of smoldering rubble, sheathed my sword, leaped up a precarious building wall that threatened to cave in on itself and bury me beneath it. Hot wind threatened to blast me off the wall as I speed-climbed until I finally pulled myself up and over the rooftop's edge. I stared upward, unsheathed my sword.

The beast was headed straight for me. If it came in too low, it would certainly take out the building I was standing on, and me along with it. Every nerve inside of me bundled into balls so tight they threatened to snap.

Then I saw Crew. He saw me, too. With one hand wrapped in lion's mane, he stood on its neck. I knew instantly what he meant to do.

I breathed. Shut my eyes. Cut myself off from the hellscape surrounding me.

Ten seconds…

One breath in. I held it.

Five seconds…

The tense wire that made up my shoulders slackened a little, muscles untethered.

Three seconds…

I opened my eyes and focused narrowly on my target and nothing but my target. Crew became a fuzzy humanoid shape flying through the air in my vision's periphery. Setting my feet, I double-fisted my sword and lifted the blade high.

The blade's point pierced the chimera's abdomen as it flew only feet, maybe inches, above my head in a mad rush of tidal wind.

I held the hilt tight. The blade sunk, traveled through fur, bone, tendon, muscle, tracing a thin dark line as it tore through the chimera's entire underbelly until it finally snapped free. Dark liquid dripped from the warm metal.

Crew hit the building's rooftop at high speed next to me, rolled, slid, clawed for purchase. I dove, grasped his wrist before he flew off the building's edge.

The flayed chimera crashed between two buildings, sending them both crumbling to the ground. Other buildings around them collapsed like a massive, terrifying game of dominoes. The entire world sounded like it was placed deep within the throat of a roaring hellhound.

Then, almost at once, the roaring wave of crumbling buildings stopped. The chimera lay on a pile of smoking rubble below.

I stood, helped Crew pull his legs over the building's precipice, then gingerly rolled him coughing onto his back.

"Holy crap," I managed. "Holy holy holy crap. You're okay."

He sputtered a laugh, even managed a thin smile as he gripped his ribs. "We've got to teach you some real swear words," he muttered between coughing fits.

"But how did you—"

"Sloane's a good shot."

A huffing, chuffing sound came from below. When we turned, we saw the chimera's body twitch, move.

A sudden rush of rage filled me.

"Get your girl," I said with a sly wink, "then go find Jordan. I'll finish this."

Crew nodded. I helped him to his feet, then lowered myself off the building.

The chimera lay atop a tower of rubble. Warm, loose rocks shifted as I climbed quickly and steadily, sword gripped tight. The sounds of labored breathing, its chest rising and falling, was like a locomotive pulling into a station. Steamy smoke wafted around me.

I saw myself reflected in the dragon's onyx eyes as I approached. They narrowed slightly, taking in the sight of me. The chimera's body twitched. Black smoke leaked from the dragon's jaws, but its strength was gone. Black blood pooled underneath it—the same black blood that covered my blade. I held it up to my chest so the dragon could clearly see it.

Yeah. I did that.

The dragon chuffed. Its jaws snapped weakly a couple times before it released a high whine. The hoods over its eyes drooped heavily.

The ram was already dead, but smashing into buildings did its face no favors. Its twisted horns were sheared off unevenly. The rest of it was hardly recognizable.

The lion was… gross. Its head looked like it had a blood faucet in the form of Jordan's hatchet attached to it, turned on full blast until it drained. The eye with Crew's haladie sticking out of it was completely mangled. Its black tongue dangled lifelessly out of one side of its jaws between sharp, dead fangs.

The dragon chuffed again, made a sound like an old car unable to start. It would probably die if I left it here. Looking up, I noticed multiple different species of flying things that I did not want to meet up close begin to circle like vultures high above the chimera's body. Or, maybe it wouldn't die. I knew nothing of chimeras really, other than what I'd learned over the last few minutes in a literal crash course. The last thing we needed was to rescue Adam only to be met by a wall of dragon flame the second we left the building where he was being held.

Plus, we don't know Jordan's status, yet. This thing, this awful beast, could've killed him…

A new wave of hot anger warmed my chest.

Leave nothing to chance.

I circled to the dragon side of the chimera. It snapped its jaws again.

"It's not personal," I said, raising my sword high above my head. "Except, well, yeah, it is."

———

I ROUNDED a corner onto the wide road, saw Crew gingerly helping Sloane to her feet. She was still gripping her waist where the chimera had pinned her down, and apparently couldn't put much weight on her right ankle... but both of them were alive. All things considered, that was pretty much a miracle. Their eyes grew wider than silver dollars when I plopped the heavy, leaking dragon's head on the dirt. Crew smiled.

Then an icy wave of relief washed over me. Someone approached Crew and Sloane from behind, covered in thick, gray dust.

"Jordan." I rushed toward him, almost threw myself onto him, but held up at the last moment, unsure whether he was suffering from any injuries. I settled for slapping him on the bicep.

"It is *really* good to see you," I told him. "I thought... we were worried... that tail—"

"I'm good," Jordan said, "luckily. Got knocked out for a while back there, though."

"I wanted to come dig you out, make sure you were okay— we all did," I said, gesturing toward the others.

"You were a little busy," Jordan said, and the corners of his lips pinched together. "You sure you killed it?"

"Oh yeah," I said. "It's most definitely dead. Like, *dead* dead. I... wait a second..." Each of them were looking at me like they were barely able to hold in fits of laughter. "What?" I asked.

Sloane snorted.

"I wish we had a mirror," Crew said. Jordan cocked his head and nodded.

"Why?" I asked.

"Girl," Sloane said, releasing herself from Crew's helpful grip. She limped over to me and placed a hand on my shoulder. "You look like you took a bath in chimera blood."

I looked down at my arms. Sloane wasn't kidding. They looked like they'd been dipped in a barrel of maroon paint. Embarrassment warmed my cheeks, but if my face looked anything like the rest of me, the others wouldn't notice.

Suddenly I felt a little nauseous.

Sloane chuckled, ripped off a piece of her slashed-up shirt, and wiped my face. "Here you go," she said, carefully wiping around my eyes, the bridge of my nose, my forehead and cheeks. "There she is. That's better."

"So gross," I managed.

"Yeah. Pretty badass though," she said, stepping back. I felt a small smile creep across my lips, then I handed Sloane the arrow I'd dug out of the chimera's paw.

"Are you okay?"

"Just got to walk it off," Sloane said. "I'll be fine."

It was the first time I'd really felt love for her—for all of them. When I handed back their weapons one at a time—Crew his haladie, Jordan his hatchet—the feeling nearly overwhelmed me. Miraculously, we'd faced a forest full of demons, shadow wolves guarding the gate to Pandemonium, a chimera, and somehow all of us stood here a little worse for wear, but alive.

They'd risked their lives for me, for each other.

For Adam.

My eyes wandered to the tall building.

"No rest for the bloody," Crew said, folding his arm around Sloane.

"Let's go get your man," Sloane added.

"*Our* man," I corrected.

"Yeah," Jordan said, "but mostly your man."

My cheeks warmed again. Sloane and Jordan were smiling wryly. Crew, though, hung his head.

"You okay?" I asked him. He cleared his throat, straightened up, apparently shaking off whatever it was that had suddenly bothered him.

"Yeah," he said. "Let's get this over with."

26

There was no door to the tall building that held Adam. In fact, I don't think there were any doors to any of the buildings—just holes of varying sizes to crawl through. One oval hole in the wall hovered a couple feet above the ground. We crouched and stepped through. The searing pain in my guts told me we were very close.

The air was rank, dusty, thick with nervous energy. Two narrow stairways curved along the edges of the building's insides, one leading up, one leading down. Otherwise, the building was hollow, vacuous. No demons in sight.

"Which way?" Jordan asked me.

"Down," I said. I wasn't sure how I was so sure, but I'd learned long ago not to question the particular instincts that led me toward Adam.

Crew went first, then Sloane. I fell in line, and Jordan brought up the rear. Light dissipated as we descended each questionable stone step. None of the steps were the same size, and it felt like the entire staircase could give way at any moment, but we pressed forward, downward. The gray, soupy light from outside the building began to disappear, replaced by a soft, reddish glow that flickered somewhere below.

My guts tied themselves in knots, then tied those knots in knots, then dipped those knots in kerosene and threatened to light a match. The thought of what we could find around the next corner...

We reached a landing, a room. A small, lit torch attached to a crude metal fixture cast dim, flickering light against the wall. It was the only thing lighting up what I guess you could call a basement. It smelled dank, foul.

"We should've left someone outside on watch," Sloane said. "We're sitting ducks down here."

"Something tells me we're going to need all hands down here," Crew responded. "I have a bad feeling."

I could hardly hear their words. Other than us, the room was empty. It took every ounce of strength and will not to double over and puke. Adam was here. But not *here*. The high-powered adrenaline I'd been feeling ever since walking into Pandemonium was replaced by raw desperation.

"Hey," Sloane said, breaking the rush of panic in my ears. "You look really pale."

"Hold up," Jordan said, then climbed a few stairs and retrieved the small torch, brought it down. "Yeah, you do look pale. You all right?"

"No," I snapped. "Scan the walls. Find an opening. He's here somewhere."

Jordan hesitated for a beat or two, then followed my orders. It wasn't more than a few seconds before he found a hole about three feet high and wide, like the kind mice make in the baseboards of old houses but much larger.

I seized the torch from Jordan. "Come on."

The others crouched low and followed me through the hole's entrance, down a long, claustrophobia-inducing tunnel.

"Hannah, slow down," one of them said. I did not slow down.

"You don't know what's waiting for us on the other side."

Yes, I do.

Despite not being able to fully stand in the narrow tunnel, I was running before I realized I was running. Every single molecule that made up the air around me vibrated. With every step, my very soul hummed in rhythm and time with what I now knew could only be the one other soul mine was infinitely linked to.

At the end of the tunnel, the inner vibrating hum ceased. I held the torch high and forward. What I saw shattered me into a million shards of sharp glass.

The room was small—no bigger than my old bedroom when we lived with Aunt Sarah. In the exact middle, a large stone slab rose like a gravestone to the height of my chest. And across the stone slab, Adam lay, splayed, naked, his wrists and ankles bound by heavy chains.

I wanted to simultaneously scream in horror and shout for joy and cry in shock, but then I saw the eyes.

Three large demons hovered along the back wall, hissing at the light of my torch. Compared to the utter darkness that had blanketed this room, the flames must've seemed like the sun itself had entered. But the torch's flame was a mere candle wick compared to the bonfire roaring inside my chest.

I dropped the torch with a clatter to the ground and pulled my sword, glaring each demon in its sick yellow eyes.

"You'll pay."

One of them screeched, which I took to mean it volunteered as tribute to explode first. I took it up on its offer.

Swiftly, I flew past the stone slab that held Adam. The demons—Reapers—each pulled crude weapons from their robes, but I did not care. Sloane had once told me never to take on a Reaper on my own, but now, I could've faced every Reaper in Hell and come away standing on a pile of their smoldering ashes.

The closest Reaper swung its weapon. I blocked it, knocked it away, then buried my blade through its neck. Another Reaper raised its weapon the moment its comrade exploded into a billion pieces of golden light. It hesitated at that, which was a mistake. I spun low and cut the Reaper down.

The last Reaper was a coward. When its two friends dissolved, it backed away along the wall.

"No!" I shouted when I noticed it was backing right into a waiting Jordan, his hatchet pulled back, held high. "It's mine." Jordan lowered his weapon and stepped away.

"Did you do this?" I said to the Reaper, motioning my blade toward Adam. My throat felt lined with hot coals.

The Reaper, of course, didn't answer. It only raised its weapon—a long, dark spike.

I licked my lips, launched myself off the wall with one foot, and with a final, primal scream, sliced off the skeletal hands that held the spike, then drove my blade up and through its head. The Reaper shook, rattled, sucked in on itself, then exploded.

Red rage had nearly overtaken my vision. My chest was a bellows. Sloane picked up the torch I'd dropped and held it over Adam's body.

I forced my eyes shut for an eternal beat, regained my breath before opening them again, then approached the slab.

"Get these chains off," one of the boys said. They scurried to unwrap them from around his wrists and ankles.

Long, dark hair blanketed Adam's face. Slowly, gently, I brushed it aside with a trembling hand. His face was pale, eyes and mouth closed, yet his skin was warm to the touch. I held my flushed, wet cheek against his.

"Adam," I whispered. He didn't move, didn't stir. "Adam, please."

I brought two fingers to his neck, searched for a pulse, but my hands trembled too violently to find one. A flood of raw emotion welled up from the deep. My breath ceased. My vision became a blurry, wet pane of glass.

"Look at this," Sloane said as she slowly scanned his body under torch light. I wiped wetness from my eyes, then nearly recoiled in shock when I saw what Sloane was illuminating.

Black, tattoo-like markings covered almost the entirety of Adam's body. I traced a couple with my finger. They were symbols, almost like the kind that Malum had branded us with before we'd finished our Dark Trials together. But these symbols weren't mere rings that fit on the back of our wrist. Some were small, yes, but others were big, taking up large portions of his chest, stomach, legs and arms. Each symbol was unique. Some were crude—slashing, intersecting lines that could resemble the scars someone would take away from a chimera fight—while others were intricate—circles intersected by sharp, crisp lines and what looked like some ancient form of lettering.

They looked altogether alien.

Sloane, Jordan and Crew shared a knowing glance.

"What is it?" I asked. "What do these markings mean?"

Each of them tightened their lips and dropped their gaze from me. "These are brands, right? Like the kind each of us got when we sold our souls."

Crew was the only one to raise his head. "Not exactly the same, but in a way, yes. They're sigils."

Not exactly the same? Sigils? One tiny wrist brand was enough to wreck my whole world before completing the Dark Trials—what would an entire body full of them mean?

The avalanche of questions formulating in my head was dashed when Adam released a low, quiet moan. His head turned ever so slightly, his chest rose and fell with new breath.

"Adam!"

Carefully, I cupped the back of his head in my hands, kissed his fluttering eyelids. "We're going to get you out of here." He groaned, moved one unchained wrist.

"Cover him up," Crew said.

"Over here," Jordan replied. He was crouched in one corner, held up what looked like shreds of filthy fabric for a few seconds before I realized they were what remained of Adam's clothes. Jordan carried over the largest shreds of fabric he could find—

large sections of Adam's black shirt and jacket—and tied them around his waist.

"Come on," Crew said. He and Jordan grabbed Adam under each arm and slowly lifted him to a sitting position. Adam moaned again. His head lulled almost lifelessly to one side. But then one of the most beautiful things I had ever seen in my entire life happened.

Adam's eyes fluttered open. His cobalt blue irises reflected the torch's flickering flame. He saw me, and I saw him. We connected for a single heartbeat, and my soul burned. He shut his eyes again, but in that moment, I knew deep in my being that *he* knew that I was there for him. Something inside me unwound, and I let out a long, relieved breath.

I wrapped my arms around his bare, symbol-covered middle. "Let's get him out of here."

DESPITE BEING STRAPPED WITH MUSCLE, Jordan and Crew struggled to carry Adam's fully limp body through the tunnel. The euphoria of finding Adam, watching him being carried from the dank dungeon that held him quickly wore off as the sharp thought stabbed at the back of my mind: What if we have to fight our way out?

Now that the Chimera was gone, demons of all kinds were free to roam the roads and alleyways of Pandemonium. Those devilish creatures floating above the city where the cavern's ceiling smoldered wouldn't hesitate to divebomb the Dantes as we made our way out of town and up the stairs to the Borderlands. Adam was in no state to defend himself. He couldn't even stand. Crew and Jordan were carrying a two-hundred-pound rag doll.

We squeezed out of the tunnel and reached the bottom of the steps when I noticed, in the dim light that seeped in from outside, that Adam still had his dagger. It lay firmly within the sheath strapped to his leg.

You'd think they would've taken it from him...

Something rumbled like thunder outside, which could've meant a number of things, all of them bad. Sloane and I led the way up the steps. Crew and Jordan used a fireman's carry, held their breath and groaned, taking each step slow and steady.

Adam wasn't the only one of us not in fighting shape. The rest of us were beat up, on our last legs. The adrenaline that masked our injuries had dissolved. Our bodies screamed. That's how I felt, at least—muscles completely burned out, threatening to melt off my bones.

Jordan groaned under Adam's weight. I was hurting, yes, but he'd been whipsawed through a whole building. Stealth wasn't much of an option either. Not while trying to carry someone. We reached the last step, neared the makeshift doorway in the wall that would lead us again into Pandemonium, into Hell.

Sloane took a deep breath and pulled her bow off of her shoulder, nocked her arrow, and shot me a glance. I didn't like it. She had always been so steady, so confident, like nothing in the world above or below stood a chance against her, which I would've believed not long ago, but now...

I gripped the hilt of my sword.

"I'll go first," I said. The old Sloane would've disagreed, insisted. This Sloane only nodded.

I swallowed, cracked my neck, readied myself to move quickly. The last thing I wanted was to peek my head out just to have it lopped off by a Reaper.

You die down here, you die forever.

I sucked in a breath, held it, then burst through the hole in the wall sword first. What faced me on the other side forced the breath back out of me.

Hundreds—no, *thousands*—of demons, from Phantoms to Reapers to full on Vessels, stood in the streets, the alleyways, around corners and on top of rooftops. The city was an ocean of black robes. Not only were there demons, but other creatures I had never seen before; Two-legged humanoids with dead black eyes and four-legged creatures of various sizes, some with wings, others with fangs, most with both. Every single one of their noxious eyes were focused in one singular direction, on one single thing.

Me.

Sloane followed close behind. When she came through the hole in the wall, her silence was deafening. Not because I couldn't hear it, but because I *could*. Despite being completely surrounded on every side, I could hear her breathing, her heart beating against the inside of her ribs like a desperate prisoner begging to be released from its cell. The only other sound was the stiff, warm wind sweeping through Pandemonium.

Sloane swallowed hard.

"Well," she whispered, but may as well have screamed, "I guess this is it."

"Guess so," I said, white-knuckling my sword's hilt.

Jordan backed out of the hole, lifted Adam through by the backs of his arms, followed by Crew. Both of them shared the same reaction: Shocked silence. With one arm wrapped around Adam, each of them slowly pulled their weapons with their free hands. I'd expected this to cause the Reapers to pull their own weapons, the creatures to growl and bear their fangs, but... no. They merely stared.

Stared at Adam.

Only at Adam, I realized. The entire population of Pandemonium didn't give a damn about the other four of us. They were fixated on Adam, propped between Jordan and Crew, with a singular, intense focus that made my guts clench.

I noticed a small ripple of movement from the back of the crowd of demons and creatures. Squinting, it looked like some of them were moving to one side, others to the opposite, forming a path for something else to walk through. Loathing filled me as I imagined what that something else could be.

Finally, the last of the demons and creatures moved to each side, creating a visual that only Moses and his people had previously seen. The sea of underworldy entities was parted. A narrow, winding path lead through Pandemonium, to the iron gate, the black bridge, the dark stairs that climbed to the black door and opened into the Borderlands. Nothing—no demon or creature of Hell—stood in the path.

None of us spoke for an eternity. I'm not sure any of us were breathing. Every creature of Hell remained utterly, unsettlingly silent.

"I think they want us to leave," Jordan finally said.

But it made no sense. Why? In both worlds, we, the Dantes, were their primary enemy, their worst threat. We'd slain hundreds if not thousands of their equals in worlds above and below. Here, now, they had a chance to end us for good, and they could do it so easily. So why let us through?

The Chimera, was my first thought. The beast that sent them all into hiding as it stalked the streets. We took it down. Maybe they were, in some strange way, grateful?

No, that didn't make any sense either. Demons are demons, and creatures are mindless. They don't feel anything, much less gratitude.

A soft, dragging sound as Crew and Jordan sheathed their weapons and pulled Adam toward the black throng, toward the narrow pathway.

"Wait," I pleaded. I imagined the sea of demons collapsing onto the three of them after they'd entered the path, destroying and devouring all three in less than a heartbeat.

They acted as if they hadn't heard me.

"There's no other way out of this, Hannah," Sloane said, resting a hand on my shoulder. "Whatever it is they're offering, we have to take it. I won't pretend to understand it, but now isn't the time for questions." She let go of my shoulder and turned to follow the boys.

I stepped forward intending to leapfrog the other Dantes and head into the path first, sword drawn. But movement among the mass of black robes froze me in place. As Crew and Jordan approached with Adam's arms slung around their shoulders, the demons at the head of the path moved, shifted, then did something I couldn't comprehend.

Each of them lowered their hooded heads, then lowered the rest of their robed bodies, some to their knees. Each of us stopped dead in our tracks.

It was like a large wave rippled through Pandemonium's population. Black robes rustled as each of the thousands of demons in turn bowed and knelt and stayed on their knees, apparently intending to remain there until we passed.

My mind swam with questions, my nerves crackled as my body wrestled between fight or flight.

"Move," Crew said. He and Jordan passed the first few, kneeling demons and entered the narrow, winding path toward the iron gate. No demon or creature flinched as they passed. "You don't need those," he added, glancing back at me and Sloane. Each of us had our weapons pulled. I looked at him skeptically, but his eyes conveyed sincerity.

My mind could not wrap itself around the current reality. They really were allowing us to pass.

Slowly, I sheathed my sword. Sloane quivered her arrow and rested her bow across her shoulders. The last thing we needed was to screw up this impossible scenario by acting trigger happy. Crew nodded, thankful.

"We could move faster with a little help," he said. Sloane and I stepped up, passed the boys, and both of us grabbed one of Adam's limp legs and rested it on our shoulders. The four of us carried Adam's body through the throng of demons and Hellish creatures like pallbearers carrying a coffin toward a hurst. Snapping fabric was the only sound, as warm, unnatural wind whipped their black robes. We made our way silently through the city following the narrow path of parted masses.

The iron gate, which was only open by a sliver when we'd

first entered, was now swung wide. The neon green, bubbling, poisonous river even seemed calmer than it had when we'd crossed the black bridge the first time, reflecting almost serenely off the rocky walls, the cavern's ceiling, the narrow bridge as we stepped across.

Shadow wolves materialized from the darkness and flanked the bridge's far side, red eyes glowing, as if the shadow simply replaced the two we had killed. Neither of them moved—they didn't even make a sound—as we walked past them toward the stairs. They only watched.

When we had entered through the black door and descended to Pandemonium, the stairway was blacker than pitch. Now, the way leading to the Borderlands was lit by flickering torches along the walls. Again, I had to bat away the flurry of uneasy questions assaulting my brain and step, one stair at a time, toward the open door above.

Every single time I'd ever entered the Borderlands from any direction, a storm was brewing in the angry red sky. But not this time. As we stepped out of the black door and into the Circle— out of breath, muscles screaming—the air was calm. No wind rustled the dark forests that surrounded us on all sides. No lightning flashes carved up the sky. Even the massive volcanic mountain in the distance seemed still.

None of us spoke.

After a moment's rest, we moved toward the trees in the direction we had come, toward the portal. I imagined the flying creatures attacking from their invisible perches in the forest's canopy, but the trees were still. No laughter came from above or around us. The only sound was our labored breathing as we climbed the slope.

Finally, the portal came into view. A small slit, like a tear in the fabric of reality, shimmered. I thought to stop, to take stock, to talk about what in the hell was going on. The knots forming in my stomach tightened at the unignorable idea that something was *very* wrong. But the others pressed on, and I kept my concerns to myself.

I glanced behind me, taking in the most unique view of the Borderland's I had ever seen. All was calm, quiet. A lump formed my throat when I noticed the unsettling scene at the black door in the middle of the Circle. Demons and creatures of all kinds poured out of the door like ants out of an ant hill, blanketing over the desert mudracks in black cloaks. Thousands of slitted, yellow eyes fixated on us. I couldn't hold it in any longer.

"Guys," I said. They paused, followed my gaze down the hill, and took in the scene.

"It's like… like they're saying goodbye, but don't want to see us go," Sloane said.

It gave me shivers. The others didn't speak, only stared as more demons poured out of the black door like a faucet, flooding the Circle just to get a glimpse.

A glimpse of what?

Pressure on my shoulder. Crew stepped forward, urging us on. We were only feet from the shimmering portal now; feet from pulling Adam out of this place, away from his torture and pain.

"You two first," Crew said. Sloane and I carefully lowered Adam's legs from our shoulders. Sloane readied her bow and arrow, then slipped through the portal. It pulled her through with a soft sucking sound.

I turned, pulled my sword, held it tight and followed her through. Sloane was waiting for me in the Gray. We turned, backed away to make room for the others, which was a good idea because the first thing that pierced the veil between worlds was one sharp point of Crew's deadly haladie. He and Jordan heaved Adam through the portal. Here, in the Gray, his—what did Crew call the markings? Sigils?—somehow seemed to glow, to emanate light even though they were black as night.

"We've got to get this portal closed," Crew said, "before the army of demons that followed us out decides to follow us here, too."

He and Jordan carefully propped Adam against a flat section of rock wall. He moaned, tried to lift his head. His eyes fluttered slightly. He was coming to, and the realization was a wave crashing over me.

He was safe. He was here, with me, alive, awake.

I rushed to him, crouched at his side.

"I should've never let you leave that night," I whispered into his ear, holding his head gently against my chest. I traced my finger lightly across his skin, outlining a marking that looked like an oblong drawing of a black sun covering his shoulder. Tears dampened my flushed cheeks.

Adam, what did they do to you...?

The answer to that question wasn't important. Not right now. The only thing that mattered was the fact that he was alive and free from the literal Hell inflicted on him. We could figure the rest out later.

Adam moaned again, opened his cracked lips. "H... Hannah?"

The breath caught. I struggled to speak. "Adam! Adam, I'm here. I'm here." His lips parted again, but I shushed him. "Don't talk. It's okay. You're going home. With me. You'll be okay."

"R... Ryan," Adam managed.

My stomach turned. "I know," I said. "That's all over now."

An uncontrollable urge to hold him against me completely, to feel all of him so I'd know it was real overwhelmed me. Every single emotion I'd kept bottled up for the last couple days—each day the length of an entire year—broke over the surface. I pressed my forehead against his.

His eyes flittered open. Those same blue diamonds that stole my breath that fall day in the parking lot of Eagle Ridge High stole my breath now. I pressed my hand softly against his bare chest and felt his heartbeat quicken. The corners of his lips spread into a small smile. With my thumb, I caressed his lips, running along every dry peak and valley. My fingers spread over his cheek, his hard jaw, behind his ear, then held his neck.

"I love you," I managed to whisper between hitching breaths. "So much."

"I love you too, Hannah," he whispered back. The ghost of a smile graced his lips. He parted them, intending to say more, but I gripped the back of his neck and pressed my lips firmly, gently, against his, exploring the curvature of his lips. Stars exploded behind my eyes and I knew then and there that if Adam had had the strength, I would've given myself to him entirely. His lips moved slowly as he kissed me back, yet his arms, hands, the rest of him did not move. He didn't have the strength to pull me into him like my body and mind suddenly, desperately craved.

In that moment, all other worlds melted away. I'd forgotten where I was, who I was with, why I was there until, after seconds or minutes or hours, I pulled back, released him and rested my forehead against his again.

"I will never let you leave me again," I whispered, eyes shut.

He didn't answer. He didn't have to. The heart pounding against my palm spoke in a volume and language I understood completely. Suddenly, his hand brushed my arm, then came to rest softly on the back of my neck. But, just as quickly as it had come, his strength melted away. His eyes fluttered closed, his head came to rest on the rocky wall behind him. That was the moment I finally allowed the sense of relief that had been knocking at the door to come rushing in, to chase the anxiety and, yes, fear, away.

He's going to be okay.

I smiled, stepped back, remembering suddenly that, oh yeah, we weren't alone.

In the background, Crew spoke words I had never heard in a language I definitely did not understand—Latin, maybe. Didn't matter. Once he spoke them, the portal seemed to pulse with energy, sending ripples of bright light bouncing off the cavern walls. From the top of the portal's opening, he slowly pressed one of the tips of his haladie inside and pulled down slowly. The haladie acted like a zipper. Every section of the portal above where he'd pulled his haladie closed until, after a few long seconds, he reached the bottom. When he freed the haladie, the place where the portal had been released a small *pop* sound.

Then it was gone. Closed.

"Hannah," Crew said, still facing the place where the portal had been. His chest was heaving, like he'd just climbed a small mountain, and his eyes were glued to the floor. "I need to talk to you about something. About Adam."

I didn't like the reticent tone in his voice.

"What?"

Crew swallowed hard, as if he fought to keep his next words in his chest. I glanced up toward Jordan and Sloane, but they each kept their heads down, their eyes away like they knew what was coming and didn't want to watch. Something wasn't right. Instinctively, I stood between Adam and the others.

"Do we have to do this here?" Sloane said, an eerie panic lacing her voice.

"Do what?" I demanded, glaring between the three of them. "What haven't you told me?"

"Sloane's right," Crew said, finally meeting my eyes. He lifted his haladie and motioned toward his sheath. "Let's put these away and talk outside the Gray."

"Better idea: Let's talk now," I said. That hot anger had begun to rise inside of me again. I hadn't risked the depths of Hell and the city of the damned for Adam only to have the other Dantes threaten him. And that *is* what this started to feel like—a threat. My muscles tensed. My heartbeat accelerated. Something was very wrong here and I didn't like the way the others wouldn't meet my gaze, or the way they constantly glanced toward Adam as if he was a dangerous, wild animal in a cage—one that needed to be put down. "Is this about the markings—sigils—all over his body? Just... whatever it is you have to tell me, tell me now."

"Hannah," Jordan offered. He lowered his hatchet so it

hovered just above his sheath, prompting me to follow his lead. "We're just going to talk."

Sloane had already slung her bow over her shoulder, dropped her arrow into her quiver and left the Gray. I pulled in a breath, sighed.

The rest of us put our Borderlands weapons away and entered reality. Somehow, even though the moon had risen higher in the night sky surrounded by a sea of stars, the world outside seemed even darker than when we'd entered the portal.

"Hello there," a low voice came from just outside the cave. The sound of it stopped my heart. I knew that oily voice. The others spun in surprise to face the woods outside. The trees, rocks, formed shadows cast by the moonlight. I peered through the darkness, into the trees until the form that had spoken the words began to materialize.

Not form. *Forms.*

My eyes adjusted. My hand rushed to cover my mouth.

The man I'd known as Michael, whose real name I'd learned was Damien, stood in the woods outside the cave's opening. He didn't bother to wear his white mask anymore. Ryan, on the other hand, wore his white mask firmly, and I couldn't blame him. I wouldn't want to show my traitorous face to anyone ever again if I were him. In one hand, Damien held something black, metallic. A gun. But it's what he held in his other hand that stole my breath and threatened to rip my entire world to shreds.

His other hand was wrapped tight around my crying sister.

27

They had found her. Somehow, they knew, and suddenly I hated myself for leaving my sister in any way vulnerable to any of my enemies—supernatural or otherwise.

"I see you were successful in your quest. That's wonderful." A slick smile crept along Damien's mouth as he nodded toward the side wall of the small cave, toward Adam.

Thoughts bubbled up to the surface of my mind, but they were foreign. Not mine. Not my inner voice. They'd broken through my mind's defenses and invaded.

What's wrong? Is it Em?

Adam began coming to again. One hand spread across his black marked chest, his head lulling side to side as he struggled to prop himself up straighter, releasing breathy moans. His eyes, though, remained closed.

"So good to see you," Damien said, his words traveling to the rocky wall where Adam rested. His sardonic smile widened, curled the edges of his lips. Damien made it sound like they knew each other. Like they were old friends.

It took every ounce of strength inside of me to not cut the distance between us and punch Damien in the mouth. The ribbons of muscle in my arms and neck tightened as I turned to Ryan standing next to him. "How could you?"

Ryan's masked chin rose defiantly. "I'm sorry, Hannah," he said. "I really am. But this… this is bigger than us." My jaw tensed so tightly, it nearly broke. I focused on Damien.

"Let go of her right now." I reached down to pull my sword, leaving any threat Ryan could make outside of the Gray.

Damien clucked his tongue. "Now, now," he said, "that weapon of yours will do you no good against this." He waved the gun toward me, then in one terrifying motion, pressed it hard against the side Em's head.

"No!" I screamed. Nesting birds rushed out of the trees. I pulled my hand away from where my sword rested. "Don't you dare hurt her!"

Em's chest began hitching. Tears streamed in rivulets down her cheeks and across Damien's hand that covered her mouth.

"It's okay, Em," I said, but my rattling voice belied my attempt at confidence. A hand grasped my arm. Crew stepped forward.

"Tell us what you want, Damien."

Damien rolled his eyes. "Don't play games with me, Crew. You know exactly what I want. Look," he said, then held Em forward, "I'm even willing to make a trade. Straight across."

Crew sucked on his teeth for a moment, contemplating. "You know we can't do that, Damien."

"Ah, well, then…" He pulled Em roughly against him again, pressed the barrel of his pistol harder against her temple. Em's eyes cinched shut. Her wet cheeks trembled as she whimpered.

"Stop!" I screamed out again. "What is it? What do you want? Whatever it is, I'll give it to you. Just…," I forced my breathing to regulate, lowered my voice into a lower register, held a pleading hand toward him. "Just let go of her. Give her to me."

Damien's face screwed up in puzzlement for a beat. His eyes raked over me before his studying gaze shifted between me,

Adam and the other Dantes. Then he released a low, caustic laugh.

"Wow," he said. "She doesn't know, does she?" The question was directed at Crew, but Crew didn't answer. He stood still, staring forward, but I sensed it wasn't because he was angry with Damien. More like he wanted to avoid my gaze.

"Sorry, Damien," Crew finally said. "No deal."

A soft *click* as Damien pulled back the hammer. Em's muffled screams became louder. A black tunnel squeezed the edges of my vision. Before I realized what I'd done, Crew was in front of me, his back pressed hard against the cave wall, my hands pressed heavy against his chest.

"You," I started, trying to formulate the words exploding in my mind and arrange them into a coherent sentence. "You don't get to negotiate when my sister's life is on the line. You don't get to say, 'no deal.' That is not your call."

Damien laughed again, distantly. I directed all my ire in his direction.

"You'll put that gun down now if you want to keep your hand," I seethed.

"Feisty," he said, then lowered his gaze, leveling me. "I like them feisty…"

"What's the deal?" I demanded.

"It's very simple," Damien said. "A trade. I hand over your sister to you, and you hand him over to me." Damien pointed toward the space behind me where Adam leaned heavily against the wall.

Slowly, Adam had become more conscious, more coherent, seemingly out of breath. His chest heaved. His hand was pressed firmly against the cave wall as if he meant to use it to prop himself up to his feet. I turned back to Damien.

"Why is Adam so important to you?"

He rolled his eyes again. "Is that his name? Adam? Adam is not important to me," he said, impatience creeping into his voice. "Adam is merely a tool. A Trojan horse, nothing more. You would know this if your so-called friends here were honest with you."

I scanned each Dante's face one by one. Sloane's lips tightened as she lowered her gaze to the ground. Jordan at least met my eyes, but his were guilt-ridden.

A bass drum pounded inside my head.

My heart threatened to rip itself out of its bony cage.

Hands on my temples, my scream seemed to shake the cave walls. "Someone tell me what is going on!"

"He can't leave, Hannah," Crew finally said, low and calm.

Behind me, Adam began coughing, retching. The sound his throat made... it was like something was trying to claw its way out. Something... alive.

"Those sigils?" Crew continued. "Each one represents a different demon."

The vast ocean of tattoo-like markings across Adam's exposed body seemed to glow even brighter. The marks varied in size from the size of a fingernail to the largest of them all—a full circle filled with scrawled, intersecting lines and markings which covered his entire chest. There had to be dozens of them. Maybe over a hundred.

Adam retched again, but I fought the urge to go to him. I needed an answer.

"He was tortured," I said. "Demons left their mark. What difference does that make now?"

Crew let out a long sigh. "Each one represents a different demon *inside* of him, Hannah."

Crew's words ricocheted off me, my comprehension blocked behind a triple-locked door.

In... inside of him?

"Hannah," Crew said softly. He stepped forward, leaned in. "He's possessed."

Suddenly, I was at the bottom of a bottomless ocean. Hundreds of thousands of pounds of pressure pressed in on all sides, threatening to crush my body like a soda can.

"He's okay, though," I said weakly. Even to me, my voice sounded a hundred miles away. Then I remembered our kiss. His heart beating, reaching out to touch my hand on his chest. The way he said 'I love you.' That *was* Adam, and no one—no*thing*—else. I would know. "He's okay. And if we have to do… something… to fix him, we'll do that but… he's okay."

"We have to take him in, Hannah," Crew said. "That thing inside of him… if it gets out…"

"That thing?" Damien called, then clucked his tongue off the roof of his mouth. "Have a little respect, Crew."

I snapped my head from Damien back to Crew. "What does he mean?"

Crew's jaw tightened.

"Tell me. Now."

"That mark on his chest," Crew said, leaning forward. "The big one. It's the mark of an Arch Demon. The most powerful of them all."

"And we just pulled it through a portal from Hell," Sloane chimed in. "Led it straight into our world."

"We had to," Crew snapped. "You know that. Better that he leave Hell under our control than his." He motioned toward Damien.

"Hannah," Jordan said softly. "If an Arch Demon gets loose in this world… I mean, it's game over. We're finished. The world as we know it will never be the same."

"Which is exactly what they want," Crew finished, nodding toward Damien. "They want to release the Arch Demon from Adam's body. Wreak havoc."

Everything became fuzzy—my vision, my thoughts.

"But that would kill Adam," I managed.

No one disagreed.

"Taking him to the Ring, though. Why? An exorcism?"

"Of sorts," Crew said. "Look, I'm not going to lie to you. He's dead already. No one can survive extraction of a demon that powerful. No one. But if the Ring does it, we have a fighting chance of doing it in a way that would cast the Arch Demon straight back to Hell. If they do it?"—Crew leveled a shaking finger at Damien's smug face—"Adam dies *and* the Arch Demon gets loose." Each Dante seemed to draw closer, closing in around me like a net around a fish. "I'm sorry, Hannah. But I just can't allow that to happen. We have a higher cause. Hundreds of thousands—maybe millions—of lives are at stake. This is bigger than us."

'This is bigger than us.' These words came from Ryan first, now Crew. Both of them were ready and willing to sacrifice the two things I loved more than anything in this world. Each of them had pledged to some bigger, higher cause, and each of them were ready to use Adam or Em, or both, as sacrificial pawns in their game.

I could not lose one of them.

I was about to lose both of them.

Damien tightened his grip around Em.

"You all done?" Damien called. "All up to speed now, young lady?" Apparently, he was speaking to me. Every sound seemed filtered through thick cotton. "So, what'll it be, then? Do we have a deal?"

I needed a plan.

I couldn't think.

Let her go.

'I will never let you leave me again.'

"You have our answer, Damien," someone said. "No deal."

Squealing tires. Crashing, warping metal.

Mom. Dad. Where are you?

Help me.

"It's her *sister*, Crew," someone else said.

"We can't risk the lives of millions to save one."

Help.

Hannah.

A voice, far away, but close. Closer than any voice I'd ever heard that wasn't my own. My eyes were shut. When did I shut my eyes?

Where is Em?

Where is Em?

"Seems like you all think I'm bluffing, which is unfortunate," Damien's voice crawled along the cave walls, narrowing my world into sharp focus again. My eyes shot open.

Crew, Sloane and Jordan ceased arguing about the fate of my sister and my... and Adam. Damien's gun was still pressed hard against Em's temple. She'd stopped crying. Even in the moonlight it was clear the whites of her eyes had turned rose-colored, her skin bone white.

"You think I won't kill? You think I would leave the fate of our world, the fate of my master, to a bluff?"

Jordan stepped forward, hands outstretched. "There has to be a way around all this," he said, glancing back at me. "You wouldn't kill her sister."

Damien laughed. Then the world exploded.

A sound much louder than the loudest crack of thunder split the air. A flash as bright as the sun itself exploded from the gun's muzzle. Time ceased to exist.

My crackling nerves crackled no more. Numbness bloomed inside of me, overtaking my body with each millisecond that passed. Blinding white blanketed my vision. The ringing in my ears screamed like someone was steadily turning up the volume.

The bright white began fading. The ringing in my ears remained.

Someone screamed.

Footsteps pounded.

Jordan's body collapsed to the ground.

Jordan.

"Jordan!"

His eyes were saucers, staring upward as if tied to the stars. Opening, then closing, then opening his lips, trying to suck in air. Dark blood began trickling from the corner of his mouth.

Sloane was already there, kneeling by his side. "No, no, no, no no!" She screamed.

An uneven, dark pattern beginning exactly where his heart lay bloomed outward, across his chest, soaking his shirt.

Sloane pressed down hard on the gunshot wound. Not a second later, she pulled her hand away, her palm soaked.

I rushed to his side opposite Sloane, held up the back of his head. "Look at me, Jordan," I said. "Stay with me." But Jordan's breathing became labored as he pulled breath through an ever-shrinking straw. "Jordan," I said, pleading between hitching sobs. "Please."

His eyes descended from the stars, made contact with mine.

"S... S...," he attempted.

"Shh, no. Don't talk." But Jordan's eyes grew even wider, more resolved.

"Sis... Sister," he said. "S... K... Keep her... Safe..."

Those were his last words to me. To anyone.

His eyelids fluttered shut. His breathing ceased. His body lost all strength.

"Oh my God," Sloane whispered, drawing a shaking hand to her face, streaking Jordan's blood across her cheeks and jaw. She looked down at him, yet somehow beyond him, unfocused as the effects of shock took hold.

The world became still, silent.

My inner silence broke when the voice in my head, not mine, came again, low and dark. *Where is Em?*

I didn't have a chance to answer it before the outer silence broke.

"You son of a—" Crew growled but couldn't finish. The sound of the gun's hammer being cocked back again seemed somehow louder than the shot that killed Jordan.

Killed. Jordan. The thought refused to land. My mind told me it was not real. But his lifeless body, lying awkwardly against the cave wall, was.

Louder still was the *click* sound the gun made when Damien

pressed it once again against my sister's temple. His eyes flashed wild, insane, deadly.

Em. She's there. He'll shoot her. He will kill her.

An eternal beat of heavy silence passed.

No, the other voice responded. *He will not.*

Behind me, Adam rose.

His long hair hung in drapes across his face as he pressed himself slowly upward, bracing against the rocky wall. Each of the black markings that covered his body seemed to pulse, none more so than the largest mark that covered the expanse of his heaving chest. He pressed his body off the wall, stepped forward. The first step was a struggle, and it appeared it might send him crashing down to his knees. He steadied himself, raised his head and met my gaze.

I couldn't explain it. When we locked eyes, it was like he reached into my chest and slowed my rushing heart, setting it back like an analog timer to a period of calm. His expression didn't change when, as he stepped forward and stood beside me, he looked down and saw Sloane, bloody and kneeling over Jordan's lifeless body. His emotions did change, though. They became a whirlpool of descending calamity—anger, hatred, sadness, rage all blending together in a cocktail that he buried inside. I knew this because I felt it too. I felt it with him. I felt *him*.

The pounding of our heartbeats rushed forward, increasing in speed and depth. Then, Adam turned, saw Em. Damien's grip tightened, but Em ceased whimpering when she and Adam locked eyes. No words were said between them, but they didn't need words to speak volumes.

"Master," Damien said, low and slithery. "It is time. Come with us. We are here to finish the mission, the ultimate design. It is our destiny and privilege to release you from that mortal cage and set you free on this world."

Damien was not speaking to Adam, but to the Arch Demon and others inside of him. They heard Damien, but so did Adam, who turned his head to me. On the outside, he was a marble sculpture, calm and still. On the inside, though, an absolute war for control had broken out. His soul battled against hordes, none more powerful than that Arch Demon who vied for control of not only his body, but his mind. I felt it, as if he wanted me to.

As if he drew strength from *my* soul, drew it into him and fortified his defenses.

Still, the Arch Demon rose.

The cave, the world outside, became ice cold. Our breath became plumes of crystalized clouds. I felt less of him, and whether that meant he'd pulled all of the strength from me he needed or that he'd been overcome by the dark entity within, I couldn't know. Suddenly, I was only aware of my pounding heart, my rushing adrenaline as it widened my veins and set all my nerves tingling. I was on my own.

So was he.

As if lifting heavy weights, Adam's hands and arms curled inward and upward. The markings pulsed outward from his chest, down his shoulders, his arms, feeding into his hands.

Adam's eyes bled to black.

Damien laughed sardonically, though the hint of nervousness that laced his voice didn't escape me. "Yes," he said. "Come with us, Master."

Adam's black marble eyes stared forward. His hands rose, seemingly pulling some form of energy or power produced by the markings and into his palms where, suddenly, glowing black flames erupted, danced along his palms and fingertips.

A low, pulsing hum rose from below our feet.

The ground vibrated in time with each pulse. No, not just the ground. Every atom, every molecule of oxygen, every form of matter vibrated. The world pulsed, the pulses increased in speed and depth, and suddenly I felt like I needed to vomit, like I wanted to fall to my knees and palm my ears and vice my eyes and yet…

And yet, I couldn't look away.

The capering black flames in Adam's hands rose. Slowly, he turned them away from himself, toward the world outside the cave, toward Damien and Ryan, toward… Em.

Fear escaped from my inner cage and I tried to scream, tried to tell Adam, "No! Don't! You know her! That's Em! Don't lose control! Don't forget who you are and who you love!"

But no words were allowed in this new reality, whatever this new reality was.

Those pulses of energy emanating from the markings across Adam's body increased simultaneously with the pulses of energy that permeated the air and everything around him.

Adam opened his jaw, released a gritty, low scream.

Then, the world broke.

Cracks in the Earth, along the cave walls as the rumbling beneath our feet intensified. Massive tree trunks split as if struck by invisible bolts of lightning. The ground swelled, moved, shifted, rumbled to life as if an ancient giant lived below, beneath the trees and rocks and dirt, shrugging them all to one side as it woke.

The giant that made the earth crumble was not beneath the dirt, though. It was beneath skin and bones and pulsing black markings. Adam's body trembled as he stretched forth both hands, pressing both flaming palms forward, the earth quaking more violently with each millimeter of trembling air they passed.

The cave began breaking apart. Huge boulders sheared off from the walls and ceiling, crashing down around us. Crew dove from the cave as one broke free just above his head. Sloane shielded herself and Jordan's body as best she could as the cavern walls split and cracked like lightning all around them. The rumbling, shifting ground sent me hard to my knees.

Outside, Damien's laughter ceased. Ryan fell to his back, yelling, screaming, covering his ears. Damien shouted something, but whatever it was, the words disappeared into the ether. Somehow, he was still standing. Then, I realized the reason.

There was only one small patch of dirt that seemed to be

immune from the quaking earth—the patch where he and Em stood.

Suddenly, the rumbling intensified, the cracking trees crashed and rolled, and Adam stretched forth his hands. The flames burned bright black, then formed into twisting horizontal tornadoes. In a blast, they flew from his palms. They molded around Em, never touching her, as if she were shielded by some invisible barrier.

The flames rushed into Damien.

His mouth, nostrils, eyes became darkness. His gun dropped to the quaking ground below. His grip on Em disappeared as his body trembled and shook in time with the pulsing world around him. Lifting his face to the sky, he screamed a terrible inhuman scream as the black flames seemed to ignite him from the inside. His feet left the ground, and for one terrifying moment he floated low in the air, hovering, arms outstretched.

Then Damien fell to the ground in a smoking husk.

Slowly, the earth stopped rumbling. Trees stopped cracking, falling. Boulders stopped rolling. The cave stood still. Em was the only person left standing. She trembled, stared forward, cemented into place by shock.

Adam's arms drifted lower until they rested at his sides.

I rose to my feet, approached him slowly. Though the markings ceased pulsing and his hands held no dark fire, his eyes were still marble black.

My body trembled, the aftershocks of a world shaken. "Adam," I managed. Slowly, he turned to me. I reached forward, brushed his arm. His head cocked to one side, studied me as if I were something new.

I realized too late that it was not Adam who was studying me, not Adam who's arm I touched.

He gripped my shoulders, stepped forward, and slammed me hard against what was left of the cave wall. Stars exploded in the back of my vision until the only things visible were those ink-black eyes, that deathly stare.

"You," he said—not Adam. The voice that left Adam's body was ephemeral, lower than low, like the humming pulse that shook the earth.

"Adam, stop," I managed, wheezing . "Listen to me. This isn't you. Don't let it take you over—"

Adam squeezed my throat, cutting off my words. Eyes wide, I tried mightily to suck in air, but none was allowed to enter my lungs. Adam's hand squeezed impossibly tighter. Pressure rushed to my eyes, my pounding ears. Then the low voice that was not Adam's spoke again.

"You're mine."

28

My lungs screamed.

My vision tunneled, the tunnel shrinking narrower, narrower...

Tension suddenly released. Oxygen cascaded down my throat. Adam's head faced downward. He said something, coughed.

"No," he struggled to say, "I won't."

His chest jerked forward, like something punched him hard in the ribs, but from the inside. His breath caught. He released my shoulders, bracing himself on the cracked, rocky wall with hands on either side of my head.

"Hannah?" A small voice came from behind Adam. "Adam?"

Adam released a gritty, gravely moan, as if whatever had trapped itself inside his body was trying to claw its way out.

"Help me," he cried out. My fear of him dissolved as he glanced upward and met my eyes. Instead of marble black, his had returned to cobalt blue. I reached, tried to wrap my arms around him but not before he clutched his bare chest, then fell to his knees.

Em stood quietly a few feet behind where Adam now knelt. I

braced him, pulled his head into my waist, then reached out for Em.

She rushed to me, nearly knocking all three of us over when she wrapped her arms around my middle.

"I shouldn't have left you in that car, Em," I said, voice quivering. "I'm so sorry."

"You had to," she said. "You had to bring Adam back."

Adam, and something else... Something that could destroy our world as we knew it...

Adam cleared his throat, propped up on one leg and reached. I helped him to his feet, checking the color of his eyes for good measure. His chest heaved, still begging for breath.

"Whatever I did," he said softly, taking in the dystopian scene surrounding us, "I'm sorry."

"You saved our lives," I said. Adam glanced past me to where Jordan still lay lifeless. Lightly, I turned his chin back toward me. "That wasn't you. That was Damien."

Adam let out a weighty sigh. Whether he remembered or understood the circumstances surrounding Jordan's death, it didn't matter. Like me, Adam had lost a friend, a brother, a Dante.

Curiously, Sloane wasn't near Jordan any longer. Crew wasn't in sight, and neither was Ryan. I'd lost track of all of them during the time it took for Adam to break our small corner of the world into pieces. Suddenly, I felt very exposed.

"We need to leave," I said. "We're not safe."

"No one is," Adam said. "Not as long as I'm alive." His words were anvils on my shoulders.

"Hey," I said, forcing him to look at me. "We're going to figure this out. We always do." His eyes drilled mine, searching for any cracks in the foundation, but there were none. I'd meant what I said.

Something made a cracking sound in the shadows between those few trees left standing in our immediate vicinity, jolting me back to reality.

"We've got to go," I said. "Now."

Only a few steps out of the cave and I realized that Adam still hadn't regained much of his natural strength. Holding Em's hand, I wrapped my other across around his back for support. Normally, he'd protest, play tough, but not this time. He leaned on me like a crutch. We hobbled as quickly as we could past Damien's smoking, black husk of a corpse and into the dark woods, but not before I scooped up his gun. The metal was hot to the touch. I shoved it hard into the back of my pants.

I wasn't sure which direction to go, but I knew my car was a no-go zone. Whoever wanted to catch me—catch Adam—would be waiting there for us for sure. The parking lot was a long way away to the east. We moved as quickly and quietly as we could in a straight line to the north, and I prayed we'd find a road or an empty cabin or somewhere safe and out of sight to...

A shape materialized in the darkness ahead of us, dark, backlit by the few silver rays of moonlight that managed to slice through the tree branches. I swerved, tried to hide the three of us behind a thick tree.

"Don't bother," the shape said. Though it came across as raspy and strained, it was a voice I knew all too well. My heart clenched.

"Stay here," I told them both, but Em wouldn't let go of my hand. With a sigh, I bent down. "Please. Stay with Adam." Her eyes pleaded, begged, but ultimately realized like I had that the only way out was through. There was no scenario in which we could outrun someone—not in the condition we were in.

Adam tried to stand tall and straight but winced, grabbed his ribs.

"Stay with her," I said. "I've got this."

Em wrapped her arms around Adam. Adam held her close, nodding to me, sharing a wordless look that meant so many things, but more than anything to be careful and come back. I returned the nod, glanced one last time down at Em.

I wrapped my hand firmly around the pistol grip and prayed

both that it was still loaded and that I wouldn't have to use it, then slid out from behind the tree

The figure was standing exactly where it had been before. The moonlight, though, had shifted slightly. Even though I didn't need the light to know who was waiting there, I was glad for it.

"You know I shouldn't let you go, right?" The voice came as I stepped forward. "That this whole thing, this whole shit show, is so much bigger than just us, right?"

"You saw what he did," I said. My fingers tightened around the pistol's grip. "He used the power of... of whatever's inside of him for good. He saved us."

"He saved you." The figure took a slow step forward. "He saved you, and he saved your sister, and he saved himself. But let me guess, you think you can fix him? Save him?"

"Yes," I said, but the confidence I'd felt before began to wane. Doubts crept up like the undead digging themselves from their graves.

The figure laughed, stepped closer. I pulled the gun.

"That's close enough," I said.

"Really? After all we've been through?"

A sharp sliver of moonlight cast itself across Sloane's face. Jordan's dry blood streaked her cheeks, her face turned up in a skeptical glare. I aimed the gun straight between her eyes. It rattled in my hands.

"Please don't make me do this," I pleaded, and meant it. "I will if I have to." I meant that too. The image of when the hot gun in my hands was last used sliced through my mind like a muzzle flash. The shock made me want to drop it, kick it away, smash it into a billion tiny fragments. But if my only choice was between pulling the trigger or letting the Dantes take Adam to the Ring... well, I had made my mind up the moment I scooped the pistol from the ground.

Sloane released a sigh, raised her empty hands. "I know what I should do," she said, slowly, as if talking to herself. "I know the stakes. Letting you go—letting *him* go"—she nodded toward the tree concealing Adam and Em—"might very well mean destroying thousands or millions of lives. I mean, the last time an Arch Demon got out, in Haiti… a quarter of a million people were killed in that earthquake…"

Slowly, the gun barrel lowered as I sensed what was coming.

"But what if you're right?" she said after a long, silent beat. "What if you *can* save him?"

Sloane reached behind her and I raised the gun swiftly.

"It's okay," she said, "just… trust me."

I kept the gun aimed squarely at her chest. "I don't know if I can," I admitted. Then Sloane pulled something from her back pocket—something small, metallic, glinting in the moonlight.

Car keys.

"My car is parked on the side of a road about a hundred yards behind me," she said. She tossed the keys to me through the shadows. I caught them one-handed, stared at them.

"Why would you help me?"

Sloane sighed. "I've already lost one brother today." Emotion choked her words. "I don't want to lose another one."

I nodded, holding back my own sudden onset of grief. "Jordan," I managed. "What will happen with him?"

Sloane's gaze dropped to the ground. For a few long seconds, she didn't speak; only shook her head, visibly fighting the urge to rub the moisture threatening to cascade from her eyelids. "We'll take care of him," she finally whispered, then cleared her throat. "You need to listen closely. There's someone you need to see—someone who can probably help Adam."

I lowered the gun and held it loosely at my side. I needed all the help I could get. "Who?"

"His name is Cade. Last I heard, he was hiding out in Vegas. I was sent to find him before getting reassigned to this sprawling metropolis." She gestured to the dark woods surrounding us. Sarcasm, apparently, was her coping mechanism.

"He's a Dante?"

Another long sigh. "The Ring wants him for the same reason they want your man over there."

It was a gut punch. "There's someone else like him? Someone..."

Don't say possessed. Adam is not possessed.

Sloane nodded. "He's been on the watch list for a long time."

Watch list...

"How would I find him if you couldn't?"

Sloane grinned at that. "Something tells me he'll find you once you roll into town with Adam." She nodded again toward the tree.

Vegas wasn't far—maybe a six, seven-hour drive. Some mixture of relief and nervous dread settled in my chest.

"What happened to Crew?" I asked.

"We split up," she said. "He followed your ex that way, toward the parking lot. He'll be waiting up there in case you show up."

"How did you know I wouldn't head that way."

"Because you're not stupid."

I nodded appreciatively, flipped the keys around my finger once and palmed them.

"You've done so much, but I need to ask you one last favor," I said. Sloane didn't reply, only raised her eyebrows. "The other campers are a couple miles that way." I pointed toward the direction of Craig's Mesa, like the sign on the main cabin's door said. "There were a lot of demons and other things out here tonight. We had a run in with a counselor-turned-Vessel. Em's best friend is out there..."

"I'll check on them," Sloane said. "Make sure they're safe."

Slowly, I walked toward her, shoving the pistol into my waistband. I wrapped my arms around her neck and thanked her.

"Go," she said, "before I realize the error of my ways."

I released her and backed away, grateful.

"Don't make me regret this," Sloane said. She turned, headed in the direction of Craig's Mesa, melding into shadow.

I returned to Adam and Em, peeled them away from the tree trunk. Adam was fading quickly, his strength all but sapped. He leaned on me more heavily than before. We snaked our way through the trees, across the hundred wooded yards to Sloane's car. The jet-black muscle car was stashed on the dirt road's low shoulder. The road was barren, dusty, and dark in each direction.

I helped Adam into the back seat. He clunked over on his side before I could finish wrapping a seatbelt around him. The memory of his marble black eyes, the voice that was not his... The thought of whether it was a good idea to place myself and my sister in the same car as a man who carried an Arch Demon inside of him did cross my mind.

Arch Demon or not, I loved that man. And he loved us too. That had to count for something.

For everything.

Em slid into the passenger seat and fastened her seatbelt. I slid into the driver seat, tossed the pistol into the glove box, checked that her belt was fastened tight, then thumbed her cheek. "We have a lot to talk about," I said, then keyed the ignition, "and a long drive ahead of us."

Suddenly, I became keenly aware of our situation, though I couldn't pretend to understand the extent of its complications. Adam was infected—I refused to use the word *possessed*—with an Arch Demon, not to mention however many dozens of lesser demons. Each had left their mark when they'd entered his body. They were powerful, dangerous. Yet, in some way that I didn't fully comprehend, Adam was able to control that power, use it against Damien, but in a way that protected Em.

I had something to do with that. It was like he drew strength from my soul, connected with his, so as not to allow the power to overtake him. Our soul circle connected to form a deeper link than simply sharing memories, pain, even thoughts. Much deeper. The implications terrified me.

Em placed her hand over mine on the shifter as I hesitated behind the wheel. She was a whole other bundle of mysteries to unravel. Her ability to see beyond this world and into the next was nothing short of a curse she didn't deserve. I was grateful that the bond between her and Adam shielded her from the power that incinerated Damien from the inside out, leaving him charred and smoldering. I don't know whether that bond has something to do with the supernatural, with the soul circle bond Adam shares with me. If I had to venture a guess, it would be that the love Adam has for her was power enough.

I twisted the key. The engine rumbled to life.

Adam had new enemies now, which meant I had new enemies. The Dantes—Crew, at least, and probably all the others except for Sloane, wherever they were in the world—would stop at nothing to turn him over to the Ring for exorcism, which will most definitely lead to Adam's death and might—*maybe*—end with casting the Arch Demon back down to Hell. The Order of the Snake was destined to hunt Adam down for the same reason, to exorcise and kill him in order to release the Arch Demon on the world to bring about some form of Hell on Earth. And finally, the Arch Demon itself, waiting for the moment in which its host was no longer living, no longer able to keep it caged. Certainly, it would do anything and everything in its power to hurry that process along.

It was us against the world. Us against the underworld.

I slammed the car into drive and accelerated up the dirt road's shoulder, swallowed hard, then turned the wheel in the direction where I could only hope answers awaited.

I revved the engine, pulled onto the road, and headed south.

To Vegas.

JOIN THE CLUB

Hi - TJK here. The best thing about writing is creating relationships with my readers. I hope you enjoyed DANTES. If so, then check out the T. James Kelly spam-free, cancel-any-time newsletter to learn more about future releases, get special offers and bonus content. You can sign up on my website, and while you're there, please say hi. I'd love to hear from you.

Visit my website at: TJamesKelly.com

HARBINGER
THE THIRD AND FINAL BOOK OF THE DARK TRIALS SERIES

Coming soon

**Sign up at TJamesKelly.com to be the first to get an exclusive
look at the first chapter (and more).**

ABOUT THE AUTHOR

T. James Kelly is an emerging author of thrilling stories. When he's not writing, you can usually find him enjoying time with his family, playing guitar, or escaping into the Utah mountains.

Connect with him on social media (@TJKAuthor) for news about upcoming releases and giveaways.

ALSO BY T. JAMES KELLY

The Dark Trials Series:

Book 1: THE DARK TRIALS

ACKNOWLEDGMENTS

Thank you, first and foremost, to my wife, who was instrumental in bringing DANTES to life. Your help and support can't be measured.

Thanks to Christian Bentulan of Covers by Christian for the amazing book cover design.

Finally, thank you for reading this book. If you enjoyed it, the greatest compliment you could give would be to tell a friend.

Made in the USA
Columbia, SC
24 September 2021